This book belongs to:

..................................

..................................

..................................

# OXFORD CHILDREN'S CLASSICS

Anne *of* Green Gables
Flambards
Little Women
Party Shoes
*The* Adventures *of* Tom Sawyer
*The* Hound *of the* Baskervilles
*The* Jungle Book
Treasure Island

# OXFORD CHILDREN'S CLASSICS

## Noel Streatfeild

# Party
# Shoes

**OXFORD**
UNIVERSITY PRESS

# OXFORD
### UNIVERSITY PRESS

Great Clarendon Street, Oxford OX2 6DP

Oxford University Press is a department of the University of Oxford.
It furthers the University's objective of excellence in research, scholarship,
and education by publishing worldwide in

Oxford   New York

Auckland   Cape Town   Dar es Salaam   Hong Kong   Karachi
Kuala Lumpur   Madrid   Melbourne   Mexico City   Nairobi
New Delhi   Shanghai   Taipei   Toronto

With offices in

Argentina   Austria   Brazil   Chile   Czech Republic   France   Greece
Guatemala   Hungary   Italy   Japan   Poland   Portugal   Singapore
South Korea   Switzerland   Thailand   Turkey   Ukraine   Vietnam

Oxford is a registered trade mark of Oxford University Press
in the UK and in certain other countries

British Library Cataloguing in Publication Data

Data available

ISBN: 978-0-19-272010-8

1 3 5 7 9 10 8 6 4 2

Printed in China

# CONTENTS

# A LETTER TO THE READER OF THIS BOOK

*During the war my niece, Nicolette, was given a party frock and shoes from America. A lovely frock of the sort that nobody had because of clothes rationing. Blue organdie over a silk slip. It was Nicolette's first long frock and she could hardly wait for the right occasion to put it on. But no occasion turned up. There was at that time almost no transport. So little heating that if it was a winter party something warmer than organdie would have to be worn. Food was difficult, and every grown-up person too busy to arrange a party of the making-do sort it would have to have been. The frock hung in the cupboard, and hung in the cupboard. A most depressing place for a first long party frock. Worst of all, Nicolette grew. Even the most optimistic person had to wonder, if there ever was a party, would the frock be too short and too tight?*

*I am glad to say that Nicolette did wear the frock. If it was a bit tight it did not show. She looked exactly as somebody of thirteen ought to look at a party. But I remember the months of anxiety when the frock hung in the cupboard. How awful to have been Nicolette. How many more girls had party frocks and shoes sent them from abroad and no party? So, for Nicolette in England, and the givers of the party frock and shoes in America, I wrote this book.*

Noel Streatfeild

# CHAPTER ONE

———•◆•———

## *The Parcel*

The parcel came while the family were having breakfast. It caused confusion because, although it was marked 'unsolicited gift', the postman had to have a lot of money before he would deliver it. Mrs Miggs, who came in to help with the housework, had not arrived, so Miss Lipscombe, who was boiling instruments in the surgery, answered the bell. Miss Lipscombe had, when she was younger, been Matron in charge of a workhouse. People say to Matrons, 'Yes, Matron', whenever they speak, which makes it difficult for Matrons when they retire. If for years and years people have said 'Yes, Matron' in respectful tones it is hard to get accustomed to people saying a plain 'No'. To make up for all the respectful 'Yes, Matrons' that she did not get, Miss Lipscombe made a favour of everything that she did in the hope that people would remember how important she was. That was why it was awkward that it was she who answered the postman's ring.

The family were sitting round the table eating breakfast, which that day was cereal and sausages. They heard Miss Lipscombe say, 'Nonsense. No parcel is worth so much. No, I certainly can't disturb the doctor at breakfast.' Mr Bins, the postman, could not be heard at first, but presently he lost his temper and then his voice roared into the dining-room. 'I've no time for argufying with you. I've got work to do, if you haven't.' At the breakfast table the children looked at each other in a hopeful sort of way. Mr Bins was a very old friend, and he had said the one thing that was absolutely certain to make Miss Lipscombe angry. Doctor Andrews got up.

'I had better save bloodshed.' He opened the dining-room door and called out in a casual voice, as though he had not heard the argument going on, 'Morning, Bins.'

The dining-room door being open the children could hear everything. Miss Lipscombe and Mr Bins talked at the same time. Mr Bins said he was not going to be put about by a cantankerous female that didn't know her place. Miss Lipscombe said what the world was coming to she didn't know when creatures like Bins could so far forget themselves. Then Doctor Andrews cut in:

'Sorry you've been taken from your work, Miss Lipscombe, perhaps you would get my instruments packed. I shall be off in a minute.' And to Mr Bins, 'What's the damage?'

There was a pause after that. Obviously money was being paid out. Then Mr Bins said, 'Good morning, Doctor.'

As soon as the money was paid all the family, from Mrs Andrews down to Benjamin, thought about the parcel.

Mrs Andrews wondered whether it was for her. Could it possibly have some of that glorious flannel in it that made shirts for the boys?

John knew it was not for him but wondered about the stamps. He collected Dominions only. He hoped it was from Canada and had a very expensive stamp on it. He had only started his collection in the summer just before his first term at Marlborough, and it was not up to much yet.

Selina prayed hard that it was for her. It might be because she had a godmother in America. It was true that her god-mother did not usually send presents for proper occasions. She never remembered Selina's birthday was in October. If a present came now, even though it was late, it would look like a present for Christmas. All the same, just once she might have kept an occasion for a change. She sent lovely presents when she did send them. Selina hoped, if it was a present, it had in it something like sweets that could be shared round, because, on the whole, she got more parcels than anybody else in the family, and that made things a bit awkward when you were just a cousin and everybody else were brothers and sisters.

The twins, Christopher and Sally, had an especial interest in the parcel. They guessed it came from America and was for them. It might say 'unsolicited gift', but they knew that they had written a letter to Uncle Bill in Washington, which, if it had got by the censor, would mean that Uncle Bill had been shopping. Christopher wanted skates. He wanted skates so badly that he dreaded a cold winter because he had not any. When it comes to not wanting ice and snow things are pretty bad. The maddening thing was he had saved the money to buy skates, but there were no new ones being made, and none of his size were ever advertised for sale second hand. He had not exactly asked for skates in his letter to Uncle Bill, but he had said, 'It would be pretty decent if there was ice this Christmas, if I had any skates, but there are none made now.' Sally felt she could no longer live without silk tights. She had written, 'There is a chance that I may dance the lead in the ballet we do at school at Easter, if I had silk tights which I have not. There are no silk tights at all here now.' Later on in the letter they had said, 'We have saved enough money to pay for skates and tights when we can get anyone to get them for us.' They were a little nervous about saying this as it was the sort of thing the censor might stop, but, on the other hand, they did not want Uncle Bill to think he was expected to fork out the money, because he had only his pay as a Colonel and their father said that did not go far in Washington.

Phoebe hoped there was material in the parcel that Mum would make into a party frock for her. She had no proper party frock. She had expected to come into Sally's pink one by now, but Sally remained so terribly small for twelve and a half. It was particularly sickening this Christmas that she had not got a party frock because she had a party to wear one at. It was the only party this year and was for children of ten or under. It was all very well for Mum to say she looked a pet in that white thing; she looked simply awful in that white thing. It was much too short and much too tight, and other children who were nine and a half did not wear, for best, a dress which their sister had worn five years before.

Augustus had not paused in his eating while Miss Lipscombe and Mr Bins were arguing about the parcel, but, as he ate, little quick pictures of what might be in the parcel

4

jumped in and out of his brain. Once a parcel had come from Australia with sort of crystallized fruits in it, at least that was what Mum had called them. There had been gorgeous parcels from America from Selina's godmother, with enormous sweets on the end of little sticks. Once there had been a parcel from Canada with a great tin of nuts in it. He did not know what to hope was in this parcel. He just saw a nice mixture of what had come in other parcels.

Benjamin had taken advantage of the parcel distracting everybody's attention to hum, which he was not allowed to do at table. He made little words to his humming. 'It's a 'normous parcel. It's a present for Benjamin. It's full to the very top of ice-cream.'

Doctor Andrews came back into the dining-room. He was carrying a large box done up in brown paper. He held it out to Selina.

'It's for you, niece. It says, "Miss Selina Cole, unsolicited gift." I hope it's something you want because there was three pounds, eighteen shillings, and fourpence to pay.'

Mrs Andrews nearly dropped the teapot.

'Three pounds, eighteen shillings, and fourpence! Good gracious, Jim!' She turned to Selina. 'I hope it's something useful, darling, after the Customs charging all that much.'

The doctor sat down and went on with his breakfast.

'I hope it's something she likes.'

Selina read the declaration form. She looked up, her eyes shining.

'It's a dress and shoes. Oh, Aunt Ann, I do hope it's velvet. I think I want a red velvet dress almost more than anything else in the world.'

5

Mrs Andrews laughed.

'Put the parcel in the armchair until after breakfast, darling. I know it seems awful to be expected to wait to open it, but you can't risk getting sausage on to a new dress, and you easily might sitting next to Benjamin.'

Benjamin stopped humming. He had a hoarse, deep voice for somebody of four. He leant across to his mother.

'My dear! I never upset my food.'

His mother pulled his plate closer to him.

'Not more than once a day; eat up, old man.'

It was hard for Selina to swallow the rest of her breakfast. Nobody, however hungry they are, could be really interested in breakfast when a parcel marked 'New dress' is lying unopened in the armchair in the corner. Especially a person who has not had a new dress for a year because of needing an overcoat, shoes, a gym tunic, and underclothes. It was hard to sit still and not fidget while the others finished eating. Uncle Jim was very strict about sitting still. He was so often called away in the middle of a meal to attend to a patient that he was afraid his children would think that was the normal way to behave. He would never let anybody get up for any reason at all until the last person had finished eating, and he never allowed them to say, 'For goodness' sake hurry up.' If anyone fidgeted he just took longer before he got up himself, or would let Aunt Ann get up, to show that the meal was over. Fortunately for Selina the surgery bell rang just as Augustus, who was always slow, finished drinking his milk. The doctor got up and breakfast was over.

Aunt Ann helped Selina untie the string. All the family

wanted to help pull off the brown paper but Aunt Ann held them back.

'Don't be mean. It's Selina's parcel.'

Inside was a box. It was tied up in the lovely way Americans tie up parcels, with yards and yards of fine scarlet and green ribbon. When that ribbon was taken off the box and the lid lifted there was a card lying on top of tissue paper. The card said: 'I have just remembered that you are now 'tween-age, and must be ready for this. I hope you'll have a good time in it.' Selina laid the card on one side and lifted the tissue paper. There lay the frock. She held it by its shoulders and gaped at it, and so did everybody else. It was long. Down to the ground. Cream organdie over a cream satin slip. It had ruched square shoulders and short puffed sleeves. After a moment Phoebe said in a whisper:

'There's still things left in the box.'

Selina undid three smaller parcels. In the two biggest were one each of a pair of satin shoes, and in the other was a blue sash for the frock and a blue bow to wear in her hair. Aunt Ann seemed to find all this glory too much for her legs. She sat down suddenly.

'Selina, my pet, your godmother has the most inflated ideas about what is worn in English villages at the end of a long war.'

Sally took the sash from Selina and put it round herself. She turned to her mother.

'She'll have to wear it fairly soon or she'll have outgrown it, and then it'll come on to me.'

Mrs Andrews was looking sadly at the frock. If only it had been made of velvet or serge or something useful.

7

'Even if it passed on to you, darling, what could you wear it for?'

Phoebe spoke very fast, her words falling over each other.

'If nobody ever is going to wear it, couldn't it, oh couldn't it be cut short and me wear it for the party next week?'

John saw how aghast Selina looked at the suggestion. He gave Phoebe's curls a tug.

'The present was for Selina, not you. Of course she'll wear it.'

Selina was grateful to John, but she did not think he quite appreciated the position.

'When?'

John turned to his mother.

'Isn't somebody getting married or anything like that? It could be worn as a bridesmaid.'

Sally stroked the blue sash.

'Everybody who was going to be married has been married, and anyway, you can't just say "I've got a frock, can I be a bridesmaid?"' She turned suddenly to her mother, her eyes shining. 'I tell you what, couldn't we give a party so's she could wear it?'

Mrs Andrews looked miserable.

'Oh, I do wish we could, but who would come to it? You see, the sort of party for that frock would be an evening one, a dance, and nobody could get here in the evening. There isn't a bus after seven. That's why the Smiths' little party next week for people under ten is in the afternoon, and even then it's been an awful job to get twelve children together.'

John did not care if he never went to a dance, but he did feel it was pretty sickening for Selina to get a present that she could never use. He knew just how he would feel if somebody gave him a motor bike and it had to stop in the garage.

'Selina's got to wear it. We'll have to think of a way. Can I have the stamp, Selina?'

Selina was trying on the shoes. Even with wool stockings they looked gloriously partyish. She felt so low that she could only nod. Mrs Andrews got up.

'If anything they're too big, which is a comfort. Rack your brains, darlings. Perhaps together you can think of something.'

Christopher was so disappointed about the skates that he had not until that moment thought about Selina. Now, looking at her feet, he felt sorry for her. Suppose it had been skates, and then there was never any ice.

'Let's think until teatime and then after tea let's have a family committee. Everybody must have an idea by five o'clock.'

Mrs Andrews went towards the door. A family committee did not include her or the doctor. It was a thing held by the children. Selina had been counted as family since she had come to live with her Andrews cousins.

'It's getting late, we may as well get the chores done. Twins, it's your day for clearing the table; don't forget, when you've swept up the crumbs, to give them to the birds. I found a whole lot on the floor yesterday. Selina, when you've finished helping with the bedrooms write a nice thank-you letter to your godmother.' She glanced anxiously towards the window. 'I do hope Mrs Miggs is coming.'

The frock and shoes were back in the box. Selina folded the brown paper. Sally picked up the string and wound it into a little skein.

'Cheer up, Selina, we've never had a family committee yet when we didn't think of something.'

Christopher was piling the breakfast plates together.

'Five o'clock in the schoolroom, and everybody's got to come with an idea.'

# CHAPTER TWO

— ◆ ◆ —

## *The Committee*

The schoolroom was only called the schoolroom when the family remembered. It had always been the nursery. When John was eleven he had asked some boys to tea one Saturday afternoon, and without thinking he had said, 'Come up and play in the nursery.' On Monday when he went to school he found lots of boys saying, and even singing, 'Andrews Major plays in a nursery.' This was such a humiliation that John had to speak to his father about it. Doctor Andrews spoke to Mrs Andrews and it was decided that in future the nursery was to be called the schoolroom.

The family met in the schoolroom at five o'clock as arranged. It was a bit difficult for them to be there at the right time because tea was at half-past four and at five o'clock they were still sitting round the table. Augustus and Benjamin took a long time over their tea. It was the last meal they had before going to bed, and they seemed to remember this, filling up cracks in their insides with slice after slice of bread and jam.

11

Phoebe also ate a good deal at teatime, but she did not need to eat as much as Augustus and Benjamin because she had a cup of cocoa and a slice of bread and margarine when she went to bed. John, Selina, Christopher, and Sally, who were going to have a proper supper at half-past seven, got very bored watching Phoebe, Augustus, and Benjamin eat. Tea was the one meal that the doctor and Mrs Andrews did not eat with their family. Mrs Andrews said, 'I was brought up to have tea in the drawing-room, darlings, a very uncomfortable meal which none of you would like, but it's the one bit of civilization, as I knew it, left to me so I'm clinging to it.'

The rule about nobody fidgeting or getting up until the last person had finished eating officially existed in the school-room as well as the dining-room, but in the schoolroom it was not so strictly kept. Sally, as the eldest girl of the Andrews family, was in charge at teatime, with John and Christopher to back her up. Nobody actually got out of their chairs until tea was over, but there was a good deal of 'Hurry up, Slowcoach.' 'Did anyone ever see a tortoise eat a buttercup?' 'Augustus, we don't want to sit here all night, if you do.' It was actually ten minutes past five before Christopher and Sally had cleared the table and John was sitting at the head of it with a piece of paper to take down the minutes, and the meeting could begin. John wrote 'Committee', and the date at the top of the paper, 'December 30th, 1944', and underneath that 'Ideas'. He looked round the table to make sure everybody was attending.

'I shall put our ideas down, starting with Selina and going down to Benjamin and finishing with me, and then we'll all vote on the best one.' He looked at Selina. 'You first.'

Although Selina had lived with the cousins for five years and five months, she still felt a little odd with them. They were quicker than she was, or at least they seemed quicker. As a family they got interested in things very fast, and had a vivid, exciting way of doing what they did. Even ordinary things, like making beds and washing up, they did not do in an ordinary, dull way. They had hair inclined to curl and they were all dark, varying degrees of darkness, from Phoebe, whose hair was almost black and who had enormous brown eyes, to John, who was brown-haired. Selina had straight hair; it was not fair and it was not dark. When it was first washed it had red lights in it, but usually it looked just plain mouse-colour. She had grey-green eyes, and a pale face with high cheekbones, and she was very thin. The Andrews family had bright-coloured cheeks and eyes which danced and sparkled, and very red lips. Sometimes, when it was cold weather and Selina's nose was red, or when it was hot and she looked even paler than usual, she would think that to outsiders, seeing her beside her cousins, she must look rather like something that had been left out all night in the rain. All the cousins were, as a rule, nice to her, but sometimes she was conscious they thought her dull. It made her put forward ideas with diffidence. It made her answer John now in a nervous voice.

'I wondered if, perhaps, at Easter, when it's fine, we could get up a dance to be held out of doors—or perhaps . . .' she looked round and saw that nobody looked enthusiastic, 'or perhaps it would have to be in the summer holidays when it's light later. We could have the gramophone, I thought, with that loudspeaker that they use for book drives and things. Perhaps some of the Americans would come over from the camp. We could charge to come to the dance and give the money to a charity . . .'

The cousins' faces were so unresponsive that her voice tailed away.

Christopher said:

'Well, of . . .'

Sally said:

'I think . . .'

Phoebe said:

'If it's got to be a . . .'

Augustus said:

'I can't . . .'

John held up his hand.

'No criticisms until we've got all the ideas down. Benjamin, don't hum. People don't at meetings.' He looked at Christopher. He was five minutes older than Sally. 'Well?'

Christopher folded his arms and leant on the table.

'I was thinking that last year when the Women's Institute had that fair and exhibition they had a baby show. We might suggest to them that this year, instead of babies, they had a show for the best decorated bicycle. Selina could wear her frock and get her bicycle up in bows to match, or something.'

As John had said there was to be no criticism until all the ideas were written down nobody spoke, but Sally and Phoebe gave Christopher such scornful looks it was as good as speaking, and Selina's expression of horror was just like words. You could see her mind saying, 'My organdie on a bicycle!' John paid no attention to any of their faces. He wrote down Christopher's suggestion and looked at Sally.

Sally spoke so fast that her words fell over each other.

'I've thought of a ballet.' John's ruling there was to be no criticism or not, this was more than any of them could stand.

For every suitable and unsuitable occasion Sally thought of a ballet. There were rude noises all round the table. Sally looked proud. 'There's no need to be hateful. It's an awfully good idea, really. A girl goes to sleep and dreams, and while she's dreaming she sees the pictures in the room come to life, history pictures, like Queen Elizabeth and Charles the Second, and all those sort of people. In the end she wakes up and finds it's only a dream. Selina would be the girl, of course, who dreamt; there wouldn't be any dancing as she can't dance much, but she could wear her dress.'

Phoebe was so eager to explain her idea that she could hardly wait until John had written down Sally's.

'I think that sometime when there are lots of people about Selina should put on the dress and stand on a tub or something, and then the dress could be raffled.' She looked at Selina's horrified face. 'We'd choose a time when there were lots of people about so they could see you in the frock.' She turned back to John. 'I think the raffle tickets oughtn't to be very expensive, because everybody hasn't much pocket money.'

John wrote down this suggestion and looked without much hope at Augustus.

'Have you any ideas?'

'Could she wear it to church?'

John scribbled down the word 'Church', then laid down his pencil.

'Benjamin won't have any ideas so I'll give you mine.'

Benjamin sat up. He beat on the table with his fist.

'I have got an idea. It's a lovely idea. I thought we could borrow a pony and have a circus and Selina could be the lady who jumps through a hoop like in my book.'

John took up his pencil again and pretended to write this down. Actually he only wrote down 'Circus'. Then he leant back in his chair.

'Here's mine. When I was out this afternoon I met Colonel Day. He says they're going to sell the Abbey. He said, as they've got no children, there is no point in keeping it on; it's going to be sold this autumn. I said wouldn't he mind it going, and he said yes, because the Days have lived there for generations and it's old and all that, but now there's no one to look after it, so he and Mrs Day would be much more comfortable in a cottage. After I said goodbye to him I was thinking about the Abbey, and suddenly I wondered if we could borrow the garden and do a show there for charity next summer. I'd thought of any old show where Selina could wear her frock, but when Sally was talking about her ballet, I had another idea. Why shouldn't we do a pageant and let Selina be the girl who dreamed it, like in Sally's ballet?'

There was a pause while everybody took this idea in. Selina's eyes were shining.

'Who will write the pageant?'

Phoebe sprawled across the table.

'I will, if you like. I'm awfully good at poetry. I wrote a poem about a violet last term. I think it's beautiful:

> "You tell me stories of the present,
> Yes, and things that shall be yet,
> I would take thee as my model,
> Modest little violet."'

There were unpleasant sounds all round the table. Phoebe

stuck her chin up. 'There's no need to pretend to be sick. I write very good poetry for nine and a half, everybody says so, and if I don't write the pageant I'd like to know who else will. None of you write poetry as far as I know.'

It was not much good trying to silence Phoebe by squashing her. Almost every day they did try and silence her that way, but it never worked because she was of an unsquashable nature. The only real way to finish an argument was to make her see reason. John said patiently:

'Why should the pageant be written in poetry?'

Phoebe hesitated. She had never seen a play in a real theatre and John and Selina had. She had always thought plays were written in poetry, but from the way John spoke he might be going to put her in the wrong and she hated that.

'When we saw those plays at the Village Institute they were all in poetry, and that Shakespeare is a sort of poetry.'

John had Phoebe exactly where he wanted her.

'You're talking about something you know nothing about. You were too young to go to plays before the war, so you've never seen one, but I've seen *Treasure Island* and that wasn't poetry. You saw *Peter Pan* and *Where the Rainbow Ends*, Selina, were they in poetry?'

Selina tried to remember.

'I'm sure they weren't. The only thing I ever saw that was in a sort of poetry was *Dick Whittington*. I think it was all poetry, anyway it finished up in poetry, "And now we've had enough of this and that. Let's say farewell to Whittington and Cat."'

John turned back to Phoebe.

'You see, they're not written in poetry. Except pantomimes and we're not doing one of those.'

Sally had been dreaming, during the argument, about her ballet. She was wondering how much talking there'd got to be and how much dancing she could squeeze in. In the pause, as John finished speaking, she burst out:

'How much writing has there got to be?'

Christopher jumped because he had a good idea.

'I say, I know what we'll do. Let's have a pageant with four scenes in it, and let's each write our own. John can write one, Sally one, me one, Phoebe one, and Selina can write her bits at the beginning and the end about the girl.'

'One would think,' said Augustus, 'that people might remember other people who are sitting at the table.'

Sally, who was next to him, gave him an affectionate nudge.

'Don't be an ass. You know it takes you simply ages to write "Dear Granny, thank you for the present, love, Augustus." It would take you weeks and weeks to write down a scene in a pageant.'

Christopher was so aflame with his idea he hated being interrupted.

'Anyway I hadn't forgotten Augustus. What I was going to say was that each of us, when we write our scene, should write parts for any of the others which they need, and particularly for Augustus and Benjamin.'

'They'd be very useful,' Phoebe pointed out. 'They could be the children in every scene. We could dress Benjamin up as a little girl.'

Benjamin's face grew red.

'My dear, nobody will be able to dress me up as a little girl.'

'Nor,' added Augustus, 'is anybody going to make me wear white socks.'

18

John behaved like a proper chairman. He tapped on the table.

'Who is going to see Colonel Day about the Abbey?'

This called for thought. Christopher summed up the position.

'He likes you, he lets you fish there, but he's more likely to say yes to Phoebe. It's Phoebe that he always says he wishes was his daughter.'

'Gosh!' Sally exclaimed. 'He wouldn't say it if he knew her.'

John spoke quickly to prevent an argument.

'I don't think Phoebe can go alone if it's important. How would it be if Phoebe and I went together?'

Phoebe pushed her hair back with a proud gesture.

'One way and another you've all been very unpleasant and I don't think I will go.'

'Right,' said John. 'You come, Selina; after all, it's your pageant.'

Phoebe had not expected this. She kicked at the table leg.

'Well, I don't want Colonel Day to say no, so perhaps . . .'

John, looking like a director at a board meeting, drew his piece of paper nearer to him.

'I think that's all. We're going to do a pageant. We want to do it at the Abbey. Selina and I will ask Colonel Day for permission. Christopher, Sally, Phoebe, and I will write a scene each, and Selina will write the bits at the beginning and the end where she wears her frock and shoes. We've all, except Selina, got to write in parts for Augustus and Benjamin. I think we ought to ask Colonel Day if we can do it right at the end of the summer holidays. That means we've got the rest of these holidays and next term to write the scenes, and the Easter

19

holidays to give out the parts and plan what we're going to wear. Then all the summer holidays we can rehearse.'

Selina leant forward.

'Don't you think we ought to ask Aunt Ann and Uncle Jim if we may do it? And what are we going to do it for? I mean, there would be tickets and people paying.'

Everybody sat up at this. They all had a pet charity. John fancied the Air Force Benevolent. Christopher and Sally Naval War Libraries; Selina thought it should be the Red Cross; Augustus was a strong supporter of Our Dumb Friends' League. Benjamin misunderstood the argument and said, 'I've got five pennies in my moneybox.'

John wrote the charities down.

'Let's show the list to Dad and Mum and let them decide. It'll make them keen on the pageant to choose what it's going to help.'

Christopher nodded.

'I think Selina's right, but oughtn't we to find out about having the Abbey before we ask Dad and Mum about the pageant?'

Sally said:

'If we don't do it at the Abbey I don't quite know where we'd do it; we haven't got a place here to make a stage and there isn't room at the vicarage. The Abbey grounds would be just perfect. Do you think that if Phoebe is going to be sensible she might go with John to Colonel Day? He doesn't know Selina very well.'

Selina felt grateful to Sally. It would be so awful if Colonel Day said no just because she asked badly.

'It would be better.'

They looked at Phoebe. Phoebe was torn. She would have

liked to have been grand and said 'Go and see about the silly old pageant yourselves,' but she wanted to be the person to arrange it. She compromised by looking haughty but saying fairly nicely:

'All right. I'll go.'

John pretended to be busy with his sheet of paper. Actually all he did was to draw a bomber.

'That's all then. Except which comes first. Dad and Mum or Colonel Day.'

'Well,' said Sally, 'Mum is likely to argue a bit. She'll think the clothes are going to be a nuisance.'

'I should think she wouldn't mind if we promised to do them all ourselves,' Christopher pointed out. 'After all, they know we're thinking of some way for Selina to wear her frock and shoes. I should think they'd be jolly thankful we don't want to give a dance, because this doesn't mean eating anything.'

Selina felt that as the pageant was being planned entirely so that she could wear her frock and shoes she was going to be held partially responsible for it.

'I do think we ought to ask them first.'

John got up.

'All right, we'll tackle Mum now. And Dad after the surgery. Meeting's over.'

Phoebe looked at Selina.

'You better be careful, my girl. The end of August's an awful long way off. You watch out you don't grow. I'd be sorry for you but I couldn't help laughing if by the time we did the pageant you found the shoes were tight and the frock wouldn't meet.'

# CHAPTER THREE

*Asking at Home*

I t was not until suppertime that there was a chance to tackle the doctor and Mrs Andrews. The moment the meeting was over the family rushed over the house looking for Mrs Andrews, but she had gone on her bicycle over to the farm with whom they were rationed to fetch the eggs. Phoebe, Augustus, and Benjamin had to go to bed without knowing whether there was going to be a pageant or not. Augustus and Benjamin did not mind, but Phoebe was furious. When Selina and Sally had bathed and tucked up Augustus and Benjamin, and came to fetch her to bed, she was in a bad mood. She made one excuse after another to loiter.

Sally said:

'Oh, hurry up, do.'

Phoebe raised her eyebrows.

'Speak to me once more like that and I'll take another half hour.' In the end she was got into bed but still under protest. As Selina and Sally were leaving the room she spoke in a spitting-cat voice. 'All right, ask them when I'm not there and you'll see what'll happen. You'll make an awful mess of it and they'll say no.'

At first it looked as if Phoebe's words were only too true. Mrs Andrews's bicycle had punctured and she only got back just before supper. Nobody feels their best when they have sat at the side of the road mending a bicycle puncture. Doctor Andrews was particularly tired. He had seen more patients than usual at his evening surgery. Just as he was thankfully showing the last of them out Miss Lipscombe had said:

'Mrs Peters isn't so well. Her boy says her pains are awful and could you see her tonight?'

Doctor Andrews had made a grunting noise.

'I bet that fool of a woman has eaten a large meal, and how she thinks she's going to get over food-poisoning if she doesn't stick to my diet I don't know.' Then he had looked at Miss Lipscombe. 'You pass the Peterses' cottage on your way home, could you pop in and see what's wrong?'

Miss Lipscombe had given a martyred sigh.

'I suppose I never need any rest,' and then she had added, 'And just as I was looking forward to a nice little bit of supper before a warm fire.'

Doctor Andrews knew that if he annoyed Miss Lipscombe he would never find anyone else to help him, so he had been forced to smile, though he did not feel like it. He had patted her shoulder and said:

'All right, I'll go.'

Having to be nice to Miss Lipscombe when he did not feel nice, and having to go out again after supper had made him on edge. He was not in a good mood when he came in to supper.

When there is something that all the family want to ask the grown-ups about there is a good deal of nudging and looking at each other, each look saying, 'You start.' 'No, you.' In the end Doctor Andrews caught one of these nudges as he was passing a plate of spam.

'What's the excitement?'

It was Christopher's nudge at Sally the doctor had noticed, so one of them had to answer. Sally had been dreaming of her ballet ever since the committee and she knew she could not bear it if it never happened.

'We wanted to ask you something. We've got the most gorgeous idea. We want to do a pageant to help the Naval War Libraries.'

John leant towards his father.

'Or the Air Force Benevolent.'

Selina said:

'Or perhaps it better be the Red Cross and St John's.'

Mrs Andrews was helping the vegetables and seeing that everybody had plenty of winter greens, which she thought were good for children. She laid down her serving spoon.

'A pageant, darlings! But where would you get the clothes?'

They all answered her at once.

'Don't worry, we'll make them.'

Mrs Andrews looked quite pale.

'Out of what?'

'Oh, any old thing,' said John. 'There must be tons of bits of stuff that nobody wants.'

Mrs Andrews went back to helping the winter greens. She did not sound sarcastic, just sad.

'There has been clothes rationing since 1941 and all of you grow and grow, and everything that we had at the beginning of the war has been worn out. There isn't sufficient material in this house going abegging to make a pageant costume for a mouse.'

Sally refused to let her dream ballet vanish.

'But we could use unrationed materials. There must be some, aren't there?'

Doctor Andrews had been eating calmly through the clothes discussion. Now he laid down his knife and fork and looked at Sally.

'What are you going to do for money to buy unrationed materials, supposing there are any?'

John saw the whole discussion was getting out of hand.

'It's because of Selina's frock. You told us to think of some way she could wear it, and this is a way. Not a grand pageant, just two or three scenes from history, written by ourselves. We thought we'd ask Colonel Day if we could do it in the Abbey grounds. Selina, in her frock, will be the beginning and end of the pageant. She'll sort of dream it.'

Doctor Andrews loved history. He looked less tired.

'Written by yourselves? There isn't much history attached to the Abbey except rebuilding after fires, is there?'

'We're going to find out from Colonel Day,' Christopher explained, 'and if there isn't we can pretend things happened there.'

The doctor turned to Selina.

'And you're going to dream it all. Are you going to write it?'

Selina looked shocked at such a ghastly idea.

'Oh, no, it's only the explaining bits that I shall do. The

others are going to write a scene each. All except Augustus and Benjamin.'

'And we're going to write parts in for them,' John added.

'And when is this pageant to take place?'

The family were thrilled. The doctor had said 'this pageant'; that meant he was thinking of it as happening.

'The end of the summer holidays,' said Christopher. 'We thought we'd write the scenes before the Easter holidays, and give out the parts in the Easter holidays, and then learn them. Then we'd have all August to rehearse and get the clothes.'

Mrs Andrews said, more to herself than to anybody at the table:

'Get the clothes!'

The doctor believed in children having ideas and carrying them out themselves. He also thought that writing a pageant would be good for their history. He looked at Mrs Andrews.

'The clothes could be hired, I think. If they don't cost too much we might manage that. There's no chance of a summer holiday; it would keep all the family busy. What d'you say?'

Mrs Andrews found eight eyes glued to her face. Eight terribly eager eyes. She knew that hired clothes would not fit; she knew the pageant would make a terrible lot of work, but she could not bear to see the eight eyes look disappointed. She knew, too, that if she said no the doctor would agree with her.

'All right, darlings. If Colonel Day lets you use the Abbey grounds I won't say no.'

# CHAPTER FOUR

## Asking at the Abbey

John and Phoebe went to the Abbey the next morning. Selina and Sally took a lot of trouble making Phoebe tidy to go. Mrs Andrews was busy, which was a good thing, because she would have thought that Phoebe would be all right in her old winter coat, gum-boots, and a beret, whereas Selina and Sally knew that Colonel Day was a man who liked little girls to look very little-girlish.

'What you've got to do,' Sally explained to Phoebe, 'is to take off your coat the moment you get into the house. It's a pity it's such a mucky morning, but you certainly can't wear your gum-boots. You must wear your brown shoes and white socks.'

Phoebe was delighted to be dressed up, but she made a fuss about it because you never knew what luck might come out of making a fuss.

'It's all very well for you. How would you like to get up in a jersey and skirt, and as soon as you'd eaten your breakfast change into a frock?'

Sally watched Selina twisting Phoebe's curls round her fingers.

'It's all in a good cause. The jersey you had on this morning is terribly darned and your skirt's got an ink-stain. You looked so awful Colonel Day would be certain to say no.'

John, too, took a little trouble. He had cleaned his shoes and put on a clean shirt. As it happened, it was a bit of a waste being so tidy under their coats because they met the Colonel in the Abbey drive. It was queer really that it seemed necessary to tidy up a bit when going to call on the Colonel because he was not at all dressy himself. If everybody had not known he was Colonel Day they could quite easily have thought he was a tramp. He was wearing a very old pair of corduroy trousers, which he had possessed for so long that all the ribbing of the corduroy was rubbed away, and the material was down to its underneath skin, as it were. He had on his Home Guard boots. He was not wearing an overcoat, but three jerseys. The bottom one was green, the next was grey, and the top one was brown. They had holes in different places, so you could see all three jerseys at the same time. The Colonel was strolling along with his four dogs at his heels, and his stick in his hand. Now and then he stopped and had a look at his rhododendron bushes. One of the many nice things about Colonel Day was his quiet sameness. Some grown-up people behaved one way one minute and another way the next, but Colonel Day was always the same. Winter or summer he walked about with his dogs at his heels, prodding his plants with his stick; he gave a feeling that he had been doing just that for hundreds of years and would go on doing it for hundreds of years more. He spoke, which was his way, as if he had expected to meet whoever he was talking to on that very spot at that very moment.

'Mornin', John.' He laid a hand on Phoebe's shoulder. 'How's Phoebe?' They walked up the drive, one on each side of the Colonel. 'Nasty nip in the air this mornin'. If we go round to the kitchen door, shouldn't wonder if we got a cup of somethin' hot. My wife says that when we had a staff lookin' after the Abbey they always had a bit of a meal at eleven in the mornin'. Now there's only herself, Partridge, and Mrs Mawser, she says she doesn't see why she shouldn't have a meal at eleven too. We might join 'em.'

The Abbey had once really been an Abbey. It still had a cloister left which led up to the front door. There was, too, a high-walled garden, where, before Henry the Eighth turned them out, the monks had exercised. There was nothing of the original building left, but there was the most enormous kitchen, which Colonel Day's ancestors had built on at some time. It was, as Mrs Day said, a dreadful trial now. It had been intended for the days when there were head cooks and second cooks and third cooks, and scullions and spits for roasting large animals whole. It had a stone floor which, when the kitchen was built, would have been kept clean by some of the minor scullions. A lot of the Abbey was closed because Partridge, the butler, Mrs Mawser, the housekeeper, and Colonel and Mrs Day could not use fifty bedrooms, but they could not close the kitchen because it was the only one there was.

When the Colonel, John, and Phoebe came into the kitchen, Mrs Day, Partridge, and Mrs Mawser were sitting at one end of the huge kitchen table having cups of cocoa and rock-buns. The Colonel looked at his wife.

'Can you find three more cups, my dear?'

Mrs Day was thin and tall and looked her best on a horse. She had never been taught to do housework, and was not really good at it, but she tried very hard. Trying very hard in her case meant doing things fast, but not always in the best way, so that she usually had at least three burns and four cuts on her hands. She had three fingers tied up now; she held them out to John and Phoebe as she went to get them some cocoa.

'Fat. Tipped it over. Told me to be careful, didn't you, Partridge? Never was good at taking advice.' John said he hoped her fingers were not painful. Mrs Day had, at one time or another, broken most of the bones in her body hunting and thought nothing of a few burns. 'Don't hurt at all. Waste of the fat we mind, isn't it, Mawser?'

Partridge and Mrs Mawser had been in service at the Abbey since they were children. Mrs Mawser had been trained as a housemaid in the time of Colonel Day's father. Partridge went back even further. He could just remember seeing what he called 'the old gentleman', who was Colonel Day's grandfather, when he had first come to the house as boot-boy at the age of twelve. Both Partridge and Mrs Mawser were used to what they called 'the old ways'. When there had been a large household of servants there was a great deal of etiquette attached to life in the servants' hall, and both of them had been important people. Partridge had sat at the head of the staff table and carved, and everybody had called him Mr Partridge and looked up to him, and, as was the custom of the time, he was considered too grand to eat his pudding with the rest of the staff; he carried that into the housekeeper's room and ate it alone with Mrs Mawser. Both

Partridge and Mrs Mawser had liked it better when Mrs Day kept to what they called her own side of the house. It was not, in their opinion, at all a good idea her sitting at the kitchen table having snacks with them. Even if it made more work they would rather that she let them take the covers off the drawing-room furniture and had sat down in there and done nothing. Actually they both thought privately it would not make more work; they would at least know she was not breaking things or coming to any harm if she was sitting on a sofa.

'One that needs tidying after, Mr Partridge,' Mrs Mawser often said, and Partridge would nod solemnly and reply, 'Doesn't take to housework, Mrs Mawser, nor to be expected that she should.'

If Partridge and Mrs Mawser had done what they would like to have done, they would have stood up when the Colonel came in, but they had been told so often not to that they had at last learnt not to argue.

'Pack of nonsense,' Mrs Day said. 'New world, new ways, never too old to learn.'

While they were drinking their cocoa and eating their rock-buns the Colonel and Mrs Day talked about sensible things like ferrets and foxes. Then suddenly Mrs Day looked at Phoebe, who had, of course, taken off her coat.

'You two come up for anything special? Phoebe looks uncommon clean.'

John had meant to ask about the pageant when they had finished eating, but after Mrs Day saying that, it was no good hedging, they had to explain. He gave Phoebe a kick to tell her to get on with it. Phoebe was very good at asking favours, she leant on the table and looked up at the Colonel with what the family called her 'puppy-asking face'. She told him about Selina's frock and what they had planned. At the end she clasped her hands.

'Could we, oh, could we do it in the grounds of the Abbey?'

The Colonel did not answer her directly, he looked at Mrs Day.

'Philip has always said the lower lawn was a natural theatre.'

Mrs Day nodded.

'Ought to know. Done nothing but produce plays since he was in his cradle.'

Partridge cleared his throat.

'Do you think Mr Philip will return to the theatre after the war, madam?'

Mrs Day lit a cigarette.

'Certain to.'

Mrs Mawser sighed.

'Such a lovely little boy, he was. I remember, sir, the first time Miss Silvy brought him here. She held him up to you, sir, and told you to have a look at your nephew, and you said he was the cut to make a Guardsman. Such a pity, I always thought. The theatre seems a queer way of life for a gentleman like Mr Philip.'

John and Phoebe tried not to look impatient though they felt it. They knew all about the Colonel's nephew, Philip Day, who was a Squadron Leader in the Air Force. It seemed a waste of time to talk about him when they were here to discuss the pageant. The Colonel evidently sensed what they were feeling. He looked at John.

'What's this pageant goin' to be about?'

'We had thought, sir, it could be things that had happened at the Abbey.'

The Colonel was silent for a moment.

'Happened here? There was that business of turning out the monks, but nothing much else. This is one of the few houses which Queen Elizabeth never slept in.'

John frowned, trying to find the right words to explain what he meant.

'But it's been here so long, at least some sort of house has, history could have happened.'

The Colonel had very blue eyes. When he was interested they shone as if a lamp were lighted behind them. They shone now.

'That's true. True of every house if it comes to that. Your house is pretty new, but even it has seen history.'

'Ours! It's Victorian.'

'But a lot's gone on. Somebody left it to go to the Boer War; the family in it at that time went rejoicin' on the village green at the relief of Mafeking. They certainly felt quite a shock at the passing of Queen Victoria.'

Mrs Day broke in:

'Young Frank, old Dr Frank's son, got decorated in the 1914 war. Old Dr Frank saved half the village time of the influenza epidemic.'

'Then there was your bit,' said the Colonel. 'You were only a baby, John. But you were around when George the Fifth died. That's a bit of history all right. Then there was the short reign of Edward the Eighth and the crownin' of this present King and Queen.'

'God bless them.' Partridge spoke devoutly.

Mrs Mawser nodded.

'And the dear Princesses.'

The Colonel smiled at John.

'You've seen enough history in this war to make a pageant on its own. Dunkirk, formin' of the Home Guard. Never thought to see a khaki overcoat behind every door in the village, did you? Then there were the road blocks. And the removin' of road signs, and all the rest of it. You've seen some history all right, old man, and you too, Phoebe. You'd be surprised if you could come back in a hundred years. You'd find your part all written in the history books.'

John was interested, but this talk was not fixing up about the pageant.

'But we wanted dressing-up history, you know, knights and things. I suppose they might have come to the Abbey, mightn't they?'

The Colonel pulled his chair away from the table and crossed his legs.

'Sure to have. Boys your age would have been sent to the monks for a bit of schoolin'.'

John was thrilled.

'There aren't many horses in the village just now, but we could think of a pretty good scene in which a boy who had been at school here was fetched away by his father . . .' He broke off, ideas forming in his head. Perhaps he could think of a way for the boy to give a display of jousting or whatever it was. Pretty good idea really. You could borrow anybody for the father and stick in a monk or two. All the talking could be done by the boy.

Partridge cleared his throat.

'There is the affair of the monks being expelled, sir.'

The Colonel frowned.

'Yes. But the children won't want to be messin' about with curses.'

John stopped thinking about the boy knight. The Days never spoke very much about the curse on the Abbey. Now was a chance to get the story straight.

'Do you think there really is a curse? I mean, however angry you were at being turned out, could you make a curse last for ever?'

The Colonel pulled one of Phoebe's curls.

'You're not interested in curses, are you, Phoebe?'

'I dote on them. I like all those sort of things. I like witches and ghosts and murders and blood.'

The Colonel continued to play with Phoebe's hair. He spoke as though he was thinking out loud.

'Pretty good fellows those monks. They lived very comfortably, you know, rich; they'd taken their vows, cut themselves off from life; must have felt bitter when everything was taken from them and they were turned out into the world. The Abbot who watched them go must have been a worried man. A lot of them would have been old. Many of them must have spent years in the Abbey. Can't blame him if he felt like puttin' a curse on the place.'

Mrs Day tapped her cigarette ash into a saucer.

'Unfair, I always thought. Curse should have gone to the person who turned the monks out, not the people who came after.'

'Don't know about that,' said the Colonel. 'It was a curse on the buildin' really. Neither the Abbey, nor any building after it, was to stand. They should be destroyed by fire or water until such time as the place should be returned to God's service. Pretty comprehensive curse.'

John was so interested he had forgotten the pageant for the moment.

'And they all have been destroyed by fire or water?'

The Colonel nodded.

'Mostly fire. This place has been burnt and rebuilt, and burnt and rebuilt. If the curse doesn't manage on its own it seems somebody's bound to help it along. There was a nasty fire started in the Georgian wing about twenty years ago. Matter of fact, the fire was noticed early and was bein' got under, but, my word, the damage all those fire brigades did with their water!' He looked at Mrs Mawser and Partridge. 'Do you remember?'

Mrs Mawser made clucking noises.

'Oh, yes, sir. The white drawing-room! Well away from the fire too. It has never been the same room.'

'Nor the guest-rooms over it,' said Partridge. 'Just careless-ness, I always said so.'

The Colonel pulled himself away from his thoughts.

'Don't know what I'm telling you about this for. There's one thing I don't want, and that's any scene of the old Abbot and his cursin' in your pageant. It's twenty years since we had a fire. We'll let sleeping dogs lie. Thought for certain we'd have had some incendiary bombs.' He looked at Phoebe. 'This pageant will be a lot of work, you know.'

'I know, but lots of fun.' Phoebe leant against the Colonel. 'Please say yes. If we don't have it here there's nowhere else for us to do it.'

The Colonel looked across at his wife.

'What d'you say, Dora?'

Mrs Day stubbed out her cigarette.

'Good idea. Make a nice wind-up as we're clearing out in the autumn.' She got up and patted Mrs Mawser's shoulder. 'Had a lot of fun here, haven't we, Mawser? Do us good to have something to take our minds off the move.'

John got up too.

'I say, thanks awfully. I'm afraid it'll mean our being here rather a lot in August for rehearsals, you know, but, of course, we needn't come near the house.' He held out his hand to Phoebe. 'Come on. Let's go and tell the others.'

# CHAPTER FIVE

## Writing

There is something about the spring term which, in spite of its name, makes it look long and dreary before it starts. The spring term looked especially long to the family this year. The night before John went back to Marlborough the doctor had a firm word with them all.

'I'm not going to have this pageant business upsetting your school work. I know that you all plan to write your scene, or finish it, during the term, but if I get news that any one of you is slacking the pageant's off.'

The doctor saying this made John call a quick family committee before bedtime. At least, it was before Phoebe's bedtime; Augustus and Benjamin were already in bed. They met in John and Christopher's bedroom. John sat on his box, which had been packed that afternoon. Selina and Christopher and Sally sat on one bed, and Phoebe on the other by herself. John kept his eyes fixed on Phoebe while he was talking.

'Look here, it's up to everybody to see the pageant isn't off! I should think the best way is some kind of a fine if anyone's losing a place in their form.'

Phoebe, who was sitting on the side of the bed, bounced up on to her knees. She leant on the foot-rail.

'Everybody won't be able to keep their place in form. It depends a lot on the other girls. It won't be my fault if Felicity Jones gets one of her working fits on and gets above me.'

Sally looked as severe and elder-sisterish as she could manage.

'Everybody knows that you can be somewhere near the top of your form if you like. Felicity Jones only gets above you when you don't work.'

Phoebe beat the bed-rail with her fists.

'I'm the only member of this family who is at the top of any form, and none of you know how hard I have to work to keep there. Look at Selina. She and Sally are in the same form and Selina is more than a year older than Sally, and all she manages to do is to keep one place above Sally, and then they're only thirteenth and fourteenth in the form. Anybody can manage to go on being thirteenth and fourteenth without working at all.'

The fact that Selina had to fight hard to keep above Sally was one of those things which it was considered bad form to talk about because it was throwing misfortune in Selina's face. It was not her fault that she had been what the mistresses called 'badly grounded'.

Sally spoke quickly.

'Shut up.'

Christopher had an idea.

'Let's do it the other way round. I mean, let's all try and go up one place from where we finished last term, and then Dad can't say anything at all. We might give a prize to anyone who does. We might all put some money in a general box to be shared amongst the prize-winners.'

The idea was good, and after discussion it was decided that they would each put half a crown on one side. Christopher had a moneybox which would do to keep the prize-money in. It was on the top of the cupboard. He fetched it down.

'It's a tin that I made for collecting for the Cottage Hospital, and then there were enough real collecting boxes and we didn't use it. It can only be opened by cutting it.'

The family could not provide the half-crowns that night because, of course, being the end of the holidays, they were poor. John had his going-back money, but he could not spare half a crown from that at the moment. Selina had two shillings which she fetched and put in. John managed a shilling, Christopher and Sally one and sixpence between them, and Phoebe fourpence. Christopher wrote these figures on the paper which was round the outside of the tin. The box made quite a nice rattle.

It was not the writing of their scenes in the pageant which made losing places in form dangerous; it was the thinking about scenes. Selina loathed geometry, and the mistress who taught it to her form had one of those droning voices which made it very difficult to listen, especially when you were not interested anyway. Often when she should have been thinking of an isosceles triangle, or something equally serious, she was seeing herself coming out between the shrubs at the back of the lower lawn at the Abbey, and walking towards the audience and saying—what? She had tried ever so many openings but none seemed quite right. Geometry lessons could have become the half hours for trying out new ideas. 'Ah me! 'Tis sad to be a ghost.' 'Ladies and gentlemen, I am the spirit of the Abbey.' 'For nigh six hundred years . . .'

Christopher bicycled to his school. It was three miles away. He always meant to start early and have a bit of time in hand at the other end before school prayers, but it was one of the things he seldom managed. He was always forgetting something. He would just be getting on to his bicycle when Mrs Miggs would shout from the kitchen door, 'You've forgotten your elevenses,' or he would remember that he had left in his bedroom something he meant to swap with some other boy. Or his mother would call from the window, 'You must take your mackintosh, darling, you can see it's going to rain.' In the ordinary way it was possible to make up time on the road, but this term Christopher found that difficult. He started off bicycling hard and fast, and then suddenly, as he was coasting down the first hill, he would be thinking of the pageant, and the next thing he would notice was that he was dawdling along the last lane that led up to his school, and he would have to spurt like mad to get to his place in time for roll-call.

The trouble with Christopher was that he could not make up his mind what he wanted to be in the pageant. He was not fussy about period. He had it in his mind that he would like to be somebody most frightfully funny. The trouble about being funny was that he had to have somebody to be funny with, and he could not think whom. He felt sure none of the others would like those sort of parts where they kept saying dull things in order that he could make funny answers. As he ambled along on his bicycle he pictured every sort of person: a very fat man who was drunk; a Court jester; an acrobat at a fair; a sort of Friar Tuck person; a funny bandit.

He knew, from listening to the wireless, the sort of scene he wanted. He wanted to be funny like Bob Hope or Charlie MacCarthy, but he found, when he came to imagine himself in any of the parts, that he did not know many original funny things to say. He kept thinking of funny things to do, like making a speech on a chair and falling through the seat. It was all very worrying.

Sally always was a dreamer, which was lucky for Selina, because if Sally had attended to what she was doing she would have passed Selina easily in form and, in fact, gone up into the form above her. This term it was particularly hard for Sally to concentrate on her work, for there were two things to think about so much more interesting than lessons. One was the end of term ballet. Always at the end of the spring term the school held a Commemoration Day, at which the girls gave a display of work they had done throughout the year. There was singing, a scene from a classic, and a ballet. The girls' school was keen on ballet.

At Linkwell, which was three miles away, there was a real ballet school. The head of it was a Russian and she sent a teacher twice a week to hold ballet classes at the girls' school. The classes were on Wednesday afternoons and Saturday mornings, and it was an honour to be allowed to attend them. You had to be picked from the ordinary school dancing-classes as being suitable, and then you had to be approved by the teacher from Linkwell. Sally had been picked to attend the ballet classes when she was nine and a half. It had not been easy because money was scarce at home and the ballet class was an extra, and as well it meant extra clothes as well as block shoes. It was only after Mrs Andrews had been over to see the ballet class and talked to the teacher from Linkwell that she and the doctor decided they must manage to let Sally have the lessons. Mrs Andrews had said to the doctor:

'Apparently Sally has got talent. She'll have to earn her living when she grows up. This teacher from Linkwell says that even if the child is no good for stage-work she will certainly be able to teach.'

Sally did not know about this conversation, but she did know that Miss Faulkes, the teacher from Linkwell, thought she was getting on well and had her in mind for the solo in the Commemoration ballet.

Then, of course, there was the pageant ballet. It was disappointing to Sally to think that she would not be able to do any point work, but that would be impossible on grass. Instead she was working out something rather like the *Midsummer Night's Dream* dances. She could not quite see how to fit a fairy ballet into a pageant, but she knew for certain that fairies would look lovely on the lower lawn at the Abbey. There were plenty of children in the village who could be taught simple things like running in time and dancing in rings.

She would have got much nearer to making up her mind about the ballet if, in the second week of the term, she had not had a horrible fright. When the week's marks were read out Selina was still thirteenth, but she had fallen to sixteenth, which was only three from the bottom. By the most extraordinary good luck the doctor did not ask that week what her place was in form, but she felt sickish all the week in case he would, and was only really comfortable inside when the next marks list was read and she was back at fourteenth. Sally was not the only one who was frightened; so were Selina, Christopher, and Phoebe, and Christopher and Phoebe told Sally what they thought about her. After that fright she managed to push both the school ballet and the pageant to the back of her mind during lessons, but since lessons and homework took so much of the day her pageant thinking did not get on very fast.

It was quite true Phoebe could be top of her class if she wanted to. To make quite certain that she won the prize-money, for the first three weeks of the term Phoebe worked hard and did become top of the form.

'I need the money so badly,' she told Selina and Sally. 'You ought to have seen me at that party I went to with Augustus and Benjamin. I saw myself in a long glass. There were big spaces at the back of my frock between the buttons, and my skirt was so short that, though I had on those tiny pants, every time I leant over my whole bottom showed. If I had the money I could go to Mum next time we get a clothing book and say, "Give me the coupons and I'll buy the dress."'

After three weeks Phoebe got tired of working so hard, and some weeks she let Felicity Jones beat her. In those weeks she got a lot of her part in the pageant written. She had decided to be Anne Boleyn as a child. She planned a scene in which grown-up people round the child, Anne, could see how wonderful she was, and how one day such a child was sure to be a queen. She wrote parts for Mrs Miggs, Miss Lipscombe, and Partridge. The scene opened with little Anne giving orders to her staff. Miss Lipscombe spoke first. Phoebe had given her the part of Anne Boleyn's very bad-tempered governess.

> 'Come, my Lady Anne,
> To your books.
> Fie, fie, no sulky looks.'

Then Partridge spoke:

> 'Fie, Mistress Dogsberry,
> That is no way to name
> This child who shall have fame.'

Then Phoebe spoke:

> 'The sun is out
> And all the flowers bow down
> As if I wore a crown.'

Mrs Miggs broke in there in the part of the old nurse:

> 'Hush, hush, child,
> I declare
> You make me faint with fear.'

The pageant went on for half an exercise book like that. It was to finish with the old butler, the governess, and the nurse making a crown of flowers and fastening a train to Anne's shoulders, and kneeling and curtsying to her as she swept out.

Phoebe planned to bring on Augustus and Benjamin at the right moment as pages to carry her train.

News of John's scene came in his letters. He wrote that he had managed to get most of it done, but that he might have to alter some of it in the Easter holidays, and that his place in form was all right.

Sally got her ballet finally planned with the help of some girls in her ballet class. They were boarders and could not take part in the pageant, but they were full of ideas and frightfully envious of Sally. They suggested letting somebody be royalty visiting the Abbey, and the ballet could be a masque performed in their honour.

His form-master gave Christopher the idea for his scene. He was telling his class about strolling players, especially the old moralities. When Christopher learnt that in some moralities the devil had been a funny character and run about with a pitchfork, he saw at once the scene he would write. He would use boys from his school for players and everybody else that he could rake in as audience, and the scene would be mummers visiting the village.

By three-quarters of the way through the term only Selina was behind with her scenes. She had got a lot of words down, but could not find a proper opening line for either her prologue or her epilogue.

'The trouble is,' she explained to Sally, 'that you all talk to other people, but everything I write down I've got to say all by myself.'

Sally had just learnt the frightful news that she was not dancing the leading part in the Commemoration ballet. It was a dull, principal role of a statue of Cupid who only came to life at the end of the ballet, and then had to pose rather than dance; all the same, a principal role was a principal role and she was very disappointed. It was a difficult moment for her to see why anyone should mind doing anything as a solo, but she tried to be sympathetic.

'Couldn't you not make her say anything first? Couldn't she come on and walk slowly down to the footlights, only there won't be footlights because it's out of doors, and then explain naturally to the audience who she is and all that?'

'Well, who is she?'

'She's the daughter of the Days or the spirit of the Abbey or something.'

'I know, but it's so vague.'

It was Phoebe who made up Selina's mind for her.

'She can't possibly be a ghost in that dress, and I don't see how she could be a daughter of the Days. They haven't a daughter and everybody knows they haven't.'

Sally sighed at the stupidity of Phoebe.

'Not a daughter of these Days, but a daughter of all the Days who ever lived in the Abbey.'

Selina looked worried.

'D'you mean a sort of mixed-up daughter, bits from every generation?'

Sally nodded.

'Yes, all prithees, and fie, fies to begin with, and finish with saying "that will be wizard", or something like that.'

Phoebe gave Selina's arm a kind pat.

'Don't you listen to her, my child. I know what you are. You are England. You must write a beautiful patriotic speech and you can carry a Union Jack.'

Selina did not like the idea. She did not fancy mixing up her lovely white frock and satin shoes with a flag.

Sally only liked half the idea.

'You're thinking of Britannia, Phoebe. If she's Britannia she wants a trident and a shield and long plaits, and heaps of chest. Selina hasn't any chest. Besides, the whole idea is to wear her new frock?'

Phoebe gave a pleased skip.

'I know what she is. She's an English rose. She must have a rose in her hand, or something like that awful girl did in that concert they had for the Red Cross.'

Selina felt better. Roses would go well with her frock.

'If only I could think of a sentence to say first.'

They were in the middle of the lane which led to the village. It was a muddy, wet day and they were all carrying their homework, but none of these things disturbed Phoebe. She walked back up the lane, then turned to face the other two.

'Now you watch me, Selina; this is what you do.'

She held out her arms with her satchel dangling from one hand and minced towards them, splashing through the puddles. As she reached them, she clasped her hands, satchel and all.

'You must imagine I've got my arms full of roses.' She raised her head and spoke in a very grand voice. 'I am the spirit of England . . .'

'Let's hope Selina looks a bit better than you do,' said Sally, 'otherwise she's going to make people laugh. If you could see yourself! The moment you started to speak you stuck your tummy out.'

Selina had thought Phoebe did not look too bad. Of course nobody could look like the spirit of England in a brown school coat that was old and worn, a shabby brown beret, and muddy gum-boots, and yet there was something very pageanty about the way she had spoken. Selina, in her mind, could see the lower lawn at the Abbey, not as it was now with sodden grass and bare trees, but bright green and all the trees in full leaf, and herself in her white dress. She would not look pretty, of course, though they would be made up, which would be a help; still, nobody could avoid looking rather nice in that dress and those satin shoes, and roses were always lovely. If she was the spirit of England, even she could write a nice little speech. It need not be long, and both times that she came on she could begin the same way, 'I am the spirit of England.' She followed Sally and Phoebe up the lane.

'I think that's a pretty good idea, and I shall use it.' She hurried to catch up with Sally. 'If you were me, would you have pink or red roses?'

# CHAPTER SIX

———•———

## *The Holidays Begin*

It seemed impossible, when everybody had worked so hard, that the pageant should hang fire at Easter, but it did. By the beginning of the holidays every scene was written, nobody had lost their place in form, all the half-crowns were paid in, and Phoebe looked like winning them. She had finished the term top of her form, and, though she had not been top all the term, she had done better than anybody else, so if she did as well next term the half-crowns were as good as hers.

What delayed the pageant preparations was rumours of peace in Europe. The war had been going on so long that Benjamin and Augustus were born during it, and Phoebe had been too small to know what peace was like. The twins talked as if they remembered a lot but it was mostly talk. Selina and John could remember, but even they did not remember a celebration, for there had been nothing to celebrate since the Coronation, and, though John had helped a bit with decorating for that, he had been too small to be much use.

Now such celebrations as they had never dreamed of were planned. A monster bonfire on the hill. Fireworks. A torch-light procession and, as well of course, there were decorations. Apart from arranging how to decorate their own house, as a family they were in great demand: they gave advice and help to half the village.

The delay in the pageant arrangements drew Selina and Sally together. Even when there was peace in Europe it did not seem likely that there would be parties and dances.

'There will still be food difficulties, darlings, and transport, and, in the winter, heating,' Mrs Andrews explained. 'I don't think you should count on too much even when the war really ends and the Japanese are beaten.'

Selina knew Mrs Andrews was generally right, and, in any case, the Japanese were not beaten yet; meanwhile she was growing. Peace or war, it seemed her one chance of wearing her cream organdie and satin shoes was the pageant. Sally, with the Commemoration ballet behind her, was dreaming of nothing but her pageant ballet.

'We aren't getting on at all,' she complained to Selina. 'Nobody but me has copied out any parts, and we ought to have a committee. It's silly all of us going separately to people to ask them to act. Most of the people are going to be asked to act more than one part.'

'Couldn't you get Christopher to see a meeting is impor-tant?' Selina suggested.

They were talking in the schoolroom. Sally was using the

edge of the mantelpiece as a practice-bar. She went on exer-
cising while she spoke.

'They don't want to do anything as dull as copy parts. There's
such lots to do outside. Like going up with Mr Pettigrew's
tractor to make the bonfire, or painting "Thank you, boys" on a
board. I must say I like painting things on boards myself.'

Selina said:

'But if the parts aren't copied out and given to the people
who've got to learn them before the end of these holidays we
can't start rehearsing at the beginning of the summer holidays.
Couldn't you and I copy them?'

Sally was busy with some *frappées*.

'We could but they wouldn't let us. They'd feel too mean
making bonfires and things while we slaved writing.'

Selina was at the window swinging the blind-cord backwards and forwards.

'It's such a lovely frock. I had organdie for parties when I
lived in Hong Kong. Not long like this one, of course. I was too
little for long frocks, but I remember the lovely way it stuck out.'

Sally glanced over her shoulder at Selina. Selina seldom
mentioned Hong Kong. It was not much good when your
mother and father were prisoners there and you never heard
from them. They were all sorry for Selina, but they never
quite knew what to say when she talked about Hong Kong.
They usually said something as quickly as possible about
something else. Sally spoke in a hurry.

'I wish Mum had a sister who was my godmother and lived
in America who sent me frocks and shoes.'

Selina thought having your mother's sister in America such
a poor consolation for having a father and mother in a prison

camp that she did not bother to answer; she just went on swinging the blind-cord and feeling miserable. She had looked forward to the pageant and now it seemed as if it might never happen.

They were interrupted by Mrs Miggs. Mrs Miggs was a Londoner who had been evacuated to the village. She was supposed to come to the house every day except Saturdays to what she called 'oblige'. Actually she did not come every day. Lots of things could turn up which seemed to her more important. 'I heard there was shoes come in at Linkwell. I been waiting for shoes for months so I pop on a bus.' 'My rheumatics was cruel yesterday. Must 'ave been the weather. "No good goin' to Mrs Andrews in this state," I says.' 'I was comin' to you when I see a queue outside the shop. "Somethin's goin'," I said; "pity to miss it; Mrs Andrews will understand." '

Mrs Andrews understood only too well that Mrs Miggs might not turn up and at breakfast most days she said, 'I hope Mrs Miggs comes today.' When Mrs Miggs did come she was wonderful. She scrubbed floors at a tremendous speed; and sang while she scrubbed. Her favourite song was 'Rule, Britannia'. Oddly enough, though she sang it so often, she never got the words quite right, and did not stick even to her own inaccurate version. She was a scraggy little woman, but very gay. She looked even gayer than she was, because she always wore a hat which was never on straight but slipped to a more and more rakish angle as she worked.

Mrs Miggs beamed at the girls.

'You'll 'ave to 'op it or sit on the table. I'm givin' this oilcloth a good polish.'

All the family were devoted to Mrs Miggs, so without

discussing what they should do Sally and Selina climbed on to the table. Mrs Miggs piled the chairs on top of each other; she hummed 'Rule, Britannia' through her teeth. Because they had been talking about the pageant, Sally suddenly decided, even though she had not written a part for her herself, to sound Mrs Miggs to see how she felt about acting.

'Did you know we were going to have a pageant next holidays?'

Mrs Miggs stopped humming.

'I ought'er. None of you talked of anythin' else at Christmas.'

Sally hugged her knees.

'Did you know Phoebe had written you a big part, and Christopher wants you to act in his scene?'

Mrs Miggs was on her knees polishing. She looked up at Sally. Her eyes twinkled.

'Phoebe told me time and again, "You're to be my ole nurse," she said. Laugh! "I'll ole nurse you," I told her.'

Selina looked anxious.

'But it's a real part. It's in poetry.'

Mrs Miggs gave a wheezy chuckle.

'Po'try! I can see meself! If Phoebe wants me in the pageant she should put me on to a bit of dancin'. "Knees up, Mother Brown", that's my ticket.'

'What's that?' Sally asked.

Mrs Miggs chuckled again.

'When we 'ave what they call this VE Day you'll see. I'll be dancin' it round the bonfire.'

Selina said:

'But, Mrs Miggs, you would act a part, wouldn't you? The pageant's going to earn money for charity.'

Mrs Miggs sniffed.

'Charity begins at 'ome. What charity is it?'

Sally was quick at sensing what was at the back of a person's mind. She sensed now that Mrs Miggs had strong views on what charities she supported. Exactly what charity the pageant was to be in aid of had not yet been decided. Why should not Mrs Miggs choose? She gave Selina a nudge, hoping she would catch what she was doing.

'We haven't quite decided. It might be the Red Cross.'

Mrs Miggs went on polishing.

'I give me penny a week to that.'

'Or the Naval War Libraries.'

'Never held with readin'. Bad for the eyesight.'

'Or Our Dumb Friends' League.'

Mrs Miggs shook her head.

'Two legs comes before four legs with me.'

'Or the Air Force Benevolent.'

Mrs Miggs sat up, her eyes shining.

'Ah, now you're talkin'. There's nothin' I wouldn't do for those boys.' She wagged her polisher at Sally. 'You're a sly one, you are. Still, I might even say a bit of po'try if it done those boys any good.'

Selina and Sally told John, Christopher, and Phoebe that the charity was fixed, and that Mrs Miggs would act in the pageant. They hoped all this important news would take their minds off peace celebrations and back to the pageant, but it did not. Mr Sprig, the landlord of The Abbey Arms, the village public house, had decided to floodlight the Union Jack, the Stars and Stripes, and the Russian and Chinese flags, only nobody had a Russian or Chinese flag, so he had asked John and Christopher to go into Linkwell and see if they could buy them for him. Phoebe, who had gone to The Abbey Arms with the boys, had arranged to go back that afternoon and help Mrs Sprig and the barmaid make red, white, and blue roses to decorate the bar. When you want to do one job and ought to be doing another, the only thing to do is to get out of sight. John, Christopher, and Phoebe did just that. John said:

'That's fine. I say, Christopher, if we can't get those flags, what about buying paints and painting some? Let's go and see what colours we've got left.'

Phoebe said:

'I knew Mrs Miggs was going to act. I asked her myself, thank you. Oh, goodness, my hands are dirty. I must wash them.'

Sally looked at Selina and her face was most expressive.

'Aren't they hateful! They won't listen in case we make them copy the parts.'

Mrs Miggs proved Selina's and Sally's unexpected ally. The next morning she was cleaning the passage outside the surgery. It was a very wet day, the sort of day when, however carefully you wipe your feet, you leave sole-marks on a clean floor. The doctor, although he had been out in his car and had only walked from the gate to the door, left marks as if he were Robinson Crusoe. Mrs Miggs looked at the marks on her polish and, though she did not say anything, there was something very pointed about the sudden way she stopped humming 'Rule, Britannia'. The doctor paused.

'Sorry, Mrs Miggs. I did wipe them.'

Mrs Miggs was mollified.

'Can't really 'elp it, I dare say. Shockin' dirty in the country. Give me good old London.'

'Hope you're not leaving us. We couldn't get on without you.'

Mrs Miggs gave her wheezy chuckle.

'Gettin' very popular all of a sudden. You can't get on without me, and the children can't act their pageant without me.'

The doctor had been going into his surgery. Now he stopped.

'You're acting in it, are you? What are you going to be?'

'I couldn't rightly say, sir. Phoebe says I'm her ole nurse. I speak po'try. My grandson says I better bring the piece to 'im and 'e'll learn it me. Wonderful at learnin' is our Alfie.'

'Good idea. You let him teach it to you. Have you much to learn?'

'I don't know, sir.'

'Haven't you got the part?'

'Oh, no, sir.'

Mrs Miggs went back to her polishing. The doctor went into his surgery to plan his day's round of visits with Miss Lipscombe, but although he had a busy morning he did not forget his talk with Mrs Miggs. He had hardly sat down to lunch before he said:

'How far has this pageant got?'

There was a breath of a pause and then John said:

'Getting on fine. It's all written.'

Christopher added:

'No good rushing now. We can't start rehearsing until the summer holidays.'

Phoebe said grandly:

'My scene's all in poetry.'

The doctor went on helping everybody to cod.

'I hear Mrs Miggs has a part. Who else is going to act in it?'

Sally was delighted that the pageant was to be discussed.

'I want Mrs Day. She's to be Queen Elizabeth and I want two ladies-in-waiting. I could get two tall girls from school for those.'

Christopher said:

'I want an awful lot of people. Seven people besides me to be mummers, and Miss Lipscombe to be a witch, and masses of rabble.'

Phoebe helped herself to mustard sauce.

'Besides Mrs Miggs I want Mr Partridge and Miss Lipscombe.'

The doctor looked at John.

'Who's in your scene, old man?'

John had not meant the casting of his scene to be discussed at the moment. It was not that he was not keen on the pageant, but there were such a lot of other things to do.

'Matter of fact I wanted you. There are only three people who speak. The boy who's been at school at the Abbey. His father, that's you, who's come to take him home, and the Abbot. I want Mr Laws for him. He mostly does blessings and things in Latin. Being a parson he'll know those. The rest are just friends of the father's. They're all on horses so I thought I'd ask some of the farmers. They've only got to ho-ho.'

The doctor had helped everybody else so he took his own fish.

'Don't know if I could manage it. What's to happen to the patients?'

'We could do the pageant on your afternoon off,' Sally

suggested. 'Doctor Wilson always does any calls on Thursdays, doesn't he?'

'Does, if he's here, but he might be on holiday in September.'

Selina said:

'Could you ring him up? You could ask him when his holiday's going to be, and whatever day it isn't going to be we could do the pageant.'

Sally felt hope rising. They really were getting on. She had thought the pageant would be on a Thursday, and so had looked up dates on a calendar.

'The best day for us, Dad, is Thursday, the 20th. We could make it earlier if we had to, but the 20th gives us lots of time for rehearsals and to sell the tickets and all that, and there'll be posters to paint.'

The doctor saw that at least Sally's interest had not flagged.

'We'll ring Doctor Wilson after lunch and see what he says.'

After lunch they stood round the telephone while the doctor telephoned. Doctor Wilson's voice came in a rather growly way over the line.

'Haven't fixed up my holiday. Have to take it when I can. Probably won't get one.'

'Well, do you know any week in September when you won't be taking it?'

Doctor Wilson could be heard fumbling with his notebook at the other end of the telephone.

'Didn't mean to go away in September. Hoping to get to Scotland beginning of October.'

'Well, you put down against Thursday, the 20th of

September, "Promised Andrews to be on call". My children are doing a pageant at the Abbey. They want me to take part.'

There was a pause in which they were sure Doctor Wilson was writing. Presently they heard a chuckle on the line.

'Shall get my calls put through to the Abbey that afternoon. Wouldn't miss seeing you in a pageant for a hundred pounds. What are you going to be? Henry the Eighth?'

It was a big moment. It made for the moment the peace celebrations fade and the pageant become terribly important. The date of the pageant fixed! One ticket as good as sold! They felt a sudden surge of excitement inside. It was the first time the pageant had got off their exercise books and into real life, as it were. They could say, 'The performance will be on September the 20th.' When they asked people to act it was so much better to say, 'Will you act in a pageant on September the 20th' than 'In a pageant some time in September?'

The doctor put down the telephone.

'That's fixed. Now, where's this part?'

John began one of those roundabout explanations that sound splendid when they are in your head, and very thin as the words come out.

'As a matter of fact, Dad, the parts won't be ready till tomorrow. I mean, not all of them won't. You see, we didn't think anybody would need to begin to learn them just yet.'

The doctor liked accuracy.

'When you say not all of them, how many parts are ready?'

'Mine are,' said Sally. She came over to her father's desk and leant on it, and played with his appointment book. 'You see, Dad, in most of the scenes it's a terrible lot of writing. It doesn't matter to me because I've only got a queen and two ladies-in-waiting that speak, but Christopher's got parts and parts. It's a terrible thing to have to spend one's holidays writing things over and over again.'

The doctor glanced at his watch, decided he could spare five minutes, and sat down.

'Can't have a typist, it'll eat away the profits. How many parts really are there to write?' He drew his writing-pad towards him and took his fountain pen out of his pocket. 'How many parts in your scene, Phoebe?'

'Me, Mr Partridge, Mrs Miggs, and Miss Lipscombe. Augustus and Benjamin come in but they don't say anything.'

The doctor wrote on his pad.

'And yours are written, Sally. What parts have you got, Christopher?'

Christopher began counting on his fingers.

'Eight mummers, including me, and four people speak in the village, including a witch. I thought Miss Lipscombe could be that, and then there's the people I put down as just rabble. They only have to roar with laughter each time I'm funny; you see, I've got the funny part, I'm the devil. I shouldn't think the rabble would need a part written out. After all, you don't need to tell people to laugh when something's funny.'

They had read Christopher's script. Sally said doubtfully:

'Perhaps some of us better lead the rabble in case they don't know you're being funny.'

'And you've got myself and the vicar, John?'

'And some extra people on horses and some monks, but none of those have parts.'

The doctor looked at his pad. He made a face at what he had written.

'Nothing for it but an all-round family effort. I think the best plan is for you all to get down to it for a couple of hours each day until all the parts are copied out, otherwise term will start and no one will have their parts to learn. If you take my advice you'll get started right away. It's two now; you'll have done your two hours by teatime.'

The family sat round the schoolroom table. They were all cross. John said:

'If I'd known that it was going to muck up all the holidays I'd never have suggested the pageant.'

Sally spoke very fast.

'I like you grumbling. I've written out all my parts, and now I've got to spend two hours each day helping you.'

Christopher propped the exercise book in which he had written his scene against the inkpot.

'You had hardly any parts to copy; yours is all dancing.'

Selina felt that her uncle might have asked her if she would help the others, instead of saying in that arbitrary way that everybody was to work for two hours a day. Of course she would have offered to help, but offering is a very different thing to being ordered. She sat down next to Christopher.

'I'll do some of yours as you've so many parts.'

Christopher ungraciously moved the exercise book an inch towards her.

'You can if you want to.'

Sally sat beside Phoebe.

'Which part shall I do?'

Phoebe had been going to The Abbey Arms at two to make more roses. She was in the mood to be rude to anybody.

'You can write out Miss Lipscombe as you're so keen to do something.'

Sally took a deep breath before speaking her mind, then she let it go again. It took great self-control but it was no good starting a row; the parts had got to be written and if they wasted time today it would only mean an extra day of copying.

For half an hour there was nothing heard except the scratching of pens and occasional questions. 'What's that word?' 'Is that meant to be can't or won't?' Then Sally giggled.

'Can you see Miss Lipscombe saying "Fie, fie, no sulky looks"? What's she going to wear, Phoebe?'

Phoebe did not like Sally giggling.

'I should have thought you could have guessed that without asking me. Just a dress like they wore at that time, only very plain.'

John paused in the middle of copying out the Abbot's part in his scene. He considered Miss Lipscombe in his mind's eye.

'Will she wear her pince-nez? I don't believe she can see anything without them.'

Selina was copying Mrs Miggs's part for Phoebe.

'Have you asked Miss Lipscombe and Partridge if they'll act, Phoebe? In fact, has anybody asked anybody except Uncle Jim and Mrs Miggs?'

Christopher said:

'They ought to be jolly glad to, seeing it's for the Air Force Benevolent.'

Selina, because she was much more shy than her cousins, could imagine Mr Partridge's and Miss Lipscombe's feelings when they got their parts.

'It's Phoebe's scene they mightn't like.' She saw Phoebe bristling, so she went on hurriedly. 'Somehow poetry looks more difficult to say than just ordinary words.'

Christopher stopped writing.

'I think Miss Lipscombe will be awfully good as a witch, but I thought I'd have to talk her round into acting it. You know what she is.'

'I should think,' said John, 'Selina better do the asking. In a way it's her pageant.'

There was a murmur of agreement round the table and everybody went on writing as though the subject was closed. Selina looked at their bent heads in horror.

'I'm not a bit good at asking people to do things. Anyone would do it better than I.'

John looked at her.

'The trouble with you is you always think you can't do anything.'

Sally was looking at the part Christopher was copying.

'That's quite true. I think Selina's got what's called an inferiority complex, or else we've all got superiority ones.' She broke off. 'I say, Christopher, Miss Lipscombe won't like being called a blasted she-goat.'

Christopher scowled at her.

'But nobody's calling Miss Lipscombe a blasted she-goat.'

'I don't know why not,' said Phoebe. 'It describes her very well.'

Christopher sighed to show he found Phoebe unbearably stupid.

'It's in the play she's a blasted she-goat. She's got to forget she's Miss Lipscombe and be a witch.'

67

'Which shouldn't be difficult,' said Phoebe.

Sally wanted to see the parts delivered.

'I should think that Selina better go to each person in turn with their parts. Miss Lipscombe, Mrs Miggs, Partridge. What d'you think about Mr Laws?'

The whole family stopped writing and thought about the vicar.

'Almost anybody could get him to say yes,' John pointed out. 'But the trouble is to see that he means it, he's so vague.' He looked at Selina. 'I tell you what, when you ask him if he'll act in the pageant, offer to go and hear his part on Saturday afternoons.'

There was a murmur of sympathy round the table.

'Poor Selina.'

'Pretty sickening for Selina.'

'Selina has other things to do with her afternoons, my boy.'

Sally said:

'I could take turns with you, Selina, except that I meant to be rehearsing the village children in the ballet on Saturday afternoons.'

Selina did not so much grudge the afternoons as she was worried.

'I wouldn't mind, John, but I shan't be able to make him learn. You know what he is. If he starts thinking about the Abbot it's sure to make him think about something else and then he'll talk and talk.'

John refused to listen.

'Obviously he's got to play the Abbot. You couldn't find anyone more suitable than him. I'm not here, so one of you must see he learns his part.'

'But it's in Latin,' Selina protested. 'My Latin's awful; I'll never know if he's right.'

John shrugged his shoulders.

'Everybody must be word perfect by the time the summer holidays begin or we'll never have the pageant ready. After all, Selina, we're only doing it for you.'

Selina made no further protest. It was never any good arguing with the cousins, but it was the beginning of her wondering whether the chance to wear her party shoes and frock just once was worth all the trouble there was going to be. It was all very well for John to say it was her pageant. It would only be her pageant when anything tiresome wanted doing, like hearing Mr Laws's part. It was really everybody's pageant. It would be awfully nice to wear organdie and satin shoes and carry roses, but you could pay too high a price.

# CHAPTER SEVEN

## Getting a Cast

The surgery was over. Miss Lipscombe had boiled the last of the instruments and was tidying the doctor's desk when Selina crept in. Selina closed the door behind her. Miss Lipscombe looked at her through her pince-nez. It was a look which in the past had made probationer hospital nurses drop whatever they were carrying. Selina, conscious that the cousins were waiting to know how she had got on, was already in a fuss. Miss Lipscombe's look and her don't-bother-me-now tone of voice made her feel worse.

'Yes?'

Selina cleared her throat.

'In September—September the twentieth actually—we're doing a pageant. It's to be in aid of the Air Force Benevolent Fund.'

Miss Lipscombe gave some papers on the desk an angry push.

'A penny a week have I put in the Red Cross box since the

71

beginning of the war, though it's gone against the grain seeing that stuck-up Mrs Mawser, who behaves as if she thought she was royalty, comes for it and gets all the credit, and I buy a flag each flag-day—still, if it's for the Air Force, I might manage sixpence.' She left the desk and picked up her bag. 'I believe I've got six pennies.'

Selina shifted from one foot to the other. She had Miss Lipscombe's parts in an envelope behind her back.

'It's not money, though it's awfully nice of you to say you will give sixpence, but it's something more important. It's to ask you to act.'

Miss Lipscombe was so surprised that she straightened up with a jerk.

'Act!'

Selina supposed that Miss Lipscombe would have to make a favour of acting so she thought she would help.

'Of course you're terribly busy—and learning parts takes an awful time—and acting is difficult—and . . .'

'You are speaking in ignorance, child. You probably do not realize whom you are asking. When I was a student nurse, on two occasions I played important parts in my hospital amateur dramatic.'

Selina could not think of any answer at all. She had every argument on the tip of her tongue to persuade Miss Lipscombe not to be shy or nervous and to make her believe that she would be good, but none ready to thank an important actress for playing a part. She tried to remember what was inside the envelope. If Miss Lipscombe considered herself a good actress, were the parts grand enough for her?

'Christopher has written you a very important part. It's a

witch.' Miss Lipscombe said nothing but gave a gracious nod. 'Phoebe has written you the part of Anne Boleyn's governess.' Miss Lipscombe's face again said nothing, so Selina added, hoping it sounded grander, 'It's in poetry.'

'Where is the pageant to take place?'

'On the lower lawn at the Abbey.'

'How many scenes?'

'Little bits at the beginning and end which I do, and four in between. One each written by John, Christopher, Sally, and Phoebe.'

'What parts do I act in John's and Sally's scenes?'

'John's is all men. It's the Abbey when it was an Abbey.'

'And Sally's?'

'Sally's is mostly a ballet.'

Miss Lipscombe was putting on her coat.

'Well, where are the parts? I will read them through tonight. I might consent. I shall have to give the matter thought. With all the work I have to do for your uncle and my own house to keep clean, and fetching my rations and everybody so disobliging . . .'

Selina handed her the envelope.

'Oh, thank you, Miss Lipscombe. I do hope you will find time. It will make a great difference you being able to act—we never thought of that.' Selina knew she had said the wrong thing; she tried to put it right. 'You see, we've never thought of you like that.'

'Nor any reason why you should. I'm not one for talking big about myself like others I could mention.' Miss Lipscombe went to the door. 'I mustn't stay gossiping here. I like a little time to myself though nobody would think so.'

'Could you let me know tomorrow if you will act?'

Miss Lipscombe nodded.

'In the morning. Come to me before the surgery.'

The next morning Miss Lipscombe said yes. Selina raced over the house to tell her cousins. Phoebe and Augustus, assisted by Benjamin, were clearing the breakfast table. John was washing up and Christopher was drying. Sally was making beds with her mother. She said:

'Oh, Mum, it makes me feel so pageanty to think that three people have got parts and are learning them.'

Selina felt this was going a bit far.

'Mrs Miggs isn't exactly learning yet. Alfie hasn't started to teach her.'

Mrs Andrews tucked in a sheet.

'And if you are counting Dad as one of the three you are going too fast. He's read his part, that's all.'

Sally was disgusted.

'Mum, you're as bad as Selina. She's always so careful, never gay before things happen, always waiting to see that they do happen.'

Mrs Andrews blew a kiss to Selina.

'Thank goodness I've one child, even if she's only on loan, who keeps calm.'

The doctor and John came with Selina to the vicarage. They had not meant to, but the doctor was driving to see Mr Laws professionally, and John was passing the vicarage gate on his way to collect tins to mount on sticks for a torchlight procession. They both ran into Selina as she was opening the vicarage gate. The doctor leant out of his car.

'Hallo, niece!' Then he saw John. 'Hallo, old man! Calling on the vicar, Selina?'

Selina had been hanging about outside the vicarage, too shy to go in. The sight of her uncle cheered her immensely. If he was going to call on the vicar professionally then she would be in the way.

'It was about being the Abbot, but I won't now.'

The doctor turned to John.

'Abbot's your business, better come along too.'

It was never any good arguing with the doctor. He might sound casual in what he said, but he seldom felt casual. Not looking too pleased, because he was keen on the torchlight procession, John jumped on the running-board on his side of the car. Selina, delighted at the way things had turned out, jumped on the other. What luck, she thought. With Uncle Jim there as well as John it would be very peculiar if I had to say anything at all.

The vicar was on his lawn. He was walking up and down, half-admiring his daffodils and half-composing a sermon. He was a picturesque-looking man. He had a thin face and very blue eyes, and a lot of snow-white hair. He was pleased to see the doctor.

'Splendid, my dear fellow! Splendid! You must see my daffodils.' He stooped and held the face of first one daffodil and then another up for inspection. 'There's a beautiful specimen! The angels in heaven have not trumpets of purer gold. Here's a dear little creature, such a delicate shade.'

The doctor looked at the daffodils for a minute or two, then he steered the vicar away from them.

'We're here on business. You taking that medicine I gave you?'

'It's most interesting the use you modern men make of the old herbs. Aconite, I noticed . . .'

'Did you just read the prescription or did you drink the stuff?'

'Oh, certainly I drank some.'

The vicar showed signs of drifting back to his daffodils. The doctor moved to cut him off.

'What did you do with the rest that you didn't swallow?'

'A little experiment.' The vicar turned to John. 'An interesting experiment. You would have enjoyed it. I grew freesias for the house this year. A sad failure. All length and no flowers.'

The doctor sighed.

'So you gave them my tonic?'

'One dose daily.'

Selina forgot to be shy.

'What happened to the freesias?'

'Nothing. The tonic neither agreed nor disagreed; they remained a failure.'

The doctor made a note on a piece of paper.

'I shall send you tablets this time, and don't think, if you bury them, they will act as a fertilizer. They won't.' The vicar made another move towards his daffodils. The doctor took his arm and gently manoeuvred him, so that he faced John and Selina. 'These two have a favour to ask.'

John explained about the pageant.

'We wanted you for a part, sir. It's in the scene I wrote. I'm a boy who has been educated by the monks at the original Abbey . . .'

The vicar's attention was caught. He temporarily forgot his daffodils.

'No evidence of an early Abbey.'

John was not going to have his scene spoilt for a little matter of historical accuracy.

'The one that Henry the Eighth turned the monks out of was pretty old, wasn't it? I mean, nobody knows, it's been burned down, but there are Roman remains found in the fields.'

'Such Roman remains as have been found would not have had anything to do with an abbey; they are very early. If any of our forefathers lived here at that time they were heathens. We were heathens, you know, a hundred and fifty years after the conquest.'

Selina gasped.

'Were we? Was Harold, who was killed at the battle of Hastings?'

John nudged her.

'Not that conquest, you mutt. Mr Laws is talking about the Romans, not the Normans.'

The doctor laughed.

'Only a few hundred years out, old lady.'

The vicar did not seem to have heard what Selina said. He gazed at the sky as if he could see through it back into the sixth century.

'Missionaries from Rome. Sent out by Pope Gregory. Augustine led them. Most interesting it must have been. I have often thought I would have liked to have joined that expedition.'

The doctor ought to have been on his rounds, but he was enjoying himself. He lit a cigarette. He turned to Selina.

'Missionaries in those days didn't preach in the language of the country. Every Christian needed Latin. Wouldn't have suited you, old lady.'

The vicar caught the word Latin.

'For five hundred years Latin had been the language used in the Holy Catholic Church. Wonderful fellow Augustine, not only to have converted us, but persuaded us of the need to learn Latin. Did a lot better than I can do nowadays. Even in their own tongue I cannot persuade all this village to come to worship.'

He seemed lost in his thoughts. John felt they were not getting on very fast.

'Would you be the Abbot in my scene, sir?'

The vicar was still thinking of Augustine.

'What date is your scene? It would be wonderful to show the village the coming of Christianity.'

John had no intention of rewriting his scene.

'It's later than that. It's the end of the Middle Ages some time.'

The doctor hated his family to be lazy-minded.

'Who was on the throne?'

John had not really decided that.

'One of the Henrys, or Edward the Fourth.' He thought of an excuse. 'It depends on what clothes are easiest to hire. A boy would go to school at the Abbey in any of those reigns, wouldn't he?'

The vicar, with a sigh, gave up hope of acting the part of Augustine.

'I should conceive that even in those dark, troubled days a father would not break his son's education without good cause.'

The doctor flicked some ash on to the grass.

'I imagine knightly training came first and learning a long way second.'

The vicar shook his head.

'Not with the type of family we have in mind. The father must have cared for learning to send his boy to the monks.'

John had a queer feeling that he had not invented his boy, but that he was real.

'There was always a war somewhere. You've come for your son, Dad, to be your esquire.'

The doctor looked at the vicar.

'He's right there. When weren't we at war in the Middle Ages? I think we can allow there was a war on.'

The vicar was glancing towards his daffodils.

'Very true. Most regrettable though. A boy of John's age. Living amongst coarse, rough soldiers.'

John raised his voice.

'Will you act the Abbot, sir?'

'Very well, my boy. This is a lovely flower, Doctor. Look at the lemon tint of the trumpet.'

John gave his father a pleading look. The doctor once again held the vicar by the elbow.

'You've agreed to act the part of the Abbot in the children's pageant. It will mean rehearsals, you know.'

'Splendid. Splendid.' The vicar detached his elbow. 'There is no more beautiful sight than a border of daffodils.'

Selina made Sally come with her to see the Colonel and Mrs Day and Partridge, and to ask Mrs Mawser to be rabble.

'You see, Sally,' she said, 'it's Phoebe's scene. Partridge isn't the sort of man who likes speaking in poetry.'

Sally wanted somebody with whom to discuss her ballet and Selina would do as well as anybody. The two girls set off as soon as they had finished washing up the lunch things. Sally was in tremendous spirits. She squeezed Selina's arm.

'Isn't it simply gorgeous that the pageant really is happening at last? I'd almost despaired. I'm going to get every child who's going to dance in my ballet fixed these holidays, and I shall have rehearsals every Saturday all the term. I should think I might use almost every little girl in the village.'

Selina did not want to damp Sally's enthusiasm, but somebody had to be practical.

'What are they going to wear?'

Sally was practising a few steps. She stopped with one foot in the air.

'I've thought and thought about that. I have an idea I'll put them in grass-green as if they were all parts of the ground.'

'Grass-green what?'

'Something that looks like muslin. I suppose one could get some stuff and dye it if there isn't any green stuff without coupons, or perhaps every mother will be so excited that their child is going to be in the pageant they'll spare the coupons to buy its frock.'

Selina shook her head.

'I don't think I should count on that if I were you.'

Sally danced up the road and on the corner made two fouettés.

'I know that something will be managed and it's no good you trying to damp my feelings and make me practical, Selina Cole, because I simply don't feel practical and that's that.'

Mrs Day was standing outside the Abbey front door with Partridge. She was shouting directions to the Colonel, who was on the roof fixing decorations.

'You've got the Stars and Stripes upside down. Don't hold on to that flagpole. It wasn't safe before the war. That Union

80

Jack is a disgrace. Haven't we got a better one?' She turned to Partridge. 'Lot of nonsense. Nobody'll see our flags, unless they come up the drive, and few people do that nowadays.'

Partridge sighed.

'Things will be different, madam, when we have peace. You'll be opening up the house again and things will be as they were.'

Mrs Day turned to answer him and saw the children. Selina, because she was nervous, blurted out the object of her visit straight away.

'We came—I mean I came—to ask you and Mr Partridge and Mrs Mawser to act in our pageant.'

Mrs Day laughed.

'Only part fit for Partridge to play is an ostrich.' She turned back to Partridge. 'Never knew such a man for having his head in the sand. Things be like they used to be, indeed! Nonsense.'

Selina wondered whether they had chosen a bad day. Sally said:

'Would you be Queen Elizabeth? There's not much to say, just a sort of triumphal entry and people curtsying, and then you watch my masque.'

Mrs Day gave another laugh.

'Good gracious, child! Hear that, Partridge? Can you see me as Queen Elizabeth?'

Selina swallowed nervously. It was not possible to explain to Mrs Day that they had thought she was exactly right for Queen Elizabeth when she was old. Sally, however, had no such inhibitions.

'I think you're exactly like her. Not, of course, when she was young, but more when she got that stretched, scragged look.'

81

Mrs Day gave Sally an amused glance.

'Dare say you'll grow up to be a great dancer, Sally, but I don't think you'll get anywhere on your tact. I may look old, scraggy, and stretched, but no woman cares to hear that she does. All the same I'll be Queen Elizabeth for you. Somewhere, if I can unearth it, I've got the togs. Had 'em for a fancy-dress dance.'

Selina turned to Partridge.

'In Phoebe's scene there's a butler. He's butler to Anne Boleyn when she was a child.'

Mrs Day said:

'Ought to suit him. It's quite your style to be butler to a future queen, Partridge. Even one that lost her head.'

Partridge was looking anxiously at Selina.

'Should I have to speak, Miss Selina?'

Selina kept back the awful news about the poetry.

'Only a little.'

'Anyone else in the scene, Miss Selina?'

Selina scratched at the gravel of the drive with her toe.

'Well, there's Phoebe. She's Anne Boleyn.'

Mrs Day was looking at the roof again but she had half an ear on the conversation.

'Come clean, Selina; who else?'

Sally giggled.

'Miss Lipscombe. She's a very cross governess, and Mrs Miggs. She's the nurse.'

Mrs Day raised her voice and shouted to the Colonel.

'Russian flag's higher than the American.' She turned back to the girls. 'Scene ought to be strikin'. You asking Mawser to act?'

82

'Not act exactly,' Selina explained. 'She's wanted as rabble in Christopher's scene.'

Mrs Day peered again at the flags.

'Russia's still too high. Hardly have picked Mawser as rabble, but run along and ask her. You'll find her in the kitchen.'

Mrs Mawser was sitting in a corner of the vast kitchen sorting the contents of a drawer. Selina and Sally sat on the table beside her. Sally asked her if she would mind taking a part. Mrs Mawser raised her head; her eyes were scared.

'I couldn't fancy it, Miss Sally. I was never one who cared for putting themselves forward in any way.'

Sally was very fond of Mrs Mawser, and as well she wanted to get the pageant all settled before the term began. She slid off the table and put her arms round her neck.

'It's only a person in a crowd. You see, there's rather a lot of room on the lower lawn and we're going to need absolutely everybody we can get, or it's going to look a bit skimpy.'

Selina played with one of the spoons that Mrs Mawser had been sorting.

'It ought to be rather a pretty scene really. It's mummers, and I think you wear wimples and things like that; you know, that bit round the face.'

Sally gave Mrs Mawser a hug.

'Mrs Day is going to be Queen Elizabeth.'

Mrs Mawser showed more enthusiasm.

'And no one more suitable.' She still looked unwilling, but it was clear she felt that if Mrs Day was taking part she could not very well refuse. 'Very well, provided it's clearly understood that not a word passes my lips.'

Outside, going down the drive, Sally clasped her hands ecstatically.

'My goodness, we are getting on. Mr Laws has got his part and is learning it, or rather, he will learn it on Saturdays when you go round and teach him. Mrs Miggs has got her part, and she'll know it when Alfie has taught it to her. Mrs Day's got her part. Mr Partridge has got his part, which, thank goodness, he didn't look at before he said yes. Dad's got his, and we've all got ours. Directly this VE-Day stuff is over I'm going to start Saturday rehearsals on the lower lawn. I mean my ballet to be absolutely perfect.'

# CHAPTER EIGHT

———◆◆———

## *The Ballet*

It was June before Sally could call her first ballet rehearsal. The VE-Day celebrations had been so exciting that nobody could settle down and take an interest in serious things like rehearsals. For four whole days even Selina and Sally forgot about the pageant. They rushed about and lit bonfires, walked in the torchlight procession, took part in the sports, and went to a dance given by the Americans at the camp. After the VE-Day excitement had died down it was still difficult to get the children together for rehearsal. One Saturday it was wet and the next something was going on, and then, just as Sally had everything planned for the first rehearsal, even to having borrowed a portable gramophone from a girl at her school and bought records with the right music, the Days' nephew, Philip, came to stay at the Abbey. He had been in hospital for months following a very bad aeroplane smash. Now he was convalescent and waiting to be invalided out of the Service.

'Not this next Saturday, Sally,' the Colonel said. 'Your father thinks that Philip should be kept as quiet as possible. Nerves still a bit pulled about.'

Sally was very sorry about Philip's nerves, but still more sorry about her rehearsal. It meant visiting thirty children to tell them that it was not going to happen, at least it would have been thirty children, only, luckily, two or three of them were out of one family.

It was nice when one day in the middle of June Selina, Sally, and Phoebe, on their way back from school, met Mrs Day. She was riding, but she stopped and called to Sally:

'Philip's getting on splendidly. It'll be all right if you like to do your dancing on the lower lawn on Saturday.'

Sally was so pleased that she almost hugged the horse.

'Oh, thank you, Mrs Day. I've found thirty children and I promise we'll be terribly quiet.'

Mrs Day gave her horse's neck a pat.

'Go on, Lucky.' She looked back at Sally over her shoulder. 'Extraordinary thing, if thirty children are quiet.'

Sally had been worried about the music for her ballet. It had to be more or less of the right date. The children, if they were to keep time, needed very hop, skip, and jump music. She had discussed with the girls in the ballet class at her school using one traditional tune like 'Greensleeves', but lovely as 'Greensleeves' was she was persuaded by the other girls that the children would find it difficult to dance to. Finally she had decided on a folk-dance medley. There were lots of catchy tunes for the children, and the 'Greensleeves' air in the middle and at the end for herself.

The lower lawn at the Abbey looked as if it had been born to be a stage. It was surrounded by a hedge of different flowering shrubs. During the war years the shrubs had not been attended to properly and they were overgrown and needed pruning, but they would make a perfect background for a pageant because there were two or three spaces which only needed clipping back to form natural stage entrances. Behind the hedge were some beautiful elm trees. In front of the lower lawn ran a small path. Up the other side of the path the front lawn sloped gradually to the house. This lawn was so big that several hundred people could sit on it, and because of the way it sloped everybody could see the lower lawn. On the lower lawn side of the path, except in front of the lower lawn itself, was a thick hedge. This hedge would act as natural theatre wings. All the actors could wait behind it for their cues, and would not be seen by the audience on the upper lawn.

Sally had invited two friends of hers, Priscilla and Madeleine, from the ballet class to come to the first rehearsal and give advice. When they saw the stage they were terribly jealous. Madeleine ran to the middle of it and made some pirouettes.

'It's lovely, Sally. You can do the most beautiful things on this.'

Priscilla was wandering round the back of the shrubs. She pushed her way through a lilac and a ribes, which were in the centre at the back.

'You must have these cut away and you must make your entrance here.'

Sally was keeping an eye out for the children, who had not yet arrived. She turned and looked at the stage.

'Where do you think Queen Elizabeth and her Court ought to sit?'

Madeleine made a few more pirouettes.

'Bother them. You must poke them away somewhere, it's the masque that matters.'

Priscilla opened the portable gramophone which Sally had put down on the path. She put on the first record, and began sketching out some steps.

'I tell you what, I believe we were all wrong when we thought of one big ring. I think it should be two rings going different ways. There's plenty of room on this stage.'

'But you'll still have to find room for Queen Elizabeth and her Court.'

Sally, Priscilla, and Madeleine jumped and turned to face the upper lawn. There, sitting on a rug, was Philip. He was out of uniform, one arm in a sling. He looked thin and pale but otherwise, Sally thought, very much as he had looked last time he had been on leave and had stayed at the Abbey. Sally introduced Priscilla and Madeleine.

'This is Squadron Leader Philip Day.' She thought she ought to warn them that Philip knew a lot about acting. 'He was producing plays on a real stage before the war.'

Philip had his mind on Queen Elizabeth. He hardly seemed to see Priscilla or Madeleine.

'It's no good you thinking that you can tuck Gloriana into a corner. She wasn't that sort of Queen and everybody knows it. You'll have to give her her entrance. Fanfare of trumpets, flowers, curtsies and all the stuff, and then you've got to pop her on a dais. You see, however important the masque is to you, and even though the audience must forget the Queen and think only of the masque, you've got to have her sitting there all the time looking regal or the scene goes wrong. What people are seeing is not Sally and her friends dancing, but a masque planned and rehearsed for the visit of Queen Elizabeth.'

Sally sat down beside Philip.

'But, Philip, Mrs Day's Queen Elizabeth. We haven't got anybody to shout and curtsy and give flowers. I know you're perfectly right from a history point of view, but what the people will pay to see is their children dancing on the Abbey lawn.'

Philip lit a cigarette. He did not seem to have heard what Sally had said.

'On the left, I think, just to the left of the entrance. Quite a small raised platform easily brought on by a few villagers, a canopy, a draped chair . . .'

Sally tapped Philip on the knee.

'But a platform will take up part of my stage. I don't want Queen Elizabeth bulging all over my stage.'

Madeleine had a very good historical sense. She went down to the path and turned off the gramophone, then she walked on to the lower lawn and stood on the left of the back entrance.

'He's quite right, Sally. You can't possibly have Queen Elizabeth at all unless you treat her properly.' She joined Philip and the girls. 'If you think of that Queen Elizabeth being today's Queen Elizabeth. Suppose she was coming here. Can you imagine she'd be shoved out of the way while the village danced? Of course she wouldn't.'

Philip had attended to what Madeleine had said. He looked at her with approval.

'Quite right, my girl, and what's more, if today's Queen Elizabeth turned up, and the village half-killed itself dancing, not one soul, even if their children were performing, would look at them. They'd look at the Queen, of course, so that they could tell anyone who hadn't seen her exactly what she looked like and what she wore.'

The village children were beginning to arrive in twos and threes. Sally got up and went down to meet them.

'It's awful. I can see you're right, and I can see you're going to make me put Queen Elizabeth where you want her, but between you you'll ruin my ballet.'

It was quite a satisfactory afternoon's work. Sally had chosen small children, and most of them were nice looking. The only difficulty was that they had to dance in bare feet. The trouble started with the children of Mrs Peters. That Mrs Peters whose boy had fetched the doctor in the Christmas holidays because she would eat big meals on top of food poisoning. Mr Peters was the local policeman, and they had a family of seven children, all beautifully brought up. It was the middle three girls that Sally had asked to dance in the ballet. Margaret, the eldest, was nine and she had received strict instructions from her mother before she came out about the care she was to take of her two younger sisters.

'That Sally Andrews is a wild thing. Don't you let her go persuading you into doing anything foolish. I don't mind a bit of dancing if it's done decently and no clothes taken off.'

Sally started the rehearsal by saying briskly:

'All shoes and socks off, and for goodness' sake don't mix them up or your mothers will make a row.'

Margaret Peters stepped forward.

'My mum said we weren't to take off nothing.'

Immediately there was a chorus from the other children.

'We aren't allowed to have our shoes off.'

'Mum says it's dangerous on account of a tack or a piece of glass.'

'My dad knew a boy that cut his foot from going about barefooted, and he got lockjaw, near as nothing died.'

Sally thought quickly. She could not possibly have thirty children prancing about on the lower lawn in shoes, or the lower lawn would be ruined and it had been especially mowed for the rehearsal.

Mrs Day would not have said Sally lacked tact if she had been at that rehearsal.

'Right. Every child who is not allowed to dance without their shoes and socks can go home.'

Sally took a big risk because at least twenty-eight children out of the thirty were saying they couldn't dance without their shoes and socks, but it worked out all right. All the children wanted to dance in the pageant, and in a minute thirty pairs of shoes and socks were sitting on the path.

All the children had done a little dancing at school and they were not difficult to train. They came on and they went off, they danced in big rings and small rings, and though they were only wearing their ordinary summer frocks, Philip, Madeleine, and Priscilla, watching from the upper lawn, could see what the masque would look like when the children were dressed up with, perhaps, flowers in their hair.

At the end of an hour and a half Sally told the children they could put on their shoes and socks and go home. It was then the barefoot trouble cropped up again. Once more Margaret Peters was the spokesman.

'Mum won't half create if we put on our socks on our dirty feet.'

Sally picked up one of Margaret's feet and looked at the sole. It was shockingly dirty, a mixture of brown and green in stripes. Priscilla, in spite of being a dancer, was very practical.

'Do you think we could get a tub and wash them all?'

Sally was doubtful. Mrs Mawser was a darling, but there was a great deal to do in the Abbey; soap was rationed, towels cost coupons, and to get the children's feet clean they would have to have a kettle or two of hot water. Philip, however, was a person who jumped over difficulties.

'Of course. Ask Mawser to shove a tub outside the kitchen door. She'll give you soap and towels. Tell her she'll have to do this after each rehearsal.'

Mrs Mawser behaved like an angel outwardly, though Sally did wonder how she felt inside. She put three large basins outside the back door and some kitchen soap, and she filled the basins with warm water. She knew every child by name and was much sterner than Sally would have been.

'Now, don't push. Behave like little ladies. You can get those feet cleaner than that, Peggy. I've heard your mother talking to you, Rose, when I come round for my penny a week, and she'd never pass feet in that state.' She put some kitchen chairs out and, as each set of feet came out of the basin, she lifted the children on to the chairs and dried the feet herself. 'Now put on your socks, Agnes. Yes, Margaret, we all know what your mother will say if you go home with dirty feet, and you're not going home with dirty feet, so let's have no nonsense.'

It was rather annoying to Sally and Priscilla when they came back exhausted from washing to find Philip and Madeleine having not only a lovely comfortable discussion on the pageant, but replanning Sally's masque. Philip started to explain the moment Sally came down the upper lawn.

'I tell you what this masque of yours needs. It wants body. We'll get that ballet school over from Linkwell.'

Sally was startled to hear Philip use the word 'we'. She had never been a person to keep her feelings to herself.

'When you say "we" I'm arranging this masque.'

Philip grinned and held out his good hand to her. He pulled her down beside him.

'Didn't you know that I was convalescing here and it's bad for me to be annoyed? I think this pageant will be rather fun, and surely, as an artist, you would rather be supported by good dancers than by bad.'

Sally considered the point. Because the rest of the girls in the ballet class at school were boarders she had to dance the only solo, for there was no local girl who could dance, but the choreography had not satisfied her. A masque should have a story, and it was difficult to invent a story for a single soloist. She had, with the help of Madeleine and Priscilla, arranged that the children were fairies who stole a human and took her to Fairyland. It showed how the fairies danced with the human in Fairyland. How, finally, the human escaped and her happiness in coming back to the human world.

When Sally had been planning the masque with the other girls it had sounded fairly good, but actually she suspected that when they danced it, unless what it was all about was written on the programme, nobody in the audience would guess what was happening, and they would only say, 'And then Sally Andrews danced a bit by herself.' Madeleine leant forward, her eyes shining.

'If you have the Linkwell Ballet School ballet you could go back to the original story you had about the girl who ran after the faun who lured her to Fairyland, and you could have some really decent dancing by the fairies. Might have the Fairy Queen on.'

Philip snapped his fingers.

'I've got it. The centrepiece of this masque is the Fairy Queen. She must have red hair. She typifies Gloriana.'

Priscilla had an idea.

'We could have some solos. A dragonfly or a butterfly or something. I can see this being simply terrific, Sally.'

Sally put on her sandals, which she was carrying. She looked searchingly first at Madeleine and then at Priscilla.

'Of course I've always wanted more than anything to meet the girls from the Ballet School at Linkwell, but it's rather grand for what we thought of. Would you like to dance in front of those Linkwell girls? They're almost professionals.'

Madeleine's eyes glowed.

'I'd simply dote on it. Think what you'd learn from just watching them.'

Priscilla nodded.

'She's right, Sally. Miss Faulkes says some of them are awfully good. They must be. Why, last year two of them went almost straight from that school and joined Sadler's Wells.'

Sally fastened her sandal. She had lived so long with her ballet that it was difficult all in a minute to see it taking new shape. She had so looked forward to this rehearsal; it was the day on which she was to begin to see her ballet coming to life. All the same, Madeleine and Priscilla were quite right. It was a wonderful chance to watch polished dancing. The ballet would be less hers than it had been. Of course nobody would even consider her producing the Linkwell girls. Still, it would be worth it. Besides, with all that talent they might produce something quite beautiful. Through her mind dashed a soaring dragonfly, a butterfly twirled in the air, the Queen of the Fairies, with flaming red hair, dancing with Oberon. She got up and smoothed down her frock. She looked at Philip and, with that look, accepted him as part-producer of her scene.

'All right. You try and get the Linkwell girls. Together we might do something pretty terrific.'

# CHAPTER NINE

## The Mummers

Christopher, in his spare time, had been going round the village collecting players for his scene. He found that when there were no words to say and no dance to learn or anything like that, people gave very vague promises.

'That's all right, Christopher. September the twentieth, we'll be along.'

'I don't need no rehearsing to laugh at a good joke. You be funny and I'll laugh all right.'

'If all you want of me is poking fun at Miss Lipscombe dressed as a witch, I'll be there. It'll come as natural as falling off a log.'

Sally came back from her rehearsal bubbling with excitement because, between leaving the Abbey and reaching home, she, Madeleine, and Priscilla had invented an enormous ballet with several solos and a lot of group-work. It was only when they reached the front door that they were slightly damped by remembering that they had thought out dances for point-work, which could never be carried out on the lower lawn. Christopher listened to the three girls all through tea. He thought they talked too much, but then girls never could stop jabbering. Still, it did seem that Sally's scene was taking shape, whereas his was nowhere at all. He had asked seven boys to be mummers with him, and they had all said yes and taken away their parts, but it was extremely doubtful if any of them were learning them.

One boy who was in the same form as he was had read his part, but he had been so rude about it that Christopher could scarcely think that encouraging. He wished Madeleine and Priscilla would go home so that he could have a talk with Sally. Sally and he understood each other, and though Sally might say she thought it pretty feeble of him to have got nothing fixed except Miss Lipscombe, doubtful mummers, and very uncertain rabble, still, she would stop thinking about her ballet and be prepared to help him with ideas. But Madeleine and Priscilla had not got to be back at school until six. They leant across the tea-table and talked and talked, and ate and ate. Sally was, of course, in charge of tea, and anyway you could not be rude to guests.

Christopher tried to hurry Phoebe, Augustus, and Benjamin, and, at the same time, remind Sally that time was getting on. He said the usual, 'Did anyone ever see a tortoise eat a buttercup?' And, wearily, 'You can't possibly want more bread, Augustus.' And, 'I should have thought you were fat enough already, Phoebe.' It did not do any good. Phoebe was, of course, angry.

'It's bad enough being rude when we're alone, but when we have visitors it's terrible to make personal remarks.'

Benjamin broke in, his voice even hoarser and deeper than usual.

'I shall eat and eat until I'm absolutely full and nobody shall stop me.'

'Quite right,' said Phoebe, helping herself to another piece of bread. 'It's all right for you, Christopher, John's clothes fit you, but I'm a different shape to Sally. It's not that I'm fat, but the buttons fasten in a wrong place on me and that's why I seem to bulge.'

Madeleine looked at Sally.

'I should think she could be the one to give flowers to Queen Elizabeth.'

Phoebe spread jam on her bread.

'I don't think I could. You see, I'm royalty myself in my scene, or at least I'm going to be royal, and I don't think it would look right for me to be just handing flowers to a Queen in another scene.'

Sally turned to Augustus and Benjamin.

'You're both going to be little pages, carrying Queen Elizabeth's train; won't that be fun?'

Augustus helped himself to the last bun.

'I won't wear white socks.'

Christopher remembered suddenly that at the first meeting about the pageant they had all agreed to write parts for Augustus and Benjamin. He had done nothing about parts for them in his scene. He began, for the first time since he had written it, to try and imagine how his scene would look on the lower lawn at the Abbey. The witch being caught and dragged towards the pond. The sudden sound of music and the arrival of the mummers. The putting up of the improvised stage. The playing of the scene. The roars from the crowd. But what was the end of the scene? What really was the beginning? Miss Lipscombe was a witch, but what had she done to make all the village turn out to duck her in a pond? What sort of thing made people in a village all turn out? They had, of course, on VE Day. That was the only time he had seen it happen. Then, of course, there had been children. All the children of the village. That was what Augustus and Benjamin would be. They would just be ordinary village children, but he would probably find something nice for them to do, like throwing a piece of mud at Miss Lipscombe. He was quite surprised to find that thinking about his scene had taken him to the end of tea. Sally, still talking hard to Madeleine and Priscilla, got up. She looked at Christopher.

'I'm taking them to see my pictures of Margot Fonteyn. I know it's my day to clear, but would you?'

When she had seen Madeleine and Priscilla off Sally came flying into the hall. Mrs Andrews was playing tiddly-winks in the drawing-room with Phoebe, Augustus, and Benjamin. She raised her voice as she heard the front door slam.

'Sally, darling. Sally.' Sally was looking flushed and excited. Talking ballet for hours had the same effect on her as some tremendously exciting party had on other people. She was so gay that it seemed awful to be pulled back into the ordinary world. Mrs Andrews saw just how she felt but the work of the house had to go on. 'It's Benjamin's bedtime. See you scrub him well, his hands are dirty.'

Benjamin flicked at a last tiddly-wink, climbed down off his chair and looked reproachfully at his mother.

'My dear, that's not dirt, that's brown from the sun.'

Mrs Andrews kissed him.

'Goodnight, pet. Whatever it is Sally'll get it off.'

Christopher heard Sally coming up the stairs with Benjamin. He knew she would call Selina to help her put the little ones to bed, so before she had time he offered.

'I'll help bath Benjamin tonight.'

Sally and Christopher understood each other so well that this remark did not need explaining. Sally said:

'I'll undress him and you turn on the water.'

Christopher sat on the edge of the bath while Sally washed Benjamin.

'Of course it will be all right, really, but nobody's exactly promised they'll be rabble.'

Sally finished scrubbing Benjamin's back before she answered.

'You can draw the scenes on paper like I do for my ballet. You don't need to know exactly how many. You can make rounds or squares for groups and keep changing them for different places in your scene, and mark in things like "all raise arms" or "scream at witch".'

Christopher was watching Benjamin, who was making a celluloid duck dive under his knees.

'It won't do it, it's got a hole in it. It'll always sink.'

Benjamin held the duck up and emptied out water through a hole in its tail.

'I'll be drabble in your acting.'

Sally picked up one of Benjamin's legs and started to scrub his knee.

'You can use him and Augustus. Children would be about in a village. I don't think it'll be a difficult scene to do. Where do your mummers play their scene? In the middle of the stage or the back, or what?'

'I don't know. Would you be using the lower lawn next Saturday?'

'Not all the time. You could do yours first or afterwards.' Sally straightened up so suddenly that she dropped Benjamin's leg and he fell backwards into the water. 'I know, if you haven't got real rabble planned, why don't we keep the children after my rehearsal? You could get groups and things fixed and a sort of idea of how many people you ought to have. Could you get your mummers?'

There was a pause. Then Christopher said:

'It's seven boys at school. Could Mum do seven?'

Sally kissed Benjamin.

'I'm terribly sorry, I didn't mean to knock you over. Give me your other leg. I think she might. Of course, seven for tea all at once is rather a lot. Like a party really. Must you have them to tea?'

'They've said yes, but I think they sort of just said it. If they were asked to tea and said they were coming, and then didn't turn up, it'd be rude.'

'You'll have to make Mum see that you won't ask her to do it twice. Seven is an awful lot and Saturday's the worst day, because if you run out of bread you can't get any more. Still, we might get buns, if we were lucky.'

Christopher felt better. It was a very good idea of Sally's to use the children at this first rehearsal. If he managed to persuade the grown-ups to come they were sure to get annoyed if they were kept hanging about. Then he remembered the witch.

'What about Miss Lipscombe? Do you think she'd come?'

Sally stood away from the bath and looked at Benjamin. He seemed extraordinarily shiny and clean all over. Even his hair was a little bit washed because of the way he had fallen into the water.

'You can play for just a minute, Benjamin.' She turned back to Christopher. 'I should go and explain, or perhaps you'd better send Selina. She's done most of the asking so far.'

'She doesn't seem a bad asker.'

'She's very good. She's got a sort of natural hang-doggish don't-hurt-me look. People don't like to be unkind. It would be rather like hitting a cat.'

Christopher opened the bathroom door. He stood outside and shouted.

'S'lina, S'lina.'

Selina came running out of her bedroom looking shocked. She jumped down the steps to the bathroom.

'Oh, I am sorry. I never noticed the time.'

Christopher stopped her going into the bathroom.

'Keep your hair on. It isn't that. I helped. Sally has bathed Benjamin and now I'm just going to fetch Augustus. What we wanted you to do is to see Miss Lipscombe about a rehearsal.'

Selina looked depressed.

'I'd very much rather bath Augustus.'

'Asking's your job. After all, we're only doing this pageant for you.'

'What have I got to ask her?'

Christopher explained.

'Make her see we would think it marvellous if she came, but we don't expect she will, you know the sort of thing.'

It was surgery time. The waiting-room was full of patients and Miss Lipscombe was busy with her card index. None of the children were allowed to go into the surgery or the waiting-room during surgery hours. Selina waited in the passage outside. The patients did not ring, for the side door was left open for them, but sometimes they left it open behind them, and then Miss Lipscombe would pop out saying, 'Some people never think of others,' or 'Born in a field, as my dear mother used to say.' It was not natural for Selina to do such a thing, but when she had been in the passage a quarter of an hour and Miss Lipscombe had not come out she opened the side door. She watched a patient go out, carefully closing the door behind them, and then she softly opened it again. Miss Lipscombe was very susceptible to draughts. In a moment Selina heard her muttering to the waiting patients, 'There. She's left the door open. No wonder she gets bronchitis. No surer way to bronchial trouble than draughts.' She came into the passage. 'They ought to have more thought. Born in a field.' Then she saw Selina.

'What are you hanging about here for?'

Selina had composed a long, polite speech, but you can't make long, polite speeches to a person who is running between a surgery and a door. She changed her words.

'It's about rehearsal on Saturday.' Miss Lipscombe's face looked terribly 'don't-bother-me-nowish'. So she hurried on. 'It's practically certain you won't want to come, but Christopher's scene is being rehearsed on Saturday, not with a proper crowd . . .'

Miss Lipscombe drew herself together.

'The scene can scarcely be rehearsed without me. What time is it to be?'

'Sally is rehearsing her children in the ballet for an hour at three, and Christopher thought after that. He thought he could borrow the children for the crowd, so he'd get some idea of how many people he'd need, and that sort of thing.'

'Four o'clock at the Abbey. Tell Christopher I shall be there.'

Christopher and Sally were so impressed at Selina's success with Miss Lipscombe that they thought perhaps she had better tackle their mother about tea for the boys on Saturday. Christopher said:

'She's much more likely to do something for you than for us, and you can remind her that we're only doing the pageant to help about your frock.'

Selina for once stuck in her toes.

'I'm not going to ask things from Aunt Ann or Uncle Jim for you. They're not like Miss Lipscombe. They'd say, "If it's Christopher's friends why are you asking?" and then I'd look a fool.'

Sally saw what Selina meant.

'She's quite right. Mum would only say to you, "Don't get someone else to do your dirty work, you ass."'

That evening there was a presentation in the village hall to the woman who had been in charge of the bandaging classes all through the war. The doctor had to give the presentation and Mrs Andrews had to be there, so they did not have supper with the children, but something cold when they came in.

'It's a nuisance,' said Sally. 'If you want to know the answer before you go to school you'll have to ask Mum about having those boys to tea on Saturday, at breakfast, and breakfast is a beastly time for asking things from anybody.'

Christopher woke up all excited about his scene in the pageant. He felt as keen on it as he had done in the Christmas holidays. He thought it would be grand to be very funny. He wanted to hear the rabble roaring with laughter at his jokes.

'I rather think,' he said to Sally when they met at the top of the stairs on their way down to breakfast, 'that I shall give the children real things to throw at Miss Lipscombe. You know how things are going to look when there's real stuff flying about.'

Sally hung over the banisters and slid down that way.

'It would look better, but I should work her into it gradually. I'd only throw little stuff like grass and leaves on Saturday, and then work up to mud and stones and bad tomatoes.'

Because Christopher was seeing in his mind his scene in the pageant as practically finished and being an enormous success, he did not wait for a good minute to ask his mother about tea on Saturday. In fact, he could hardly have chosen a worse minute. Mrs Andrews said:

'Take some extra Force this morning, darlings, there's only some very small fish-cakes coming. I don't know when I knew food more difficult than it is this week.'

Christopher broke in:

'Could I ask seven boys for tea on Saturday?'

Luckily both Dr Andrews and Mrs Andrews thought that funny. Dr Andrews said to Mrs Andrews:

'If you had any thoughts of Christopher for the Diplomatic Service I hope you now realize that the idea's dead.'

Mrs Andrews poured his milk on to Benjamin's Force.

'Why seven, darling? It's nobody's birthday.'

'It's the first rehearsal of my pageant scene. We're doing the mummers, and Miss Lipscombe's coming, she's the witch, but I'm not getting the rabble along because I'm using the kids Sally's using in her ballet. She said she thought they wouldn't mind stopping on and that would save the real rabble coming until everything was a bit more settled.'

'Shouldn't keep Miss Lipscombe hanging about too long, old man,' Dr Andrews broke in. 'Not a woman to treat casually, you know.'

Phoebe was furious. What was this? Everything planned for a pageant rehearsal. Miss Lipscombe, who had only one important part to play and that was in her scene, being asked to Christopher's rehearsal. It was disgusting.

'I suppose that it didn't strike anybody that I might want Miss Lipscombe on Saturday afternoon.'

Mrs Andrews spoke quickly before Sally or Christopher could answer.

'Listen, darlings. There's one thing I won't have over this pageant and that's quarrelling. You must fix up the rehearsals so that everybody gets a fair turn at using the lower lawn at the Abbey.'

Sally bristled with rage.

'But, Mum, Phoebe never thought of having a rehearsal until she heard we were having them.'

Phoebe looked proud.

'That's all you know. I was planning to ask Mrs Miggs this morning if Saturday afternoon would be convenient.'

Dr Andrews choked over his Force.

'You shouldn't make me laugh when I'm eating, Phoebe. And I implore you, if you have Mrs Miggs and Miss Lipscombe playing in the same scene, don't ask Mrs Miggs before you've asked Miss Lipscombe, or I shall find myself without a nurse.'

Mrs Andrews moved Benjamin's plate a little nearer to him.

'Whatever you do, don't offend Mrs Miggs, she's not very regular but she's the only help I've got.'

Sally was rearranging Saturday afternoon in her mind. She knew Phoebe too well to hope that she would not have a rehearsal after having said that she would have one.

'We can't ask Miss Lipscombe to come to a rehearsal of her scene and then stay for the dancing rehearsal waiting for Christopher's scene. I should think we had better do the dancing rehearsal last. It won't make any odds to the children.'

Mrs Andrews smiled in a pleased way at Sally.

'That sounds all right.'

Sally took advantage of her mother being pleased with her to help Christopher.

'It's only this once, Mum, that Christopher wants the seven boys, who are being mummers, for tea; he isn't absolutely certain that they'll come to his rehearsal, but if he said you'd asked them to tea they couldn't stop away without being rude.'

Mrs Andrews told Christopher to clear the Force plates and to give his father the plates for serving the fish-cakes. She was turning over in her mind the question of Saturday. Tea parties were difficult in Little Muchover. The one cake shop there served the whole village. It was easy enough if anyone was going into Linkwell, there were plenty of buns there if you got to the shop first thing in the morning, but it was almost impossible in term-time to send anyone into Linkwell first thing in the morning. If people were coming to tea every

Saturday while these rehearsals lasted, it was going to come very hard on the fat and jam ration. She knew she ought to make some kind of a rule, but it wanted thinking out. It was difficult to think things out in the middle of breakfast. She looked across at the doctor.

'What do you say?'

Dr Andrews finished helping the fish-cakes before he answered:

'I quite see that there will be this business of Saturday afternoon tea all through this term. Saturday afternoon is the only time they have to rehearse, and it seems a bit inhospitable if they can't ask some of them home sometimes. All the same, can't have five, or six, or seven dropping in every Saturday. We shouldn't have a thing left. There are three scenes to rehearse, aren't there? And there'll be four when John gets home. Then there's Selina's.' He turned to her. 'I know you haven't anyone to rehearse with, old lady, but I dare say you'd like to bring a friend along from rehearsal sometimes. I would suggest a maximum of five any Saturday and,' he made a big, heavy pause on the word 'and', 'the tea will be buns and you've got to find a method of getting buns from Linkwell yourselves.'

Sally, Christopher, and Phoebe never saw difficulties until they were in the middle of them. They just saw five people coming to tea every Saturday eating buns. Sally said, 'Thanks awfully, Dad.'

Phoebe said, 'I shall want five nearly every Saturday.'

Christopher said, 'But could it be seven this Saturday, just for once?'

Dr Andrews nodded.

'Yes, provided it's buns and you lay them on and don't bother your mother about it.'

Selina looked round the table and marvelled at how pleased her cousins looked. It was very difficult to buy buns any afternoon in Linkwell, and impossible on Saturday afternoons, and they all went to school on Saturdays from nine to one. How did the others think they were going to get buns?

At breakfast during the term everybody was allowed to leave the table as soon as they had finished eating. Christopher had a scheme in his mind which to him was as good as carried out, but he realized it would need the sanction of the others. He was just rushing off to get ready for school but he made time to say:

'Family committee tonight after tea.'

Phoebe was still cross. She too had finished her breakfast. She stood outside the dining-room door and shouted:

'I'll come to the committee if I can, but I shall be calling in to see Mrs Miggs on my way home and then I've got to see Miss Lipscombe.'

The surgery door opened and Miss Lipscombe's head came round it. Mrs Miggs, who was scrubbing the floor outside the kitchen, shuffled into the front hall on her hands and knees.

'And what were you wanting me for, Phoebe?' Miss Lipscombe asked in her most matron-of-a-workhouse voice.

Mrs Miggs said:

'Wot are you creatin' about, Phoebe?'

Phoebe was not easily put out but she could see she would have to be careful what words she used. When she had shouted at Christopher she had supposed the surgery door was shut, and that Mrs Miggs had not yet arrived. It was not only Miss Lipscombe and Mrs Miggs who were listening for Phoebe's answer. All the family, except Christopher, had their ears stretched. Phoebe put on her best smile.

'I heard you were coming to Christopher's rehearsal, Miss Lipscombe, on Saturday, and we thought it would save you trouble if we did my scene at the same time.' This putting of her own scene second sounded humiliating so she added: 'Of course my scene is the biggest and most important because it's written in poetry.'

Miss Lipscombe believed in children being kept in what she called their place. She thought Phoebe astonishingly clever to have written a scene in rhyme before she was ten, but she would have considered it a sin to say so.

'Poetry is as poetry does. Well, what time is this rehearsal?'

Sally rushed out of the dining-room, her words falling over each other.

'If it was convenient we thought about half-past two for Phoebe's scene. Could you come then? And then Christopher's could come straight on afterwards, and you'd be home in time for tea.'

Miss Lipscombe was looking forward to the rehearsal. She fancied herself as an actress and she had not had a chance to show her talent for years, but she considered it was always a mistake to give in easily about anything. She frowned and made the face of a person wondering how to spare the time in a day chock-full of engagements. Actually, all that she had to do on Saturday afternoon after she left the surgery was to have her own lunch and feed her cat, but nobody knew that except herself.

'I might be able to arrange it. Though how I get through all I have to do I don't know without rehearsals on Saturday afternoons; still, I've always been one to put myself out for others, and I suppose I always will be. Very well, Phoebe, two-thirty.'

Sally kicked Phoebe's ankle to remind her to say thank you. Together they went over to Mrs Miggs.

Mrs Miggs waited until the surgery door was shut. Then she said in a hoarse whisper:

'If I'd broken the last cup in the world and was dyin' for a cuppa tea and I knew she,' she nodded at the surgery door, ''ad a cup, I'd die of thirst before I asked 'er for a borrow of it.'

Mrs Andrews's voice came from the dining-room.

'Hurry up, you two, or you'll be late for school.'

Phoebe said:

'Could you come to rehearsal at half-past two on Saturday, Mrs Miggs dear?'

Mrs Miggs winked at Sally.

'Phoebe'd dear the hind-leg off a horse.' She turned back to Phoebe. 'Our Alfie hasn't learned me all of it yet.'

Phoebe was beginning to climb the stairs and hung over the banisters.

'I knew you'd say yes, you are an angel.' She lowered her voice. 'You'll like rehearsing with Mr Partridge, even if you don't like *her*.' She paused and jerked her thumb dramatically at the surgery. 'And you needn't worry a bit about not knowing all the words. Everybody will read what I've written at the first rehearsal. Even though I've written it, I don't know everything I've got to say, and I shall have to read it myself.'

The family meeting was held that evening after tea as arranged. Tea was a little late because Phoebe had gone up to the Abbey on the way home to ask Partridge to come to the rehearsal on Saturday.

'What'd he say?' Sally asked as soon as Phoebe came into the room.

'Nothing very much. He just looked rather sad and said he would be glad to oblige.'

'Well, don't talk,' said Christopher. 'Get on with your tea. You're awfully late and we don't want to have to sit around watching you eat.'

Augustus looked up from his plate.

'Nobody need do that. Benjamin and me will be eating for hours and hours.'

Christopher took the chair at the meeting as John was away.

'It's this bun business,' he explained. 'We've got to lay on somebody to get us buns in Linkwell on Saturdays, and I've thought of a person to do it: Mrs Miggs's Alfie. He doesn't go to school on Saturday mornings, only it'll cost something. There's his fares on the bus and I should think he'd need paying. I was wondering whether we could put in the fine-money.'

Phoebe bounced off her chair and stood up.

'Really, Christopher Andrews, I think that's the meanest suggestion I ever heard. That money's practically mine. I'm the only person who's managed to stay top of their form nearly all the time, in fact I'm the only one who's been top at all, and now you talk of giving away the money as if it belonged to everybody.'

Sally was next to Phoebe. She gave her arm a pull.

'Sit down and don't shout.' She turned to Christopher. 'She's quite right. It is almost her money. I don't think it is fair.'

Christopher looked at Selina.

'What do you say?'

Selina flushed.

'I don't think it's fair. I was wondering. After all, this pageant is for my frock. I've quite a lot of money saved. Couldn't I pay for things like Alfie fetching buns?'

Christopher looked at Sally. Christopher's eyes said, 'She gets more pocket money than we do. Is it all right to let her?' Sally's eyes answered, 'I think she wants to. I vote we do.' Christopher said:

'If only one of us had a birthday, but only John has one just now, and, though I expect he'll get some money next month, we can't expect him to pay for fetching buns he won't be here to eat.'

Selina saw that they would like to have the money to help, but it was a bit awkward letting a cousin do it all. She spoke more firmly than she usually did.

'There wouldn't be a pageant and so there wouldn't be buns to be fetched if it wasn't for my frock and shoes.'

'She's quite right,' Sally agreed. 'As Selina's nice enough to offer, let's say yes.'

Christopher took a vote. Everybody agreed except Benjamin, who was humming and had not heard what Selina offered.

'Passed unanimously,' said Christopher. 'We won't count Benjamin. If a person doesn't know it's rude to hum at a committee, they shouldn't come.'

The committee broke up then. Christopher said to Selina:

'I think I'll go and see Alfie right away. Would you like to come with me or would you like me to take him some money?'

'No, you do it. I've done a great deal of asking lately. I'll give you half a crown and if there's any change it can go towards the next Saturday.'

# CHAPTER TEN

* * *

## *Philip*

Phoebe, Partridge, and Mrs Miggs stood in a huddle on the lower lawn. Miss Lipscombe, looking very matronish, explained to them about acting.

'It's no good our just standing about reading our parts, Phoebe. What we need is a producer. When I acted with the hospital amateur dramatic, we always engaged a professional producer. Who is producing this pageant? That's what I want to know.'

Neither Partridge, Mrs Miggs, nor Phoebe had the faintest idea what Miss Lipscombe was talking about. Mrs Miggs, however, always argued on principle when she heard anyone being what she called umpshious.

''Oo wants producin'? Wot's wrong with just standin' and readin' our parts?'

Miss Lipscombe's voice was crushing.

'There should be movement.'

Mrs Miggs put her hands on her hips and danced a few steps.

'Righty ho! How about sayin' it to a cake-walk?'

Partridge cleared his throat.

'If I might suggest, Miss Phoebe, if you were to stand a little in advance to the rest of us we could stand in a row, as it were behind, and step forward as we spoke our piece.'

Miss Lipscombe sniffed.

'Nonsense!'

Mrs Miggs did not like that sniff, nor the way Miss Lipscombe spoke. She was always one, as she frequently said, to stand up for the underdog. Obviously this Mr Partridge was an underdog. Funny, old-fashioned josser, speaking as if he had prunes in his mouth, and calling Phoebe 'Miss' as if she were somebody out of an old-fashioned tale.

'I don't see nothin' wrong with wot Mr Partridge says.'

Miss Lipscombe sniffed again.

'And how do we get into a row, may I ask? Do we pop up on this lawn like daisies? We have to come on. In my case I suggest I sweep down from behind those bushes there.'

Alfie was a great supporter of the pictures, particularly of gangster and Wild West films. It had given him ideas on action in acting. He had not merely rehearsed Mrs Miggs so that she should know her lines, but invented gestures to go with them. Mrs Miggs had no intention of having these effects spoilt by Miss Lipscombe sweeping in from anywhere.

'Wot I say is we all walk in and stand in a row, none steppin' forward further than the other. That's fair to all.'

On the upper lawn Selina and Sally were sitting. Selina nudged Sally.

'Poor Phoebe. Ought we to go and help?'

Sally shook her head.

'Sssh. You know what Phoebe is. She wouldn't like it.'

Phoebe, very red in the face, had raised her voice.

'All right then. Let's stand in a row. But I shall step forward if I want to. It's me that's Anne Boleyn and the most important person.'

Miss Lipscombe shuddered.

'If there's going to be any unpleasantness . . .'

Phoebe remembered just in time that Miss Lipscombe ought not to be annoyed. She swallowed before she spoke. Then she said in a more polite voice:

'Sorry. Let's go over there and walk on. You go first, Miss Lipscombe.'

The four of them went behind the hedge. Then they marched on; Miss Lipscombe leading, then Phoebe, then Partridge and, last, Mrs Miggs. Selina gave Sally another nudge.

'It looks rather queer, doesn't it? I mean, people don't walk in in a tail like that when they're going to talk.'

Sally was determined not to interfere. She frowned at Selina and again said 'Sssh.'

Miss Lipscombe stepped forward. She took so enormous a breath that her chest swelled out. She pointed a finger at Phoebe. She made her voice tremble, to show how angry she was, and she shook her finger to make it look as though she were quivering with rage.

> 'Come, my Lady Anne,
> To your books.
> Fie! Fie!
> No sulky looks.'

119

There was a pause. Phoebe was so busy being sulky that she forgot to look at her scene to see who spoke next. It was Mrs Miggs who reminded Partridge of his duty. She gave him a dig with her elbow.

'Speak up. You're amongst friends.'

Partridge spoke in a quick, polite voice, as if he were announcing dinner. He put no expression whatsoever into his words.

> 'Fie, Mistress Dogsberry,
> That is no way to name
> This child
> Who shall have fame.'

Phoebe tossed her head and held out her arms.

> 'The sun is out
> And all the flowers bow down
> As if I wore a crown.'

Mrs Miggs barely waited for Phoebe to finish before she burst in. She spoke her first line with one finger raised just as Alfie had taught her.

''Ush, 'ush, child,' she lowered the finger and folded her arms. 'I declare,' she clutched her heart and staggered backwards, 'you make me faint with fear.'

Miss Lipscombe took another deep breath and once more pointed her finger.

> 'Away now, Lady Anne,
> 'Tis not the day for play;
> Away, away, away.'

Selina and Sally were startled to hear a choking sound behind them. They looked round and there was Philip with his handkerchief stuffed into his mouth, laughing so much that tears were pouring down his cheeks.

Sally scowled at him.

'Shut up, Philip.'

Philip was laughing far too much to stop all at once, but he was tactful enough to crouch down behind Selina and Sally so that he could not be seen from the lower lawn. When at last he began to recover he kept remembering things and started to laugh again. He murmured, 'You make me faint with fear,' and 'Fie! fie! no sulky looks.'

Phoebe's scene was nearly over before he completely recovered. Phoebe was saying:

> 'Nurse, do not kneel to me;
> And yet I see a crown,
> And all the world bows down . . .'

She broke off. 'Now this is where you get the crown of flowers and put it on my hair, and one of you claps your hands and Augustus and Benjamin bring on my train and you fasten it to my shoulders. We haven't got Augustus and Benjamin so we'll just have to pretend.'

Phoebe had a vivid imagination. Even at this first rehearsal, with the part in her hand, she was feeling as she thought the little Anne Boleyn would have felt. She did not need to have Augustus and Benjamin there in the flesh. She could see them as she thought they would look when they were acting. She watched them walk on to the lower lawn, carrying a magnificent train of cloth of gold. She moved a little to allow Mrs Miggs and Miss Lipscombe to pin it to her shoulders. She thought that Mrs Miggs and Miss Lipscombe were very dense. They did not see the cloak and so did not realize it needed pinning, but this did not stop her feeling like the little Anne Boleyn, although she had to say in a whisper, 'They've brought the cloak, pin it to my shoulders.'

She looked at Partridge. He should have fetched flowers and woven them into a wreath. Obviously Partridge was not imagining himself doing anything of the sort. He was standing with his hands folded on his part, looking very like he looked when he opened the front door. Phoebe did not mind. To her he had the wreath of flowers. She gave him a nudge. 'You've got the wreath. Put it on my head.'

Partridge jumped.

'Have I, Miss Phoebe? I'd no idea.'

'Go on,' Phoebe said, 'put it on.'

Partridge, through the years, had become very experienced at putting on coats, and he was accustomed to handing people their hats, but he had never put a wreath on anybody's head. He managed awkwardly. Phoebe did not mind, she had a crown on her head and a train fastened to her shoulders, and she was a queen. She swept away, giving room for her train to fall behind her. She looked proudly over her shoulders at Mrs Miggs and Miss Lipscombe.

'You curtsy,' and then to Partridge, 'You bow.' She smiled down to where Augustus and Benjamin would be. 'The pages have my train, and now I'm going off, and as I go you speak, Mrs Miggs.'

Mrs Miggs watched Miss Lipscombe out of the corner of her eye to see how she curtsied. Miss Lipscombe had once

played in a costume play and was very good at curtsying. Mrs
Miggs did not manage so well. Her knees creaked and she
wobbled a bit. Then she straightened up and looked after
Phoebe.

> 'Ah me! Ah me! a vision we have seen,
> That child will be our Queen.'

Phoebe stopped being the child Anne and came back to
the others. She felt flat and muddled. It had been so lovely for
a minute to be a person who was going to be a queen, and so
grand as to have Miss Lipscombe and Mrs Miggs curtsying to
her, and Partridge bowing. It was tiresome to find them just
being themselves again, and herself just Phoebe in a rather
skimpy green check frock. She looked at Sally, Philip, and
Selina.

'Do you think we ought to rehearse that again?'

Philip was talking to Sally.

'Quite an actress, young Phoebe. She managed in those last
seconds to do something with that scene, did you see?'

Phoebe's question came before Sally could answer. She
looked at Philip to see what he thought. He shook his head,
his eyes twinkling.

'I'm not going to interfere with this. There's nothing that
could be done with a scene like that.'

Sally would not stand up for Phoebe in the family, but if
anybody outside was rude about the family they all defended
each other. She called out truculently:

'It's lovely, darling, we're talking about something; wait a
minute,' and turned back to Philip. 'I should have thought it

was a pretty good scene seeing that it's been written by a kid of nine.'

'So it is.'

'What do you mean then, there's nothing could be done with it?'

'Well, there isn't. It all depends what you're aiming at. If you're aiming at showing that a child of nine can write doggerel, you've succeeded, but if you're aiming at putting on a scene in a pageant, you've failed. It's a pity, because you could probably put on a jolly good scene with Phoebe acting in it.'

Sally could see what Philip meant. She tugged at a daisy root beside her.

'But couldn't you do something to help her in producing that scene? I mean, she's written it and all that.'

Philip shook his head.

'I could not. There's nothing there that anybody could produce.'

Phoebe jumped across the path and came up and joined them.

'Do you think it's all right? I think it's pretty good myself.'

Phoebe could not have said anything more tactless. Sally could have shaken her.

'Better ask Philip what he thinks.'

Phoebe, perfectly certain that Philip had nothing but praise for her, looked up at him hopefully. She put on her puppy-asking face.

'Do you think it's all right, Philip?'

Philip took Phoebe's chin in his good hand and gave it a little shake.

'I think it's good for a person of nine, and I like the bit where you put on the crown and the train, but I didn't make out who you were. Who are you?'

Phoebe's eyes opened wide. She quite obviously thought the scene made that perfectly clear.

'Anne Boleyn as a little girl. Miss Lipscombe's my governess, Miss Dogsberry, Mr Partridge is my butler, and Mrs Miggs is my old nurse.'

'Why did you choose Anne Boleyn?'

'She was dark, like me, and she was a queen when she grew up. Do you think we ought to move about a bit? Miss Lipscombe thinks we shouldn't stand in a row.'

Philip wanted to say, 'It doesn't matter what you do. It's just funny and that's that,' but Phoebe was looking at him so askingly that he weakened. He got up and held out his hand to her.

'I'll come down to the stage and see what I can do.'

Phoebe was delighted. She pulled Philip towards Mrs Miggs and Miss Lipscombe.

'He's going to help us. He thinks it's a lovely scene, but he's going to make us move about, like you wanted, Miss Lipscombe.'

Philip had to say something so he muttered:

'Do what I can.'

Mrs Miggs nodded.

'That's all we can any of us do, sir, and it's all in a good cause, to raise money for boys like you.'

Miss Lipscombe was not going to be left out.

'No matter at what sacrifice. Rushed off my feet though I am, I'm willing to spare the time to help.'

Philip smiled at Partridge.

'Fancy yourself as an actor?'

Partridge shook his head.

'No, Mr Philip. What people are going to say when they see me I cannot guess. It's not work that I care for.'

Philip was looking round the stage.

'I think you want to add to this scene a bit, Phoebe. Bring more people on. A pageant isn't like a play, you know. You don't want too much talking. Pageants should be mostly wordless.'

Phoebe gasped. Her face went scarlet.

'Do you mean waste my lovely poetry?'

Philip tried to explain.

'You see, if the wind blows on September the twentieth, at least if it blew the wrong way, nobody will hear a word. Not unless we could fix up loudspeakers. You see, we three, Sally and Selina and I, were sitting in what would practically be the front row. You've got to think of an audience stretching right away back to the house, hundreds of them.' He saw Phoebe's face. 'You'll be able to speak some of it, of course, but I think a lot of it might be done in dumb show.' The children were arriving in twos and threes. He turned and looked at them. 'I wonder how it would be if all that crown and train business happened in a singing game.' He was walking about the stage thinking out loud. 'Little Anne could be picked as queen, crowned, use a tablecloth or something as a train, and the other three might have a premonition.' He turned to Miss Lipscombe. 'Are you good at looking as though you had a premonition?'

Miss Lipscombe was not at all sure how the scene would turn out if a lot of children were put into it. She answered guardedly:

'I'll do my best I'm sure.'

Philip turned to Mrs Miggs.

'How about you?'

'There was never a woman more given to premonitions than me, sir. Only last week I broke Mrs Andrews's blue vase, and I said to her, "Two more to go before I leave," and the words were 'ardly out of me mouth before I knocks me 'ead against a shelf and down comes two coffee-cups. So I said to 'er, "May as well smash 'em first as last."'

Philip turned to Sally.

'Could we borrow some of those kids for a minute?' Phoebe was still looking angry so he put his arm round her. 'Don't be cross with me. This is only a suggestion. If you don't like my suggestions you can act your scene exactly as it was before. I'm just going to try out something for you that might be effective.'

Margaret Peters and her sisters and six other children had arrived. Sally beckoned them over.

'I don't know that you're going to act in this scene, but we're going to try something that you might do.'

Philip was muttering round the stage.

'It's lesson-time. Partridge and a footman or somebody might bring on a table. Then I suppose the child and the nurse would come on. Wonder what toys they had in those days. Skipping-rope wouldn't look bad. Then there's the governess. Might have the children singing off and distracting the child.' He turned suddenly to the children. 'Do you know a game where somebody finishes up as a queen?'

The children looked at each other. Margaret spoke for them all.

'We never play a game like that.'

'But there is a game,' Philip persisted, 'where one girl goes in the middle, isn't there?'

Margaret nodded.

'Poor Sally sits a-weeping, but she isn't a queen.'

'How's it go? Show me.'

It took time to persuade the children to play the game. It was all very well to play a game at a party or when you wanted to, but it was different to show it seriously. At last, however, they made a ring and put Margaret's youngest sister in the middle.

'Poor Sally sits a-weeping, a-weeping, a-weeping.
Poor Sally sits a-weeping
On a fine summer's day.
Pray tell me what she's weeping for,
What she's weeping for, weeping for,
Pray tell me what she's weeping for
On a fine summer's day.
She's weeping for her lover, for her lover, for her lover,
She's weeping for her lover
On a fine summer's day.'

Margaret turned to Philip and broke the ring.

'Then she chooses one of us, and in the end they're both in the middle, see?'

Philip pointed at Phoebe.

'Now then, poetess. You do your stuff. You make it poor Anne sits a-weeping, and she's weeping for a train and a crown. Could you do that?'

Phoebe liked being called poetess but she was still cross.

'It doesn't want poetry. You just have to sing "Weeping for her trai-ain," and the next time "for her crow-own." I should have thought anybody would know that.'

Philip had become interested in Phoebe's scene, and so he did not notice the tone of her voice.

'I'm not sure about this rhyming stuff. Anne was a real

child. She wouldn't have spoken in rhyme if she were speaking to her governess or her nurse.'

Phoebe lost her temper.

'I only spent most of my Christmas holidays and most of last term writing that poetry, and all the Easter holidays copying it out. Of course it doesn't matter to me a bit if you tear it up.'

Philip felt a beast.

'I say, I am sorry, Phoebe. I didn't mean that. Jolly good poetry for somebody of your age. Don't pay any attention to me. It's your scene. Go on and do it your way.'

Phoebe did not want Philip not to help, but if he helped she only wanted him to help her in an admiring way. If he was going to interfere and tear up her poetry she was not going to let him have anything to do with her scene. She spoke in her proudest voice.

'If everybody would get off the grass we could get on with our rehearsal. I don't like to be rude, but you're all in the way.'

Sally led the children off the lower lawn. Philip and Selina went back and sat down on the upper lawn. Philip made a face.

'I did put my foot in it. I wouldn't have hurt her feelings for the world. She's a clever little thing, but the scene is frightful as it is; you do agree, don't you?'

Selina tried to find words to explain what she meant.

'It was all right as it was when we first thought of the pageant, but it doesn't seem to be all right in the rather grander sort of pageant you're thinking of.'

Philip put a cigarette in his mouth and lit it with his lighter.

'When I was about the same age as Phoebe I started using that bit of lawn as a stage. I've been everything on it—William the Conqueror, Lord Nelson, Robin Hood, Henry the Fifth. I always told my aunt and uncle that I should put on a show here some day. Then the war came and now they've got to sell the place, so I never will.'

'Unless our pageant is that show.'

He smiled at her.

'I mustn't let it be. I should have hated it if someone had stepped in and produced me when I was Phoebe's age.'

'When you said there would be hundreds of people watching all the way back to the house, do you think there really will?'

'Well, a hundred anyway. People from the villages round and the American camp and so on.'

Selina pictured herself in her organdie frock carrying roses, coming down speaking to a hundred people. The lines she had written were suitable for a little pageant, but not for a hundred people to hear.

'I should think if a hundred people are coming we'd all be glad if you helped. Not perhaps Phoebe, but all the others would.'

He looked at her, his eyes crinkling at the corners.

'Temptress. If you knew how I was bursting to get my paws on it.'

'Of course I can't answer for John and Christopher, but you're already helping Sally with her thing, and if you always meant to act here ever since you were a little boy—well, this is your last chance, and I should think everybody'd agree it was only fair you should have some say.'

He was silent for a minute or two. Then it was almost as if he were speaking to himself.

'Knights, horses, kings, queens, robbers—I've had them all waiting in the wings for years. Fun, just for once, to bring them to life.'

# CHAPTER ELEVEN

───────•●•───────

## *Christopher's Rehearsal*

Christopher and his friends arrived at the rehearsal in a very knock-each-other-about mood. Christopher had got the haziest idea about mummers. He had written a part for himself in which, as the devil, he ran round with a pitchfork and the other seven boys fell over. To make this funny some of the boys were to be dressed as women. He had also put in some jokes. They were the sort in which the funny man says, 'My dog ain't got no nose,' and the feed for the funny man asks, 'How does he smell?' and the funny man answers, 'Awful.' To put it in period Christopher had tacked on a word or two. The jokes began 'Prithee, master, tell me,' otherwise they were just any jokes that he had heard on the wireless and thought funny. But as he and the seven boys who were going to be mummers came along the road from the school they began to write up their parts, until they were all roaring jokes at each other. They thought themselves so terribly funny that they could not stop laughing. The rest of the cast and

Philip and Selina could hear the mummers long before they reached the upper lawn. Sally looked expressively at Philip.

'You'll have to help or this isn't going to be a serious rehearsal.'

Christopher and the seven mummers raced down on to the lower lawn. Christopher shouted:

'Look for sticks everybody. We want sticks for pitchforks.'

Sally said:

'Miss Lipscombe's been here a long time and she likes a proper rehearsal. You won't just fool, will you?'

Christopher was a little damped at this reminder of Miss Lipscombe.

'We won't fool more than we have to in this sort of scene; but that's what they mostly did, fool about and shout things at the crowd.'

Sally did not answer back. Instead she said:

'Where do you want the children? And will you tell them what they've got to do.'

Christopher had no idea what the children would have to do.

'You tell them. They're just doing what the rabble will do. Running after the witch and somebody says, "To the pond. To the pond." I thought Mrs Mawser might do that, and somebody else says, "Drown the blasted she-goat." Mrs Mawser could do both really.'

Sally had already guessed that Christopher was not in a very sensible mood. Now she could see he was in a very silly one indeed. She was glad Mrs Mawser was not there.

'Mrs Mawser won't say anything, and can you see her saying things like that? You know she wouldn't.'

'Well, somebody's got to, and I don't know who else'll do it.'

'One of the real rabble will have to when you've got them. Today I'll say it. How does Miss Lipscombe come on to the stage?'

One of the boys rushed up to Christopher and prodded him with a stick.

'Have at thee, Satan.'

Christopher jumped away from Sally and her boring questions.

'Anything'll do for today. After all, it's only a first rehearsal.'

'If you won't produce your own scene, you'd better let Philip do it. He's helping with mine.'

Christopher did not at that moment care who produced his scene provided everybody got out of the way and let him and his mummers be as funny as they liked.

'Good idea.'

He brandished his stick and made fiendlike noises. He chased the boy who had prodded him round the lower lawn.

Philip proved unexpectedly knowledgeable on mummers.

'What date is it?' he asked Sally.

Sally shouted to Christopher:

'Come here a second. Philip says what date is your mummers' play?'

Christopher unwillingly left off his chase and joined Selina, Sally, and Philip on the upper lawn.

'I don't know. It was the date that they were.'

Philip laughed.

'Well, that covers a pretty big field. Practically from the Norman Conquest up to the present day. What sort of a play is it?'

Christopher felt as if Philip had dug a pin into him. It was

133

such fun being a noisy mummer and so depressing being tied down to dates and facts and dull things like that.

'Just mummers. They always came to villages. I'm the devil. There was often a devil in them, I learned that at school.'

'Mummers?' Philip's face lit up. 'That's a pretty good theme for a pageant. You and the rest of the mummers would be people from the village performing your play. Not that we have a mummers' play here, but lots of places do. You do a sword dance too, you know. You could, of course, be Beelzebub; he did come in sometimes, but more often he was just known as The Fool. The Fool wore the skin of an animal.'

Christopher liked the sound of that.

'Did he tell jokes and make everybody laugh?'

'I'm not sure about that. I think it was more that he did things that made people laugh, he and somebody dressed up as a hobby-horse. Oh, yes, and there was a woman, or rather a man dressed as a woman. She was called The Bessy.'

'Who else ought there to be?'

'The hero, of course. He'd be a saint. And I think a funny doctor.'

Christopher looked worried.

'I haven't written parts for all those. I've just written "First mummer", "Second mummer", things like that.'

'Well, you don't need to say much in a pageant. Anyway, I think the words were more a couple or so of rhymes to introduce each person. If you wanted words I imagine we could get hold of the real thing.'

Christopher liked the jokes he had written, but he never had been certain they would make people laugh.

'I'd much rather be funny doing things.'

Philip had a sudden idea.

'I tell you what: there used to be processions. I'll have to look it up but it was something to do with St George. The affairs were organized by the Guilds of St George. I think they were called Ridings. I think they must have had all the funny stuff in and I suppose a collection for money at the end. It'd be very effective stuff in a pageant. Kind of period Lord Mayor's Show, you know. I should think we could choose any fairly convenient period. I have an idea they were going on in the eighteenth century. The seventeenth century wouldn't be bad. Good period for dressing.'

Christopher hugged his knees.

'Would that be all right for a witch? You see, I couldn't just make my mummers act and nothing else happening, so I made the village turn out and stone a witch. It's when they are chasing her the mummers come, and then everybody watches the mummers, and the witch escapes and at the end everybody's chasing after her.'

'Witch would be all right as part of the set-up. What's she done? Overlooked a pig or something?'

'What's that mean—overlooking a pig?'

'I'm not quite sure how witches overlooked pigs, but they certainly did, and the pig died. I imagine really the pig had colic or whatever it was.'

'I haven't written what the witch has done, I just have her running and being stoned.'

'Well, let's have a look at it and see how it goes. We'll soon see if there's a line needed.'

'I'm not really having only children,' Christopher explained.

'I'm having lots of grown-ups as rabble, but I thought they might get put off if they had to wait around at rehearsals.'

'Too true,' Philip agreed. 'Grown-ups are awful that way.'

It was extraordinary how quickly Philip got order. In no time he had got the mummers sorted out. He just said, 'You'll be St George. You'll be Maid Marian. You'll be The Bessy. I'll tell you about her. You'll be the Hobby-horse. You can be a Turkish Knight and you a funny doctor. You'll have to be inside the dragon and open and shut his mouth. And you will be a fat man, a blustering sort of fellow, probably a skit on somebody in the village.' He then turned to the children.

'Now, you're being the people in the village. Actually there'll be more people than this because you're being the grown-up people as well as the children now. Do any of you know what a witch is?'

Margaret Peters looked shocked at such ignorance.

'Of course. She rides on a broomstick with a black cat on the end.'

'I didn't mean that sort. I mean the sort of witches that people believed in and ducked in ponds.' Even Margaret could not answer that, so Philip went on. 'Just some ordinary old woman who had got a bad name and whenever anything went wrong, a pig dying or a child getting ill, she was blamed for it. Well, in this village, probably about three hundred years ago, it is St George's Day, that's April the 23rd, and you're all waiting to see a procession pass. You know what that is?'

Margaret Peters again spoke up.

''Course. We had a torchlight one for VE Day.'

'So you did. Well, this is a procession in honour of St George. There are going to be flags and St George and his Dragon and funny men, and then, while you're all waiting, down the village street runs the witch being chased by somebody and she's caught, and she screams. Does she speak, Christopher?'

Christopher nodded.

'Pages. Only it's written in rather big handwriting.'

'Well, she is caught and you all start to chase her off and throw things at her. Then you hear music and the procession comes on. Now, I want half of you children to go off that side and half on this side, and when I say "Now" I want you to come running on exactly as you ran out into the streets to see the torchlight procession on VE Day.' He turned to Miss Lipscombe. 'You go off up there. Who's to chase her, Christopher?'

'One of the rabble. Two really, they've got things to say.'

'Well, you had better do that for today. You and some of your mummers. You can get back into the procession afterwards.'

The lower lawn was empty. Philip called out 'Now'.

It is extraordinary how difficult it is to do ordinary things on a stage. The children came on exactly as Philip had told them, only they did not look in the least like they had done on VE Day. For one thing they never said a word, for another they kept on stopping and nudging each other and whispering, 'You go first.' 'No, you.' Then, as soon as they were on the stage, some stood so still they might have been turned into statues. Those that moved fidgeted and giggled and looked as if they did not know what to do with their hands and feet. Philip laughed and beckoned to them to come and talk to him.

'Are you going to tell me that that's how you came out into the streets to see the torchlight procession? Didn't you say anything to anybody? Now, let's try something else.' He looked round. 'Sally, Selina, and you mummers, will you get into a line and be a torchlight procession?' He turned back to the children. 'I was in hospital on VE Day so I didn't see the torchlight procession. Would you all try and remember what you said, how you looked, what you felt like and show me. Could you do that?'

There was a murmur of 'yes' from the children.

'What time was the torchlight procession?'

There was an argument about this, finally it was agreed it was eight o'clock at night.

'And were there fireworks?'

There was another chorus of 'yes'.

'Oh, dear, I did miss something. Now, off you go. I'm going to count eight this time. It's eight o'clock at night. It's Victory Day and we're going to see a torchlight procession.'

This time the children were very good indeed. It started by just two or three of them being good, and then the others heard them saying, 'Come on, the procession's just about to start,' and 'I want to see the fireworks,' and quicker than you could believe they were all talking to each other and pretending it was VE Night, and, when Sally led the others on as the torchlight procession, everybody said 'Ooh! Ooh!' just as if they were seeing a real torchlight procession.

'Yes,' said Philip, 'that's more like it. Now I want you to do that all over again, only this time you're talking about another sort of procession. You can say you want to see St George and the Dragon and the funny man, and you can ask each other whether they've brought money for the collection. But although you're saying different things, you go on thinking of it as VE Night and you'll be quite perfect.'

138

Philip took the children through that first entrance ten times before he was even nearly satisfied. They had to come on from all the different entrances, and form up on two sides of the stage, leaving a path like a village street from left to right across the stage. It was not very easy for them, because there was nothing to mark it, but by the tenth time they left not at all a bad village street, and they were no longer stuffed dummies but real children come out to see a procession.

'Now,' said Philip, 'where's that witch?'

Miss Lipscombe was longing to act her scene. Philip's rehearsing was what she considered proper rehearsing, and because he could rehearse a scene she was sure he would be able to appreciate good acting when he saw it. She looked forward to the words of praise he would give her when the scene was over. She stepped on the stage.

'I'm here. Would you please tell me what you want me to do.'

Philip looked at Miss Lipscombe with a polite face, but inside he wanted to laugh. He thought he had never seen anyone look less like a bedraggled old witch. She had on a brown coat and skirt and a very neat felt hat with a brown feather bird on it. She had got used throughout her career to wearing stiff collars and she had on a brown tussore blouse with a stiff collar. She had on good stout stockings and flat brown shoes. She peered at Philip through her pince-nez, looking so neat and so respectable that it seemed rude even to suggest that she was chased and thrown mud at.

Philip said:

'I'm afraid this may be rather a rough scene. They hadn't very gentle manners, you know, in the seventeenth century. I mean, your hair would be down and your clothes half-torn off.'

139

Miss Lipscombe, though inwardly dismayed at this picture, betrayed no sign. She looked Philip straight in the eyes.

'We must all make sacrifices in the cause of art.'

'Right. You come down here chased by Christopher and his fellow thugs. What does she say, Christopher?'

'Somebody says "To the pond. To the pond", and somebody else says, "Drown the blasted she-goat."'

The children, who had begun to lose interest in the scene, brightened up. They roared with laughter and murmured to each other, 'Blasted she-goat.'

Philip looked at Christopher.

'You've started something. Now, what do you say, Miss Lipscombe?'

Miss Lipscombe took a deep breath. She started a little weakly, but as she went on her voice rose and trembled and, where it was necessary, she screamed.

'Have pity, neighbours, have pity. I'm not a witch, that I swear, I'm but a poor old widow woman, living on weeds and carrion and such-like that I can find.'

Christopher looked at Philip.

'That's where somebody says, "To the pond. To the pond."'

Miss Lipscombe gave a tremendous shout and screamed:

'No, no. Not the pond. 'Tis death to me for my skin to touch water.'

Christopher repeated 'To the pond. To the pond.' Miss Lipscombe screamed again.

'No, no. Spare, oh spare, a frail old woman who never meant any harm. If you see me out in the moonlight it is only because I like walking at that time. Besides, sometimes I can

140

find herbs and things growing in the moonlight that I wouldn't find at the ordinary time of day.'

Philip held up his hand and stopped Miss Lipscombe.

'Are you absolutely determined that she's got to say all this, Christopher? I should have thought a few screams and hysterical mutterings would be good. And one of the crowd chasing could shout "She killed my pig" or something.' Miss Lipscombe was looking rather peculiar so Philip said, 'It's as you like, of course, but it will be child's play to an actress like yourself. Just scream and have hysterics and all the rest of it. Now, throw down that script and let's see how it looks.'

It was the sort of scene that went well from the beginning. Once the sheet of paper was out of Miss Lipscombe's hands it was easy. Miss Lipscombe ran and screamed, and though her pince-nez did not fall off, her hat went on one side. Christopher and the other boys shouted 'To the pond. To the pond,' and Mrs Miggs, who, without being asked, had joined in the witch-hunt, shouted all by herself, 'Drown the blasted she-goat.' The children enjoyed the scene so much they forgot to be self-conscious and laughed and pointed just as they would have done had they been real children three hundred years ago.

'Yes,' said Philip. 'That's fine, but now you hear something. You hear distant music. The moment you hear that, every single person on the stage, except Miss Lipscombe, forgets the witch and turns and looks up at that left-hand corner and shouts, "The Ridings! The Ridings! They're coming", and after that you jostle and push each other and stand on tiptoe and tell each other you can see the procession coming, and all the while the music's getting louder.' He turned to Christopher.

141

'We'll have to time this. I imagine you'll have to start in the sunk rose garden. You'll start just about the time Miss Lipscombe is being dragged towards the exit. It'll have to be done by my waving a flag or something. Now, you boys must all go off. Mrs Miggs, you drag Miss Lipscombe to the exit. Now, I'm going to be the music.'

The second half of the scene did not go so well. Philip beat with the flat of his hand on the back of a book and began to whistle. The children turned and, rather sheepishly and dully, said, 'The Ridings! The Ridings!' Philip did not take them back that time. He went on with his music. Then he signalled to St George, who led the procession, to come on.

It was four o'clock by the time Philip had got some life into the procession and the children showing some sort of animation. Sally came up to him apologetically.

'I simply hate to interrupt, but Miss Faulkes is here with a Madame Ramosova. I think she must be the head of the Linkwell dancing-school. She's asking for you.' She gripped his arm, her eyes shining with a mixture of fear and excitement. 'Oh, Philip, you never told me she was coming today. Don't let her see my rehearsal, please, please, swear that you won't.'

142

# CHAPTER TWELVE

———◆●◆———

## *Madame Ramosova*

Madame Ramosova was small and dark. She was nearly sixty but she did not look as old as that. She had dark eyes, which flashed with interest whenever she spoke, and a very slim figure, but the most noticeable thing about her were her hands. They were slender and white and beautifully made, and she used them a great deal when she talked. To Sally, Miss Faulkes had always seemed a slim, elegant person, but beside Madame Ramosova she looked clumsy. Miss Faulkes was usually brisk and very much the head of the dancing-class, but today she hung back behind Madame Ramosova looking, Sally thought, as shy as she felt herself. Madame Ramosova came over to Philip, her hands held out in greeting. She had a touch of a foreign accent.

'Phil-eep, I was so glad, my dear, dear boy, to hear you are getting better and have come home. And already busy! "Is that not like Phil-eep?" I said. "Others lie on invalid chairs but Phil-eep, he produces a pageant."'

143

Philip kissed Madame Ramosova.

'It's not my pageant. It's the work of the Andrews children.' He looked round and saw Sally and beckoned to Christopher. 'These are the only two about at the moment. This is Sally, the dancer of the family.'

Madame's face lit up with interest. She ran an eye over Sally.

'So you are Sally.' She turned to Miss Faulkes. 'This is the child you've spoken to me about, yes?'

Miss Faulkes nodded.

'Yes, madame. She'll do very well if she works hard.'

Philip pulled Christopher forward.

'And this is her twin, Christopher. One of the co-authors of the pageant.' He looked round. 'Where's Phoebe?' He raised his voice. 'Phoebe. Phoebe.'

Phoebe, directly after her rehearsal, had gone behind a flower-bed where she could watch Christopher's rehearsal without being seen. She had tried to persuade herself that Philip was making an awful muddle of Christopher's scene, and that Christopher would have to do what she had done and refuse to have any interference. But as she had watched the scene she had begun to doubt. It did seem as though it had improved while Philip was doing something about it. She had just decided to go home to tea when she saw Madame Ramosova arrive. Phoebe was always intensely curious. She was delighted when Philip called her. She had not wanted to come without being called, because she wanted Philip to know that she was still annoyed with him, but if he had not called her when he did she would have made some excuse to butt in. She sauntered along with what she hoped was a casual air.

'Did I hear my name?'

Philip was not fooled for a moment. He knew Phoebe must have been somewhere within earshot to arrive so neatly on the spot.

'Oh, there you are, Phoebe.' He held out his good hand. 'Come and meet Madame Ramosova, head of the Linkwell Ballet School. This is Miss Phoebe Andrews. I'm not having anything to do with her scene in the pageant, which is written throughout in rhyme and is being produced by the author.'

Phoebe shook Madame Ramosova's hand.

'Not rhyme, poetry.'

Madame Ramosova laughed.

'Dear me, that's very ambitious. How old are you?'

'Nine and eight months.'

'And do you dance?'

Phoebe shook her head.

'No. I go to ordinary school dancing-class, but not to a special one. I don't like doing anything unless I do it better than other people, so I don't dance.'

Madame Ramosova's face was grave, but her eyes twinkled.

'There would probably be fewer broken hearts in the world if everyone worked on that principle.' She turned to Philip. 'Now, Phil-eep, in what way can I help?'

Philip glanced at Sally.

'It's your story.'

Sally shook her head.

'No, you explain.'

Philip explained. He said that the children were doing the pageant on the twentieth of September and that Sally had planned a masque for her scene, to be danced in front of Queen Elizabeth. He took Madame Ramosova on to the lower lawn and showed her the entrances and exits.

'You see, there really is something here. We could get some quite beautiful effects. Of course I don't know whether we could raise any flood lighting, and do it in the evening as well as the daytime, but I've always seen this as a natural theatre.'

Madame Ramosova smiled.

'Did you act here yourself when you were a child?'

'Yes. Then, when I grew up, I meant to put on something big, but the war stopped that. It's a bit of luck really that the children planned the pageant. You know my uncle is selling the place?'

Madame Ramosova looked sympathetic.

'I've heard. Very sad for Colonel and Mrs Day. There's one difficulty that I see, the rehearsals, and even the performance, will take place in the summer holidays, when my school will be closed. But I'm holding a summer school and some of my old girls will attend it, and quite a number of my present pupils live not so far away. I think perhaps we could help.' She said to Sally: 'Can I see what you've planned?'

Sally turned scarlet.

'We've only had one rehearsal. I don't suppose the children remember. It'll all be the most frightful mess.' She looked pleadingly at Miss Faulkes. 'You know how slow I am at remembering.'

Madame Ramosova did not give Miss Faulkes time to answer.

'I do not mind at all. I'm quite used to early rehearsals. Let me see how far you've gone, and we will see how my girls can be fitted in.'

Philip pointed to the left of the stage.

'Queen Elizabeth, and, I suppose, local notables as her ladies-in-waiting and so on, will be on a dais there. We've got somehow to perform the masque in such a way that she still remains the centrepiece of the picture. There should, I think, be a crowd of locals standing round, their attention on the Queen rather than on the masque.'

Madame Ramosova nodded.

'Then, of course, the masque must be performed on a slant; that is to say, to the dais with the Queen on it and not to the audience. Perhaps it will be possible to get that dais further down stage so that the dancers do not have to have their backs to the audience.'

Philip agreed.

'Sally and I have some idea that the Queen of the fairies, typifying Gloriana, could be one of your dancers, and perhaps some other characters could be added.'

Madame Ramosova, Philip, Miss Faulkes, and Phoebe sat on the upper lawn. Selina hung about behind them, longing to join the party but too shy.

I do think it's mean of Philip, she thought, introducing all the cousins and leaving me out. Nobody would think the whole idea of having a pageant at all was my frock. In fact, nobody would think I had anything to do with the pageant.

Sally was trying to start the gramophone. But she was in such a flurried state that she kept dropping the needle. She glanced up and saw Selina.

'I say, come and put the gramophone on, Selina. And then you might see that the children are all out of sight before they come on.'

Philip remembered Selina had not been introduced. He called out to her as she was going by.

'Selina. This is Madame Ramosova,' and then, turning to Madame Ramosova, 'This is Selina Cole. She's the Andrewses' cousin, she's being brought up with them.'

Madame Ramosova had heard Sally call Selina.

'Are you going to be the stage manager? Very useful too. I always think that not enough praise or thanks goes to stage managers of amateur theatricals.' She watched Selina join Sally, then she turned to Phoebe. 'Tell me about your scene while we're waiting.'

Phoebe was charmed. Casting sidelong glances at Philip and speaking with great passion to show how much she believed in her own work, she explained her scene, giving short quotations from each part. Madame Ramosova, she discovered, was a splendid audience. She never interrupted, but just nodded her head. At the end she said, 'Dear me. I'd no idea that Anne Boleyn's future had been prophesied. I'm sure it will be a very interesting scene.'

Phoebe was so encouraged by this sympathy that she enlisted Madame's help against Philip.

'And Philip wanted to take all the words out, and put in a lot of children to dance instead. Can you imagine anything so silly?'

Madame did not answer at once.

'Of course, if all the other scenes are going to have a great many characters in them, a little scene with four people . . .'

'Six with Benjamin and Augustus.'

'Well, six. I expect Phil-eep is afraid it will look less important than the big scenes, but we shall see.'

At that moment the rehearsal on the stage started, and Phoebe, though she would have liked to have said a great deal more, had to be quiet because Madame Ramosova said 'Sssh' in the kind of whisper that expects to be obeyed.

Sally was quite right in thinking that the children would remember nothing. It was her first attempt at producing anything, and she had not thought to write down which of the thirty children came on from which side, and the long pause before the rehearsal started was due to the fact that all the children argued.

'She didn't come in on that side. She came on this side along with me.'

'No, she didn't.'

'I wasn't this side. I was on the other.'

It took the most tremendous time and a great deal of exertion to get this sorted out. Then, when the children did come on, they seemed to have forgotten everything they had been taught. Sally gave up whispering from the side of the stage and came on herself and shouted:

'Now, two rings. Now one ring inside the other. Now dance off and on again. This time right off.'

By the time she came to her own first solo she was hot and exhausted, and covered with confusion. Whatever could Madame Ramosova be thinking? It was mean of Philip not to back her up. He could so easily have said there was nothing ready for her to see yet. But Sally loved dancing, and when the lovely music of 'Greensleeves' started she forgot to be annoyed and flustered. It was nice dancing with the children and, because she was on the stage with them, the children gained confidence and began to remember what they ought to be doing. When, at the end of the masque, the children danced off and Sally had escaped from them and was supposed to be back in the world again, she began really to enjoy herself. A lot of the steps that she was doing needed practice and lacked finish, but she felt happy all over. When the masque was over she told the children to put on their shoes, but not their socks, and very shyly she went up to speak to Madame Ramosova. She expected criticism and was quite willing to have it. What she did not expect was that her ballet would not be mentioned at all. She forgot that Madame Ramosova had seen bits of rehearsals all her life, and dances sketched out, and that it would never cross her mind to give detailed criticism of something which did not concern her. She was talking to Philip when Sally reached her.

'I think the theme of the girl stolen by the fairies might stand. Of course it's very simple, but then you want something very simple for this sort of thing. I've a lovely redhead who might dance the Fairy Queen. I think that we might have perhaps twelve or sixteen dancers to accompany her. I will work out something. These open-air affairs should not be elaborate. The audience will be drawn, I suppose, from the surrounding villages and Linkwell.'

Philip laughed.

'What's left of the surrounding villages. They'll most of them be acting in the scenes, though I dare say we can use the same people two or three times over. I've got to think of something to pull the whole thing into shape. I was wondering whether you couldn't help there. You see, if we're going to use the same people in more than one scene they must have

150

time to change, and I should rather have liked to have some connecting theme joining one scene to the other.'

Madame Ramosova nodded.

'Puck, or the spirits of the Abbey, or something of that sort?'

'That's right. Somebody or something beckoning to the spirits of the past. Sort of ushering on each scene. Would you think about that?'

Madame suddenly remembered Sally.

'I don't think that my dancers need interfere with what you're planning for your little girls to do, except when you reach fairyland. I think that your dancing with them should take place on the earth, and my girls will represent fairyland. We must think out the music and how it's best for the children to bring you to the Queen of the Fairies. I like your traditional music and we can find some more, suitable for a fairy ballet.' She turned back to Philip. 'What are you going to do about music?'

Philip had to admit he had not thought. He said he supposed they might be able to get an orchestra. There was a very good band attached to the American camp, but he doubted whether it could be spared for many rehearsals. It would be worth approaching the authorities because, if they could get it, it was much better than anything local; they could do with a piano for rehearsals. He then asked Madame Ramosova and Miss Faulkes to come into the house for tea.

Sally, Christopher, and Selina looked after them as they walked up the lawn. Christopher saw that Sally was feeling in a way disappointed.

'It would be pretty good if we had a real band. We'd never thought of that.'

Sally nodded. She could not explain how she felt. She was terribly glad that Madame Ramosova was going to help, and it was simply tremendous that Philip was taking a hand and the pageant was going to be so big and important, but it did seem that the pageant was becoming less and less theirs. It was awful to think it was being discussed by Madame Ramosova and Miss Faulkes, and Colonel and Mrs Day over their tea and they were not there to hear what was said.

Christopher's seven mummers were rushing about all over the garden. Sally nodded in their direction.

'You'd better take them home to tea. We promised we wouldn't make much noise. Selina and I will be along when we've washed the children's feet. Don't be a hog with the buns. Alfie got heaps.'

Selina and Sally walked home together, Selina carrying the portable gramophone and Sally the records.

'Of course it's the most marvellous experience for me,' Sally said, 'seeing Madame Ramosova's dancers, and I suppose I'll actually dance with them in that bit in fairyland.' Sally was rapidly cheering up. Selina could feel that in a few minutes she was going to think that she had enjoyed every moment of the afternoon and everything was for the best in the best of all possible worlds. The cousins were like that. You could never be sure of anything they felt lasting for long. 'I expect the children will sort of drag me on and then I shall dance with those twelve or sixteen dancers that Madame Ramosova was talking about.' Sally stood still, her face glowing. 'Do you suppose that will mean that I shall be asked to go to special rehearsals at the Ballet School at Linkwell?'

Selina tried hard, but she did not sound very enthusiastic.

'I suppose it might.'

Sally hated lack of enthusiasm.

'You might be more interested. It would be a pretty important thing for me if I went over to the Ballet School at Linkwell. And, anyway, this is your pageant and you ought to be excited about anything that happens.'

Selina tried not to sound bitter.

'My pageant! You didn't hear what happened. Nobody mentioned me in the pageant at all. Philip forgot to introduce me to Madame Ramosova. He only remembered when you called me to put on the gramophone records, and then Madame Ramosova said that she was sure I would make a good stage manager.'

Sally was not listening. She was posed in the middle of the lane with one knee raised.

'Do you think this is a better finish than the one I did this afternoon?'

It was on the tip of Selina's tongue to say, 'I don't know and I don't care, and just for once would you think about me.' But she knew that Sally was not meaning to be unkind, she just had that sort of mind that thought nothing important except dancing. Instead she said:

'I'll tell you at the next rehearsal.'

# CHAPTER THIRTEEN

## *John Comes Home*

The end of the term seemed to them all to drag inter-
minably, but it dragged most of all for John. John was
enjoying his term, but the letters he had from home
made him restive. He had never had many letters from his
brothers and sisters, but in the last half of that summer term
they stopped writing altogether. His mother wrote to him
every Sunday, just as she had always done, and his father usually put in a note at the same time, but it was these letters
which made him restive. They were all about the pageant,
and, as is the way of people writing from home to people who
are not there, they forgot what they had told him in the last
letters, and took his knowing a lot of things for granted. So he
would read suddenly, 'Christopher is very busy now on
Saturdays. Not only do he and Philip have a rehearsal but
Christopher has to jog about on his bicycle asking people to
take part. He seems to be going to use the entire population
of every village in the county in his scene.'

155

Another time it was a letter from his father which said, 'Colonel Day is in touch with the transport authorities. He is trying to get special buses and trains run for this pageant of yours.' Then there was another letter from his mother, in which she said, 'Augustus and Benjamin are in such demand for Saturday rehearsals that I have had to say they can only rehearse two scenes on any Saturday afternoon. They get so spoilt and what my old nannie used to call "above themselves" in all that crowd.'

When John had left home the one topic of conversation had been VE Day. The pageant was going to happen but it had rather fallen into the background. In any case it had never been the sort of pageant that it seemed to be now. Whole villages taking part! Special trains and buses! All that crowd on Saturday afternoons! What on earth could be happening? He began feverishly to learn his own part. Because he had the whole term to do it in he had not bothered with it very much. Now things plainly had gone ahead so fast he must arrive home word-perfect. He wrote to Christopher in rather a lordly tone. The pageant might have got on a good way without him, but he was still the eldest and the pageant had been his idea. 'Will you ask Mr Laws, Dad, and anybody you can rake up who has got a horse, to come to a rehearsal the day after I get home. I want some monks to walk about too, but they can come to the next rehearsal. I don't mind what time the rehearsal is; ask Dad and Mr Laws what time they can manage.' At the end of the letter he put PS—'Tell Selina I hope she's got Mr Laws word-perfect and, if not, will she hurry up and see that he is.'

This letter reached the family as something of a bombshell. John's scene, which was to be the first scene in the pageant, had stopped being called John's scene. They had adopted Philip's name for it, which was 'That Medieval Affair'. Every now and again, when they were going through lists of casts, he would say, 'Don't forget, Sally, that the men in your scene will have to be monks and what-not in that medieval affair. They'll have time to change during Phoebe's Anne Boleyn doings.' Sometimes at rehearsal he would say, 'See if that fellow has a horse. Good knight type for that medieval affair.' On paper, 'That Medieval Affair', besides its leading players, had got twenty-five horsemen and forty-two monks. Christopher showed the letter to Selina.

'Does Mr Laws know his part?'

Selina hesitated and then decided to speak the truth.

'I haven't had a chance to go and hear it. Every Saturday there's a rehearsal and I'm looking after the children, or sorting people out, or turning on gramophones.'

'Well, you'd better get on with it or there'll be a row next week when John comes home.'

Christopher asked Sally what steps he had better take about John's rehearsal.

'Do you think I'd better ask all those knights and monks or let him start with a few?'

Sally was living in the clouds. Some time in August she was to go over to Linkwell to rehearse with the Ballet School. This was so absorbing a thought that it was all she could do to keep her place in form. She had no mind ever to worry about John's troubles. In fact she did not see them as troubles. How splendid for him to find twenty-five people on horseback and forty-two monks when all he had expected was a few people on horses and perhaps two monks.

'Of course ask them all. He's got to hurry. I shouldn't think Dad can manage rehearsals except on Thursdays, but you can ask him. I should think Mr Laws could come any time, if Dad fetched him. If he is left to come by himself he'll forget.'

It was not easy for Selina to miss a rehearsal on Saturday afternoon. Philip called her the SM, which, he said, meant stage manager. To Selina it seemed to mean that you were the person that everybody shouted for.

'Where's the SM? I say, do keep those kids quiet on the side, Selina. We want a chair for the dais. Well, ask the SM, Selina. Selina, will you please make out a list of everybody who should appear in any scene, and call a roll-call before the scene. If anybody's missing you might find out why. Sally, I shouldn't try and remember to bring the gramophone needles, you never do remember. Leave it to the SM. It's her job.'

In a way Selina did not mind. She was obviously very useful and knowing this had its effect on her. Because everybody was always shouting for her at once she began to feel less inferior. She knew that she was just doing all the odd jobs that nobody else had time to do, but it is impossible to be important to everybody concerned in an undertaking, and not gain confidence. Sometimes, as she was rushing about with her lists, or finding makeshift properties, or saying something polite to somebody who said they were being pushed to the back of the scene when they ought to be in the front, she wondered who would do all the things she did when it came to the real performance. Of course she would be able to help quite a lot in all the middle part of the pageant, but before the pageant she would be busy making up and dressing like every-body else, and dressed in cream organdie and carrying red roses she would not be very useful for all the sort of dirty jobs she did, such as handing out properties and carrying tables and chairs about.

She kept hoping Philip would rehearse her. Just coming on alone he did not seem to bother. But it seemed a pity, as he was being so professional with all the other scenes, except Phoebe's, that he should not do something about hers. Even if he only read the words. So few words were now being spoken that she sometimes wondered whether her speaking part was not a bit long. But you could not really come on and say 'I am the Spirit of England' and nothing else. She did one day say 'You will rehearse the Prologue and Epilogue, won't you?'

He had been very nice in a casual way. He had put his arm round her shoulders and said, 'Don't worry, old thing, it's in the bag.' Then he talked about something else.

Selina went to the vicarage the very day John's letter arrived. She had to go after she had finished her homework, so it was six o'clock. She did not need to ring the front-door bell, the vicar was in his garden. He had a pair of clippers and was cutting the dead heads off his roses. He was pleased to see Selina.

'Good evening, my dear. Come over here. Stoop down. Did you ever smell anything sweeter than this rose? I was not able to buy new rose trees during the war, but year after year they flowered. I really think they have grown sweeter with each year. Now you must let me pick you some. Which would you like?'

Selina was very pleased to have some roses. She would put them in a vase on her dressing-table, but she knew it would be hopeless trying to get the vicar's attention if he was cutting them.

'I have come to hear your part.'

The vicar stopped and stroked a yellow rosebud.

'I think I must cut you this little fellow.'

'Thank you awfully, but when you've cut it would you listen to me? I've come to hear your part.'

He was not listening. Selina remembered what her uncle had done when they had come to ask him to be the Abbot. She put her hand under his elbow, and, as he finished cutting the rosebud, she helped him up and gently turned him to face her.

'I've come to hear your part in the pageant.'

The vicar looked at her with a puzzled frown.

'What was that, dear?'

'Your part of the Abbot. Do you know it?'

Light dawned in the vicar's face.

'The Abbot. Of course. An invention of John's. Purely imaginary, I'm afraid. No history of an ancient abbey.'

He was turning away to go back to his roses, as if in those few words he had dismissed the whole pageant and it were not going to happen. Selina once more caught his elbow.

'John comes home next week. There is going to be a rehearsal. I expect it will be Thursday because it's Uncle Jim's half-day. You've got to be absolutely word-perfect. Besides you and Uncle Jim and John there're twenty-five knights on horses and forty-two monks coming. Where is the part? I'll hear your words now.' This time Selina could feel that the vicar was not being vague, he was pulling away from her. An awful suspicion crossed her mind. 'You haven't lost the part, have you?'

Even as she spoke the horrible possibilities of this flashed through her mind. What had happened to the whole of John's scene from which the parts had been copied? Had he taken it back to school with him, or had he thrown away that first, rather carelessly written, copy? If he had, would he or anyone else know what the Abbot ought to have said? There was such urgency in her voice that even the vicar felt it. 'You can't have lost it, you simply can't.'

'Not lost, my dear, I remember the occasion perfectly. Your uncle was here, and John.'

'It was daffodil time, just before VE Day. John gave you the part in the garden. Can you remember what you did after we left?'

He was clearly trying to think.

'I preached on daffodils. My text was the lilies of the field. It was inspired by my daffodils.' He looked triumphant. 'I went straight into my study and wrote my sermon.'

'And what did you do with the part while you were writing your sermon?'

'Ah! That's the problem, isn't it?'

Selina saw that he was worried. She took hold of his hand.

'Let's go into your study. Perhaps that will help you to remember.'

The vicar's study was not an easy room to remember things in. It seemed as if everybody he had ever known had at some time sent him a snapshot or a printed announcement of a birth, death, or marriage, and he had them all framed and hung on his walls. Where there were not these things hung on the walls there were bookcases. Every shelf crammed with books right up to the roof, and because there was not room for every book in the shelves, another layer of books was placed sideways on top of the books that were standing the right way up. In the middle of the room was a big roll-top desk, so placed that when the vicar was working he could see his front lawn and his best flower beds.

'Now,' said Selina, 'you'd have come in and sat at your desk, wouldn't you? I think you'd better do it, it will help you to remember.' The vicar obediently sat down. 'Now, if you had an important paper in your hand, where would you put it?'

There was quite a long silence. Then he said:

'In a book.'

Selina looked at the bookshelves.

'In which book?'

'Which book? That's the question, isn't it? Which book?' There was another pause. 'I should undoubtedly have placed it carefully in the next book I opened. You would be surprised, Selina, at the papers I lose that way.'

Selina shook her head.

'I shouldn't be surprised at all.' She had a sudden bright idea. 'What book would you have needed for that sermon?'

'None. It was not a sermon that required a reference book, though, mind you, I very nearly changed that sermon. It was our discussion on the coming of Christianity. The theme ran in my mind after your uncle had gone. I remember I was looking up the correct date, when the clock chimed. I closed the book with a snap. "I must put this matter out of my mind," I said, "and attend to my sermon."'

Selina leant on the desk and looked him firmly in the eye.

'What book would you have looked for the dates in?'

He seemed surprised at such a simple question.

'My Haydn.' He saw that Selina was none the wiser.

162

'Haydn's *Dictionary of Dates*. I still have the copy I had as a boy at school.'

He was plainly going to talk about his school, so Selina had to interrupt.

'Which book is it? Can I get it down?'

Even if the vicar was fond of his Haydn he did not seem to know where he kept it on his shelves. It took him quite a while before he found it, then suddenly he saw it. It was a thick red book, tooled in gold, with its title written on blue leather. He pulled it out. Selina took it from him and held it, pages downwards, and gave it a shake. Out fell fourteen pressed flowers, thirteen little pieces of paper and some sheets out of an exercise book. The sheets of the exercise book were covered in John's handwriting. On the top of one sheet, in big letters, was written the word 'Abbot'.

The vicar seemed to think a minor miracle had been performed.

'Well, isn't that remarkable? Most remarkable.' He stooped and picked up a very old pressed flower. 'I found this little flower during that terribly cold spell in 1940. A most remarkable example of the will to live, I thought, so I kept it.'

Selina saw that he felt that finding the part was all that mattered. She spoke in a severe voice.

'I'm coming at this time tomorrow, and you've got to know every word of this by heart. Every word.'

The vicar took the part from her. He began reading the words softly.

'Wonderful how much better a blessing sounds in Latin.'

Selina hated Latin, but this was no time for an argument.

163

'Have you understood? I'm coming at this time tomorrow to hear that part.' She laid both hands on his arm. 'Please do learn it. You see, I promised John that I would come and hear you on Saturday afternoons, but I haven't, so it's me that'll get blamed if you don't know it.'

The vicar sat down in a chair by the window.

'Very interesting. I shall argue with John about some of this, but very interesting.'

He looked away from the paper and began whispering to himself.

Good gracious! Selina thought. He's begun to learn it already. She tiptoed to the door and slipped quietly out.

John was so pleased to be home, and there was such a lot of talking to get through, that he did not at first grasp what a big thing the pageant had become. Of course there was a lot of pageant talk going on, but it was not about the sort of things which could make John see how different the pageant was now from what it had been going to be when he went away.

'All of us, except Phoebe, are getting Philip to help,' Christopher explained to him. 'We told Philip about your rehearsal, which is on Thursday, because of Dad. We thought you'd probably like him to lend a hand.'

John had exactly the feelings that the others had felt when Philip first began to take an interest in their pageant.

'It's all right. I've got the thing mapped out. Of course he might tell us if we can be heard and all that.'

'I should think he'd cut out most of the talking. He has in the other scenes.'

John was indignant.

'He certainly isn't coming to my rehearsal if he's going to mess about with what my people say. I wrote the scene. Don't want him interfering.'

Christopher reported this conversation to Selina.

'I say, you'd better see Philip and tell him to go slow. John'll be browned off if Philip interferes too much.'

Selina was, by now, so used to carrying everything to do with the pageant, including messages, that she did not argue. As it happened it was so wet for the next few days that all rehearsals had to be put off, so John did not see a rehearsal until he came to his own on Thursday. Selina had plodded up to the Abbey through the rain to give Philip his message. He said:

'Of course I won't say a word. I'll just be about to offer any advice if he wants it.'

Selina knew that it would be very unlike Philip if that was all he did, but she hoped for the best.

The doctor brought John and the vicar along in his car. He parked his car and they were about to walk down to the lower lawn when they ran into the Colonel.

'Hallo, John. Had a good term? All your people are waiting on the lower lawn. Philip's told them where to stand with their horses. Don't want to be a nuisance but can't have 'em all over the shop. Got to have the grass looking fairly decent as we're sellin' the place.'

John thanked the Colonel, though he thought he was being a bit fussy about two or three horses. Philip and Selina were on the lower lawn waiting for him. Philip behaved beautifully. He treated John exactly as he would have treated a real stage producer. The hedges at the back of the stage had been

165

clipped and there were now good, clear entrances. He waved a hand in the direction of the elm tree.

'Your men and horses are at the back there. Don't know where you want to bring them on, but it's a good place for them to mount. I've got half your monks off one side and half off the other. You can shift them round any way you want.' He looked at the doctor. 'My aunt's Lucky is there for you to ride.'

John had planned that the father and his friends should ride up to what was supposed to be the Abbey. Then the father had to shout 'Halloo there. Knock on the door, one of you.' At that moment the Abbot came out with two or three of his monks. The father then was told to get off his horse, kneel, and be blessed. He then explained to the Abbot that he had come for his son to be his esquire. The Abbot had to protest and say the boy was not through with his schooling. The father then said he did not want his son to grow up a milksop. At that moment John, as the boy, was to come out of the monastery and greet his father. John had quite a lot of talking to do, and then, to prove he was not a milksop, he was to borrow one of the horses and give what he had put down in the part as a 'knightly display'. In the end he was blessed by the Abbot. Then one of the men was to lend him his horse and he was to ride away with his father.

Inside John felt a bit nervous about this first rehearsal, but he was not going to let Philip see how he was feeling, so he said, in as competent a voice as he could:

'Right. Well, Dad, you know what you've got to do. You ride up to the monastery with your friend. I should think you'll have to come in there,' he pointed to an entrance on the left of the stage, 'because the Abbot and the monks will come in at the back, which is meant to be the monastery.' He turned to Mr Laws. 'As soon as Dad says, "Halloo there. Knock on the door, one of you", you come through those two bushes, and your monks come too. I'm not on at the beginning so I'll go and sit over there and see how it looks.'

Selina knew that Mr Laws would forget to come on at the right moment, so she took him to the back of the hedge and stood by him.

'You get the monks along,' she said to Philip, 'and push them on at the right moment.'

The men and the horses were bored with waiting and were glad that the rehearsal was going to begin. The doctor told them what they had to do and they all understood, and so when he said 'Ready' there was the sound of clop, clopping, and in one moment the lower lawn was filled with men and horses. The doctor shouted 'Halloo there. Knock on the door, one of you.' Selina gave Mr Laws a push and Philip dropped a handkerchief and on marched the forty-two monks. There was a pause then, for Mr Laws had forgotten to speak. Philip poked his head through the entrance by the path.

'Have you got the script, old man? Shall I prompt?'

It was no good John being proud. He had no more idea what to do with twenty-five horses and forty-two monks than he would have known what to do with Sally's ballet. He came down to Philip, his face scarlet.

'You tell them. I can't.'

# CHAPTER FOURTEEN

## Clothes

That evening at supper Doctor Andrews discussed clothes.

'Have any of you any idea about clothes?'

All the family looked at him in surprise. He had promised that the clothes should be hired. John reminded him.

'You said we could hire them.'

'I know I did, old man, but when I said I would hire them it was clothes for all of you and a few friends. How many people are there taking part in this pageant now?'

Everybody looked enquiringly at Selina. She did some mental arithmetic in her head.

'Seventy in John's scene. Thirty children and Sally in hers and the ballet from Linkwell. Then there's Queen Elizabeth, only Mrs Day's got that dress, but there are lords and ladies. Almost everybody in the village and a whole lot of people from other villages in Christopher's. Four in Phoebe's.'

The doctor was helping macaroni cheese. He handed out the last plate before he asked:

'Roughly, how many in Christopher's?'

Selina tried to visualize her list.

'When they all come there's a hundred and two from one side of the stage and a hundred and fourteen from the other, and the eight mummers and Miss Lipscombe.'

Mrs Andrews did not mean to, but she let a little groan escape her.

'Good gracious! I'm practically the only person in the neighbourhood who's not taking part. I can't think who's coming to see the pageant.'

Dr Andrews helped himself to mustard.

'Philip seems to have got that in hand. He's going to put posters over half the county. Of course, as you can all see for yourselves, I can't afford to hire dresses for that number. What I was thinking was this, we might have a talk with everybody, perhaps Philip will, and see how many people can manage their own clothes.'

Selina looked horrified.

'But we've told everybody they haven't got to worry about clothes, that they're coming.'

'I know, niece. I don't know what clothes cost to hire, but I do know, with a family the size of mine, it can't be managed. I shouldn't wonder if quite a lot of people in the crowds and that could rake up something for themselves.'

Mrs Andrews looked at him, rather as she looked at Benjamin when he was being silly.

'People haven't things they can rake up these days. We had an appeal this spring to help re-home the blitzed Londoners, and anybody who had anything like a bedspread or old curtains gave them then.'

The doctor refused to be crushed.

'Well, let's take John's scene as a start. The monks can all be dressed in black-out material. There must be a lot of that around.'

Mrs Andrews shook her head.

'There was an appeal to send black-out material for overalls for the children of France.'

Dr Andrews was still quite unmoved.

'You don't go into houses like I do. You'd be surprised what a lot of junk there is put away. The number of times I've said, "Can you give me another pillow?" or "Can I have a towel?" when I've been seeing a patient, and a cupboard is opened, and you see it simply bulging with stuff that's been saved. I'll take a bet that if we send out an SOS we'll get enough black material to dress forty-two monks.'

Mrs Andrews thought of her sewing-machine. It had not been new before the war, and it had done a great deal of work since, and was inclined to be temperamental.

'Who is to make the monks' clothes?'

'The wives.'

Mrs Andrews did not want to be difficult, but she sympathized with the wives.

'They haven't all got sewing machines, and most of them are terribly busy.'

'Well, let's try it out. I'll talk to the monks myself at the next rehearsal and see how it goes down. If it doesn't go down, I vote we ask the Women's Institute, they're always willing to help.'

Mrs Andrews belonged to the Women's Institute. Mrs Day

was President. Mrs Day was a darling, but not very good at getting a lot of work done in a hurry.

'It's the jam season. We make jam for the Ministry of Food.'

The doctor brushed that aside as though she had not said it.

'The twenty-five horsemen could hire their own clothes, I think. Anyway, I'll put it to them. Won't cost much if each one pays for himself. Now, whose scene comes next in the pageant?'

They all answered at once:

'Phoebe's.'

'Well, what does Phoebe want?'

He looked at Selina, so she answered:

'Dresses for herself, Miss Lipscombe, Mrs Miggs, and one for Mr Partridge.'

Christopher said:

'She ought to have good clothes for that scene. It's absolutely idiotic as it is, it'll need dressing up.'

Mrs Andrews said gently:

'Well, don't say that to Phoebe.'

Sally leant towards her mother.

'It doesn't matter saying it now as Phoebe's in bed, but it really is frightful. It doesn't seem to belong to the rest of the pageant at all.'

Dr Andrews nodded at Christopher to collect the plates.

'The idea of this pageant was that you kids should write it and put it on. It's gone a long way from that, and you've got Philip in to help, but if Phoebe wants to stick to the old scheme I don't see why she shouldn't. Fair's fair. I'll hire the clothes for those four.' He turned to Selina. 'You keep a check on this, I'll write the letter after supper. So far we've got four dresses for Phoebe's scene, and two for John's, his and mine.'

Selina felt personally responsible for the vicar.

'What about Mr Laws?'

'Black-out. One of the dresses the Women's Institute will have to make. Now, what's next?'

Sally leant her arms on the table, which was not allowed, but this was being more a meeting than a meal.

'I wanted all the children to be dressed in green. Philip thinks that there's going to be some green dancers from Linkwell between each scene; it isn't worked out yet. I wouldn't mind really what colour my children wore if they were all alike.' She turned to her mother. 'Is there any material that isn't on coupons?'

Mrs Andrews was watching John, who was putting the next course in front of his father.

'Be careful of those stewed pears, John, I made them with an awful lot of juice.' She turned to Sally. 'Off-hand, I should say absolutely nothing.'

Dr Andrews began helping the pears and custard.

'We've got to be rather clever about this. I don't suppose I could hire thirty children's dresses if I wanted to, and I certainly don't want to. They'll only be scrappy bits of stuff, not worth the hiring; we ought to be able to think of something.'

Mrs Andrews's mind was running up and down a house. Not her house, but anybody's house. She mentally picked up articles and discarded them. Dust-sheets. No, nobody could spare those. White curtains. If anybody had any they certainly could not part with them. Then suddenly she remembered something.

'Before the war we had a bazaar in the village hall one year; the end of the room was got up as a Christmas scene. We hung the whole of it with white butter-muslin. Now, I wonder what's happened to that? There must have been dozens of yards of it, and it could be dyed any colour Sally liked.'

Sally gasped.

'Oh, Mum, how gorgeous! Do you remember where it is?'

Mrs Andrews was already racking her brains without Sally reminding her.

'It was Christmas, 1938, I think. Now, whose idea was it?' Suddenly it came to her. 'I know who'll know all about it; Mrs Peters. I can see her now sitting at the top of a ladder, her mouth full of pins. If she put it up I expect she took it down.'

Sally had jumped mentally from having no material at all to having all the material in the world, beautifully dyed any colour she liked.

'How simply gorgeous! I shall go and see Mrs Peters after supper.'

Selina had found a pencil and a piece of paper in her pocket and had scribbled down the figures Dr Andrews had given her.

'I tell you what we've forgotten, Benjamin and Augustus. They're in every scene except John's.'

'I ought to be able to make something for them,' said Mrs Andrews. 'What ought they to wear?'

Dr Andrews said:

'It's Phoebe's scene. Have to ask her. I suppose she's designed something.'

174

'I bet she hasn't,' said Christopher. 'As a matter of fact, they ought to have little clothes like grown-ups had, oughtn't they, Dad? Children did.'

The doctor nodded as though Mrs Andrews had all the material and all the patterns in the world.

'Yes, I should make them small editions of the sort of thing Henry the Eighth wore.'

Mrs Andrews tried not to sound bitter.

'What of?' She felt she was being a wet blanket and she hated to be that. 'I'm sorry to keep saying depressing things, but honestly I don't know.'

Dr Andrews was determined to get the clothes question settled that night.

'Go and see Mrs Day. They're turning out of the Abbey, and I bet she's got some evening dresses that are put away and that she'll never wear again.'

Sally thought that a very good idea.

'Of course she has dozens. If she's got one of velvet and one of taffeta you've as good as got Benjamin's and Augustus's clothes.'

Mrs Andrews said resignedly:

'If I had a pattern and if the sewing-machine works. However, I will go and see Mrs Day tomorrow.'

John, Christopher, and Sally hated the word tomorrow. They all said in different ways:

'No, Mum, ring her up tonight.'

The doctor turned to Sally.

'What are you going to wear?'

Sally had been thinking that she too could use the butter-muslin, but now that her father had suggested the cupboards

175

of unworn evening dresses at the Abbey she began to have grander ideas.

'When you're choosing evening dresses at the Abbey, Mum, could I come too? What I ought to have is flowered crêpe de chine.'

'Well, you won't get it, darling. If Mrs Day has any flowered crêpe de chine she'll have it made into a nightdress or underclothes or something.'

Sally threw away the picture of herself dressed in flowered crêpe de chine, and redressed herself in taffeta.

'My dress, though it's made for dancing in, ought to be Elizabethan to look at. After all, I'm a human being. I think taffeta wouldn't be bad.'

Mrs Andrews shook her head at her.

'Don't dress yourself up until we see if Mrs Day has even one evening dress. You'll only be disappointed.'

'Then there's Queen Elizabeth,' Selina said. 'Mrs Day's got her own dress, but there are going to be heaps of courtiers and some children belonging to the courtiers. One of them presents the flowers to Queen Elizabeth.'

The doctor dismissed Queen Elizabeth and her Court.

'All well-off people. Mrs Day asked them, didn't she? I'll tell her to tell them they're expected to hire their own things.'

Sally saw Selina's anxious face.

'It'll be all right. They haven't been asked to come to a rehearsal yet. I dare say Mrs Day did tell them they would have to get their own clothes. Anyway, she can now.'

'What,' said Mrs Andrews, 'do Augustus and Benjamin wear in your scene, Sally?'

'They're Queen Elizabeth's pages.'

Mrs Andrews remembered her history.

'And Queen Elizabeth was Henry the Eighth's daughter. They can wear the same clothes in your scene as they do in Phoebe's.'

There was a gasp of horror.

John said:

'They could not. It would look so queer they're coming on all that time later, still children.'

Sally shook her head at her mother.

'You're only teasing. You know they couldn't.'

Christopher said grandly:

'Anyway the clothes had changed.'

Mrs Andrews had finished eating. She laid down her spoon and fork.

'I am not going to make two complete sets of clothes for pages. To begin with I couldn't get the stuff; secondly, I shouldn't have time to change them. Benjamin is very stupid about putting on his clothes in a hurry even when he isn't excited. He's very apt to put two feet into one leg. I hate to think what it would be like dressing him in a hurry behind a bush at the Abbey.'

Dr Andrews was drawing on a piece of paper. He drew a short gown like a little, very full overcoat. It had big puffed swollen sleeves. Under it showed puffed short breeches. He then drew a picture of the puffed short breeches with its jacket. To this drawing he added a short cloak with a high collar. He brought the pictures round the table to Mrs Andrews.

'Look. This is what the kids wear. Those are trunks, they ought to be slashed, but it doesn't matter, and the top is plain or slashed, as you like, with a white linen collar or ruffles. That cloak could be made of anything.'

'What about the legs?'

'We could paint them, I should think.' He pointed to the first picture. 'Now here's that same dress covered by the Henry the Eighth overcoat.' He pointed to the bottom of the coat. 'There ought to be fur or something here.'

Mrs Andrews said 'Fur?' She did not say anything more but it was a very expressive one word.

The doctor patted her shoulder.

'We'll get a book on costume from the county library. I'm sure you'll be able to manage.'

Christopher had been very patient but now he could bear it no longer.

'What about my scene? To make the pageant's dates move on, Philip says it can be any period between Charles the Second and George the First. They were still having Ridings on St George's Day in some places up till then.'

The doctor went back to his seat.

'Of course yours are village people and at no time in our history have villagers gone in for the height of fashion, but we've got to be careful, because of course we must, at all costs, avoid wigs. They would cost a terrible lot.' He drew on the other side of his bit of paper. 'If I remember rightly, something like this would have been worn by country people in the reign of William and Mary.'

He drew a man in an overcoat which came just below the knees. It had a big collar and huge cuffs and buttons all down the front. 'It was a rather stiff reign. Dutch influence, I suppose.' He put on his man a plain wideawake hat. 'Stockings at this date were pulled over the knee, gartered below and rolled above, that ought to be easy. They can borrow a pair of their wives' stockings.'

He added a fuzz of hair below the hat. 'We'll have to ask all the men not to have their hair cut until the pageant's over. That'll get us out of the wig trouble. Now for the lady. She'd have been plain, too, in our village. Stuff dress to the ankles, a tight bodice, puffed sleeves to the wrists, long white apron, rounded white collar. Then on her head she'd wear a kind of white bonnet thing and a hat on top.' He passed the drawings round the table. 'I should think everybody in your crowd could manage something of that sort, Christopher.'

Christopher saw no difficulties at all.

'Rather. Pretty good fun to make, I should think.'

Sally took the drawings.

'Everybody could look like that. An apron and a plain hat thing and that white bit and you're there.'

John held out his hand for the drawings. He nodded at them approvingly.

'Easy.'

Mrs Andrews took the drawings.

'Come here, Selina, you and I are the only ones with our feet on the earth.'

Selina leant on her aunt's shoulder. Together they stared at the drawings in dismayed silence. Selina saw herself explaining to two hundred and sixteen people that they could easily make clothes like that at home without using coupons. Mrs Andrews smiled up at her.

'All right, darling, don't say it. I know exactly how you feel.'

Christopher burst out.

'It's all very well for you, Selina, to keep seeing difficulties. You've already got a good frock, and you walk on in it and walk off. It's the rest of us who've got to worry.'

Selina saw this was true.

'It isn't that I'm being difficult, Christopher, it just is that I don't think they'll do it. These sorts of clothes take yards and yards of stuff.'

'I think you're worrying unduly, niece,' said Dr Andrews. 'The sort of thing they need for these clothes they probably can raise. Once more the black-out material.'

Mrs Andrews interrupted him.

'I can't help thinking that this is going to look a rather sombre pageant.'

'Quite a good idea in this scene. We'll give all the colour to the mummers.'

'Ah!' said Mrs Andrews. 'Those mummers. What are they going to wear and who's going to make the clothes?'

Dr Andrews had meant to say that half the clothes for the mummers could easily be raked up at home, but he began to think that perhaps Mrs Andrews was losing heart.

'I'm hiring those.'

Christopher bounced in his chair.

'Goody, goody. And will you hire the witch's?'

'No. She only wears rags, doesn't she? I'll have a talk to Miss Lipscombe myself about that. She ought to be able to concoct something with a bit of sacking.'

Mrs Andrews said:

'Concoct is the word, I should think.'

The doctor collected back his drawings.

'And that's the lot. What am I hiring, Selina?'

'Two dresses in John's scene, four in Phoebe's, none in Sally's, and eight in Christopher's.'

'But,' said John, 'you've forgotten us. I'm a courtier in Sally's scene, and a rabble leader in Christopher's. Sally's rabble in Christopher's scene. And Christopher is a boy holding a horse in mine and a courtier in Sally's. And Augustus and Benjamin are children rabble in Christopher's.'

'And Selina?' the doctor asked.

'Selina doesn't come in any,' Sally explained. She looked at Selina in surprise. 'I don't know why you don't.'

Selina flushed. She did not want to sound fussy about her frock, but she did know she did not want to take it off once she had got it on. She could imagine everyone fingering it when her back was turned.

'I thought as I came on at the beginning and the end it was easier to stop in my frock, and I'm more useful like that running messages and things for Philip.'

Christopher agreed.

'Philip's using her as stage manager. He said she was jolly good.'

It was the first word of praise Selina had received and she was quite overcome.

'Did he? How awfully nice of him.'

'I don't see it's nice of him,' said John. 'You seemed to be doing all the mucking about at my rehearsal while he just gave orders. I should think it's a bit of cake for him.'

Sally turned to her mother.

'She is good at it. You ought to come to a rehearsal and then you'd know.'

The doctor held out his hand for Selina's list.

'All right, niece, you're evidently too useful to be spared except for the prologue and the epilogue. Now then, let's get these additional dresses down. One dress extra in John's scene, two dresses in Sally's scene, one for John and one for Christopher, and two William and Mary dresses in Christopher's scene, one for John and one for Sally. You . . .'

Mrs Andrews knew what he was going to say.

'You needn't say it. Augustus and Benjamin's dresses can be made at home.'

The doctor smiled at her and got up.

'If everybody has finished eating I shall now go and compose a letter to a firm who hire pageant dresses.'

Mrs Andrews had also got up.

'And I shall go and telephone Mrs Day while you children clear and wash up.'

Sally ran round the table and clutched her mother's arm.

'Oh, Mum, could I listen while you telephone? It's almost a matter of life and death.'

'I thought you were going to Mrs Peters.'

'I am.' Sally turned to the others. 'Could you manage without me for a bit?'

John nodded.

'It's not my washing-up night. I'll do it for you.'

Mrs Day answered the telephone herself.

'What, my dear? Evening dresses? Must have a stack of 'em put away somewhere. Shockin' state by now.'

Sally was dancing with excitement beside her mother.

'Mum, ask her if she's got any flowered crêpe de chine.'

Mrs Andrews laughed and told Mrs Day what Sally had

said. Then she had to hold the telephone away from her ear because Mrs Day was hooting at the other end of the line.

'You ask Sally what she thinks somebody old and scragged looking would be doing with flowered crêpe de chine. You come up to tea tomorrow and bring Sally with you. I'll tell Mawser what you want. She'll know where everything is. Warn you the whole lot's probably been eaten by moth.'

Sally went dancing down the lane to call on Mrs Peters.

Her head was in the clouds. How glorious everything was being! Dancing rehearsals starting soon at Linkwell. Dancing every day at rehearsals. Then all this fun about the dresses. What colour should she dress the fairies in? Pink? Blue? No. Yellow. The yellow of laburnum and yellow flowers in their hair. They would look simply heavenly against the hedges and the green grass.

Mr Peters was out on what he called 'his rounds', which actually, as there was hardly ever any crime in the village, meant discussing people's gardens with them over the hedges. Mrs Peters and the eldest girl, Gert, were picking currants. Mrs Peters liked Dr and Mrs Andrews, and she quite liked the children, but that did not mean she wanted them calling at all hours of the evening. Her voice was a little forbidding.

'Well, Sally?'

Sally knelt beside Mrs Peters and helped pick the currants.

'Mum told me to come and see you. She said that before the war you decorated the village hall as winter.'

'So I did, too.' Mrs Peters looked at Gert. 'You're eating more than you pick. A mort of trouble it was too. Balls of snow hanging from the ceiling, and Gert here, she wasn't much more than a baby then, was dressed up as the spirit of Christmas, weren't you, ducks?'

Gert had her mouth full so she only nodded.

Sally said:

'Mum said you hung white butter-muslin all over the walls and do you know what happened to it? Because we want it for the pageant and . . .' she swallowed because she had just been going to say what they wanted the butter-muslin for, and as Mrs Peters would have to make three dresses it did not seem a tactful moment.

Mrs Peters sniffed.

'Not dressing me in it in that bit where Miss Lipscombe's a witch, I hope. Sure to rain on the twentieth, and I don't want to catch my death.'

Sally remembered her father's drawing.

'Oh no, you'll be wearing warm clothes. It's for something else.'

Mrs Peters stood up. She was frowning.

'Now, what did we do with that white stuff? It's so many years ago I mostly forget. Must have put it somewhere. There was some talk of using it as white curtains for those cottages we fixed up for the evacuee children, but we never used it.'

Gert looked up from under a currant bush.

'Teacher said we'd dye it red, white, and blue for VE Day.'

Mrs Peters made a clucking sound.

'I like her sauce. Red, white, and blue indeed. It wasn't hers to dye.'

Sally felt as if she had suddenly jumped from mid-summer into winter. Dyed red, white, and blue! Nothing could be worse. Fairies could not wear red, white, and blue. She tried to sound ordinary but her voice was very sad.

'That's that, then.'

Gert said:

'Only she never did. She had the toothache something shocking and had to go to the dentist to have it out.'

'There,' said Mrs Peters, 'getting us all worried for nothing. Where is it, then?'

'Where it was, we never touched it.'

'Well, where was it?'

Gert was a slow-thinking child.

'Where you put it after we done with it, that Christmas.'

Mrs Peters could have shaken Gert.

'Well, where did I put it? Here's Sally come with a simple question from her mum, and first you say it's dyed and then you say it isn't. You give a straight answer to a straight question or I'll give you what for.'

Gert was quite unmoved by this threat.

'In a brown paper parcel under the stage in the village 'all.'

Sally was so pleased that she almost kissed Mrs Peters. 'Oh, thank you awfully, we'll fetch it tomorrow.'

It was getting dusk as she ran home. She was so happy that she felt as if she would burst. She danced up the lane humming the folk dance music that they used in the pageant, and behind her, so clear in her imagination that she could see them, danced thirty fairies dressed in laburnum yellow.

# CHAPTER FIFTEEN

---●◆●---

## *Phoebe*

Now that the holidays had started there were rehearsals every fine day. There were never full rehearsals, because most of the people who were taking part were busy and could not come very often. Both John's and Christopher's scenes could only be rehearsed in the evenings when work was finished. John's scene was especially difficult because at least half his knights were farmers, and they could hardly ever spare time unless it was raining, and then John did not want them.

'It's all right,' Philip said. 'If they all come to a few rehearsals, and to the dress rehearsal, we'll get by.'

Sally had a rehearsal for her children sometime every day. She fixed her rehearsals before Christopher's so that the children could stay on for his scene. The children loved rehearsing and would not have minded if they had rehearsed all day. The mothers were beginning to think rehearsals a good idea. They were mostly taking part in Christopher's scene, and came to rehearsals when they could and enjoyed them. But what they liked was knowing the children were busy and happy. 'Keeps them from under your feet,' they told each other.

Either during the morning or the early afternoon Phoebe commandeered the stage for her scene. She commandeered it more often really than she needed it. Miss Lipscombe, Mrs Miggs, and Partridge were all more or less word-perfect, and both Miss Lipscombe and Mrs Miggs were beginning to grumble at being made to spend so much time on the lower lawn.

Nor was it only Miss Lipscombe and Mrs Miggs who grumbled. Dr Andrews spent his time saying, 'Good gracious, Phoebe, you can't want Miss Lipscombe again. That scene of yours doesn't take ten minutes. What are you doing all the time?'

Mrs Andrews complained about Mrs Miggs being rehearsed so often. 'She never was very reliable, darling, but you've made her worse. Must you have your rehearsals at such awkward times? It only means that you all have to do extra housework. I should have thought teatime would have been more suitable.'

Phoebe answered all the grumbles in a proud, aloof way, simply saying, 'It's a difficult scene. It needs a lot of rehearsing,' or 'It's going beautifully, but I want it to be quite perfect.'

The worst grumble started the morning after the clothes discussion. Phoebe had begun to call Augustus and Benjamin to regular rehearsals. It had been all right for the first two days. They played about until it was the moment for them to make their entrance, and the time passed quite happily. On the third day they did not want to go to the Abbey. They wanted to go with their mother to fetch eggs from the farm. The row started at breakfast. Mrs Andrews said:

'What are the rehearsals today?'

'I've got my children at eleven,' said Sally.

'And I've got my scene at two-thirty,' said Phoebe. She nodded at Augustus and Benjamin. 'So don't go out after lunch, because I'm wanting you.'

Augustus put down his spoon and leant across the table to his father, certain that he would see that justice was done.

'Me and Benjamin have gone two days to that awful rehearsal. All we do is to carry a pretend train and fasten it on to Phoebe's shoulders, and then pretend to carry it. We know how to do that now. Today Mum said we could go to the farm for eggs, didn't she, Benjamin?'

Benjamin had not been paying the slightest attention to the conversation. He was humming while he ate his Force. Augustus's appeal to him caught him in mid-hum, as it were. He looked at him with a puzzled frown. Mrs Andrews pushed his plate towards him.

'You were humming, Benjamin, that's why you didn't hear what was said.'

Phoebe leaned across the table to Benjamin.

'You like rehearsals, don't you, Benjamin?'

Benjamin sucked his spoon and gazed at Phoebe with round eyes. Then slowly he took the spoon out of his mouth.

'My dear, I loathe them.'

Mrs Andrews looked at the doctor. It was an asking look, saying, 'What are we to do about this? Are we to force the little boys to attend the rehearsal?'

Dr Andrews considered before he spoke. He wanted to be perfectly fair to everybody.

189

'Do you think, Phoebe, that you need them at every rehearsal at the moment? Of course they must come to the later rehearsals nearer the pageant, but a rehearsal every day, especially as they are in other scenes, is rather a lot in the summer holidays.'

Phoebe's face was pink.

'It's not their holidays. They don't go to school.'

Augustus was much incensed.

'I do sums and reading and writing and making things with Mum every morning, and I'm going to school with Christopher next term, so it is my holidays, isn't it, Dad?'

'And Benjamin is learning to play the piano, and he makes things, don't you, pet?' said Mrs Andrews. 'So they are his holidays.'

Dr Andrews said:

'I don't think we can say they aren't their holidays, Phoebe, they are. They're everybody's holidays. All Benjamin and Augustus do is to carry on this train. They haven't got anything to say, have they?'

'No, nothing, but they're being slow at learning.'

Augustus and Benjamin began to speak, but the doctor silenced them.

'I think we must have reason in this, Phoebe. It's the best part of seven weeks to the pageant. I think they could learn to carry a train in that time without rehearsing every day. You give them a couple of days off and try them out again at the end of the week.'

Phoebe looked at her father, her face red and her mouth a narrow, angry line. Then suddenly she burst into tears. Everybody looked at her in shocked amazement. Even Benjamin knew that

190

crying at the table was unheard of, and that crying, without a pretty good reason for it, was considered a thing that you ought to do by yourself with the door shut. To cry because somebody couldn't come to your rehearsal was likely to cause a major row. It was particularly odd that it was Phoebe who was crying because Phoebe was not the crying sort. She was often bad tempered, and almost always difficult, but she did not cry. It was, as John had once said, almost the only good thing about her.

Dr Andrews signalled to the boys to clear the cereal plates. He did not seem to notice that Phoebe was crying. Then, as John put the dish of bacon in front of him, he said:

'I don't think we want that sniffling at the breakfast table, Phoebe, you'd better go up to your room.' Then he thought better of it. 'No. Go to the surgery. I'll have a talk with you after breakfast.'

Everybody looked at Phoebe's heaving, retreating back sympathetically. It was, of course, simply idiotic to cry about a thing like a pageant rehearsal, but they were sorry for her if she was going to be told off by Dad in his surgery. He despised scenes, and he would think crying at breakfast over a pageant unspeakably silly. Quite likely he would just say that Phoebe's scene couldn't happen at all.

When the doctor came into his surgery Phoebe was sitting at his desk. She tried to look truculent, but she felt a sinking inside. Miss Lipscombe was in the room rearranging some papers. As the doctor came in she went out into the waiting-room, saying, in a voice which sounded as if she thought Phoebe was going to be hanged:

'You won't be needing me. I shall close the door.'

191

The doctor sat on his desk.

'What was all that fuss about at breakfast?'

'Everybody's mean about my scene.'

'Who is?'

'You. You keep saying you don't want Miss Lipscombe to rehearse, and Mum says she doesn't want Mrs Miggs to rehearse, and Miss Lipscombe, Mrs Miggs, and Mr Partridge never want to rehearse, and now, when Augustus and Benjamin don't want to rehearse, you back them up.' Her voice wobbled. 'Everybody's mean.'

'If you're going to cry again we'd better leave this talk for another day. I'm all in favour of anybody crying if they think it does them any good, but I've never seen why the tears should be inflicted on one's family or one's friends. Tears are one of nature's safety-valves, but not intended for use in public.'

Phoebe had control of herself.

'I won't cry.'

'Good. Then you can come and sit on my knee and let's have this matter out.'

The doctor sat on his chair and lifted Phoebe on to his knee.

'What's up? Scene going wrong?'

Phoebe had, for days, been fighting the knowledge that her scene was going to be the low spot of the pageant. It was all very well to say it was written in poetry, and all very well to pretend it was going nicely, but it was not. It was not a bit as she had meant it to be, and she had no idea how to make it any better. Meanwhile everybody else had done things to their scenes. They had let Philip help them, and he had taken out almost everything that anybody had to say, and put in huge crowds and horses and things like that instead. Now, suddenly, sitting on her father's knee, she found that she need not know all these things by herself any more. She could tell Dad. He would be very sensible.

Out came the story. How much trouble she had taken to write her scene. How nobody else had written in poetry excepting herself because nobody else could write poetry. How, in spite of writing the scene in poetry she had managed to keep top of her form, almost every week of the term, beating Felicity Jones, who had nothing whatever to do except be top of the form. The doctor interrupted here:

'Didn't I hear something about some prize money you came into for that?'

Off Phoebe went again. Yes, she had won the prize money, but she had very nearly lost it because, without even asking her, Christopher had thought they could spend the money on buns. How, in any case, it wasn't enough money to buy a party frock, which was what she needed more than anything on earth. Then she came back to the pageant. It wasn't that her scene wasn't written in good poetry. It was, but it wasn't coming out as she'd meant it to. And all the others had put lots of people into their scenes, which wasn't fair.

The doctor turned her to face him.

'I suppose now what you really need is a bit of help from Philip, which, I take it, you've refused.'

'Well, he was so proud about it. After all, it was my scene, and I knew how it ought to be.'

'But you'd be glad of help at this stage? Nothing much perhaps, just a few people added and the whole thing brought more into line with the pageant.'

Put like that, asking Philip's help did not sound so ignominious.

'John had to ask for Philip's help at his very first rehearsal.'

The doctor laughed.

'If you'd seen twenty-five horses and forty-two monks crashing on to the lower lawn, you'd have asked for help.' Then he looked serious. 'If I were you, I'd go up to the Abbey this morning and have a talk with Philip.'

Phoebe ran her fingers up and down the lapels of her father's coat.

'You don't know how difficult that is. He's all rush, rush, these days. Quite likely if I went up there and said, "Philip, I want to talk to you about my scene", he wouldn't even hear.'

'Dear me. Philip seems in a poor way mentally.' Then he had an idea. 'How about our calling in Selina? She seems to be the general factotum of this pageant. I should think she could arrange an interview, couldn't she?'

Phoebe accepted that idea at once. In fact she marvelled that she had not thought of it for herself.

Dr Andrews opened the surgery door and shouted.

Selina was making beds with her aunt.

'I'm so sorry.'

Mrs Andrews tucked the sheets on her side of the bed under with a resigned air.

'It's all right, darling. I imagine your uncle wants you in connection with Phoebe's scene in the pageant. I imagine somebody will always be wanting all of you in connection with scenes in the pageant. I dare say by the twentieth of September I shall get quite used to doing the housework alone.'

The doctor explained Phoebe's predicament. He had his back to Phoebe. He spoke very seriously but he let Selina see that he was smiling behind his eyes.

'Selina, Phoebe feels that the time has come when she could do with a little professional advice in the handling of her scene in the pageant.'

Phoebe broke in:

'Not an awful lot. I want my poetry left exactly as it is.'

The doctor went on:

'It seems that Philip is very busy just now and inclined to be distrait. Phoebe thinks that it would be better if you made an appointment for her. Could you do this?'

Selina had great difficulty in not showing how glad she was. She did not very often see rehearsals of Phoebe's scene, but every time she did see one she thought the scene needed a great deal done to it. It would be a terrible thing if the audience laughed, and as it was being rehearsed at the moment, it was very likely that they would. Mrs Miggs was really very funny. Selina succeeded in sounding serious and efficient.

'I'm going up to the Abbey with Sally at eleven. You'd better come too, and I'll talk to Philip.'

Philip had been hoping that Phoebe would see that her scene needed alteration. By now he was so interested in the pageant that he had begun to think he could do as he liked with it. He had, however, found out that he was wrong there. When one day he had said, 'If young Phoebe doesn't ask for help for that scene of hers we'll have to do something about it by force,' he found all the family disagreeing with him. John had not been home from school at the time, but the other three had spoken their minds quite forcibly.

'It's her scene,' said Sally, 'you can't do that.'

'It's nice of you to help and all that,' said Christopher, 'but the pageant was our idea and Phoebe's only doing it the way we first thought of it.'

Selina said: 'You couldn't do that, Philip. She wrote the scene and she must do it the way she likes.'

This conversation had made Philip remember his position. He had been very careful ever since. It was the children's pageant, though he was by now producer. It was quite certain that he could not do exactly what he liked. If he wanted to make any major alteration it would have to be with everybody's consent.

Philip and Phoebe sat on a seat at the top of the upper lawn to have their discussion. It was a proper meeting between equals. Phoebe started by being rather difficult.

'It's not that I want the scene altered or any of the poetry taken out, only I'd like more people and more moving about.'

Philip did not answer at once. He lit a cigarette.

'I still think we might make use of the children. Play games with you, you know, like I suggested. Of course I quite see you don't want your poetry interfered with, but in a pageant, as I told you, talking is not very effective. You see, if it's windy like it is today, people up here wouldn't know what was being said.'

Phoebe was not prepared to accept that.

'We all speak very loud.'

Philip pointed to the lower stage where Sally was directing her dances.

'You don't speak much louder than that gramophone. Can you hear it?'

Phoebe wanted most terribly to say yes, but the wind was blowing the wrong way and they caught only the music between gusts.

'I expect we speak much louder than that gramophone.'

'Have you ever seen a film?'

'Yes. Mickey Mouse and *The Wizard of Oz* and some films they showed in the village hall once.'

'I once saw a very serious film with a sad story. It was called *Mrs Minniver*. In the middle of the film, at a very sad place, the sound apparatus went wrong, the picture went on but we heard no sounds at all. The actors walked about opening and shutting their mouths, but no sound came out.'

Phoebe laughed.

'They must have looked very silly.'

'They did. We all laughed. Even though it was a sad piece of the picture. Well, that's what might happen if the wind blew the wrong way in your scene. I should hate people to laugh at it.'

Phoebe was impressed by this argument, but was not going to give in easily.

'I would simply hate it if nobody said any of my poetry.'

Philip leant down and, with the first finger of his good hand, drew the shape of the lower lawn on the gravel of the path.

'Here is the stage. Here,' he drew a little square on the left of his design of the lower lawn, 'is a thing called a rostrum. A rostrum is a raised-up bit like a small stage. The Abbot and the boy and the boy's father will speak from that rostrum in John's scene. Queen Elizabeth speaks from there in Sally's scene, and people stand on it and call out important things in

Christopher's scene. On that rostrum we're having a thing which makes voices come to the audience through loud-speakers. Now, you couldn't play all your scenes tucked away on the rostrum, but you could say important things from there.'

Phoebe looked at Philip's drawing.

'Couldn't we have things to make voices loud everywhere? Then everything that everybody says will be heard.'

'Too right. I've been all over the county asking about a decent loudspeaker outfit, but they're hard to get. That fixture on the rostrum is the best we can manage, and it won't surprise me if that doesn't work any too well. They're chancy things, loudspeakers. They crackle and roar, you don't want to use them more than you must.'

Phoebe got up.

'I have a rehearsal at half-past two this afternoon. You can come and you can see how much of my poetry we can say from that rosplom.'

Philip got up too.

'How would it be if you asked some of Sally's kids to come along? You know, for the extra people in your scene.'

Phoebe hesitated. It was a big climb-down to say yes.

'I don't think only some. I think we'll use them all.'

Philip got hold of Selina before Phoebe's rehearsal.

'Wish I knew what we were going to do with this scene. Such a bit of nonsense. There's some sort of historical accuracy about the others, but none at all about this child Anne Boleyn stuff. I wish we could switch the whole thing to some actual child.'

Selina saw that Philip would need keeping in order.

'You can't change it. Phoebe's written the thing and she's really pretty miserable about it inside. She cried at breakfast this morning, and nobody ever cries in her family. I mean, not unless it's something simply dreadful.'

Philip had a sheet of drawing-paper on his knee with the outline of the lower lawn and the rostrum traced on to it. He jabbed at the rostrum with a pencil.

'I don't want to spoil the kid's scene. Matter of fact Phoebe's the best actress of the lot. I just want to give her a better scene. You think she's absolutely determined to be Anne Boleyn?'

'She's determined to be a queen and wear a crown.'

Philip shook his head.

'Pity she's so small or we might have had her as Queen Victoria.' He began running over queens. 'Can't have her as the young Queen Elizabeth, we've got her already. She's too small for Lady Jane Grey. Pity, that. We could have staged a fine procession for her.' Suddenly he stiffened as he did when he had an idea. 'I've got the very thing. May Day revels. Jack-in-the-Green, maypole dancers, a May Queen with crown and train, pages, old Uncle Tom Cobbley and all. Just the thing for a pageant.'

Philip was just going to rush off to look for Phoebe when Selina stopped him.

'You've got Miss Lipscombe, Mrs Miggs, and Mr Partridge to use. They've rehearsed for weeks and they know all their words.'

Philip sat down again.

'Now, come on, Selina. Be a bright girl. What are Miss Lipscombe, Mrs Miggs, and Mr Partridge doing in May Day revels? They've got to say something and they'll have to say it from that rostrum, so that they can be heard, but what?'

'Couldn't Miss Lipscombe and Mr Partridge be Phoebe's father and mother? And Mrs Miggs the person who comes to tell them Phoebe is going to be May Queen?'

'The trouble with you, Selina, is that you don't see things in your mind.' Philip pointed to the lower stage. 'Today is May Day. There are stalls and cheapjacks and dancers round the maypole, and then a fanfare of trumpets and the arrival of the May Queen and her attendants. They process to the rostrum. You can't start a thing like that with somebody coming up and saying, "Good morrow, mistress, our Phoebe is to be May Queen." This isn't a play in a theatre with three acts, it's one scene in a pageant, and a pageant is spectacular, all movement, colour, life. Now, tell me, on this May Day, who are Miss Lipscombe, Partridge, and Mrs Miggs?'

Selina was quite used to Philip's outbursts by this time. She could see that her job was to keep him from mentioning May Day to anybody until he had everything clear in his mind.

'You'll have to know by Phoebe's rehearsal at half-past two, and I don't think anybody ought to know about May Day until you've talked to Phoebe. She mightn't agree, but I think she would agree when she knows about the procession and everything, and that she'd wear white and all the rest of it.'

Philip got up.

'Very well, Selina. You always do talk sense. I don't know what this pageant would do without its stage manager.' He looked at her suddenly. 'Don't you want to come on in any of the scenes?'

'No. We talked about that at home. But I don't really want to keep changing. I think once I'm dressed I may as well stop as I am.'

The rehearsal at half-past two went off better than Selina had dared to hope. Philip could be perfectly charming when he liked, and he was perfectly charming that afternoon. He never got impatient once. He very seldom got impatient out loud so that people knew about it, but he was nearly always impatient in a mutter for Selina only. 'Look at that fool. Always the wrong side of the stage. That's right, look as though you were attending a funeral. Such a help to the scene. Looks as though she was made of wax.' But at Phoebe's first May Day rehearsal he was not even impatient inside. He was nice all the time. First of all he saw Phoebe. He took her by the arm and walked her up and down the upper lawn.

'Of course it's only an experiment, Phoebe, but if you don't mind, I'm very keen to try it. It's May Day. Terrific excitement, jugglers, conjurers, cheapjacks, perhaps a performing bear if we can get a skin. Then comes the great moment. Fanfares of trumpets, wild excitement on the stage, cheers and curtsies, and we come to the high spot. The entrance of the child May Queen attended by pages and ladies-in-waiting. She processes all round the stage and finishes on the rostrum. There she watches the maypole dance and other junketings arranged in her honour. Then comes the big scene. More fanfares of trumpets and she's crowned. Of course none of it's worked out yet, it's only an idea, and you may not like it, but I should like to try it out this afternoon, if you don't mind.'

'Is this instead of Anne Boleyn?'

Philip squeezed her hand.

'Not if you don't want it to be. Just a suggestion. Gives you a much bigger scene and more scope.'

Philip then went and talked to Miss Lipscombe, Mrs Miggs, and Partridge.

'I'm trying another scene instead of this Anne Boleyn idea. Doesn't seem to me that that scene gives any of you a chance. You three will be on a rostrum, which has a loudspeaker. You won't say anything today, it's got to be worked out. You'll see the kind of thing I'm planning and you can give me any ideas you have after rehearsal.'

Miss Lipscombe said:

'Am I to understand that all these rehearsals have been wasted?'

Philip spoke to Miss Lipscombe in a you-and-I-under-stand-each-other kind of voice.

'After seeing your big performance as the witch I didn't think the Boleyn scene worthy of you.' Then he turned to Mrs Miggs. 'I rather fancy you as a comedian.' He smiled at them all. 'We'll have to work out some first-rate stuff for all of you.'

Selina admired Philip enormously but she did wonder if he had only smoothed over this first rehearsal to have a lot of trouble later on. It was all very well to say 'We must work out some first-rate stuff', but who was going to work out the first-rate stuff? So far all Philip had done was to cut down the speaking parts to almost nothing. He had never shown any signs of being a writer.

Sally was, of course, bursting with enthusiasm. More dancing. What could be nicer? Already the children knew what they had to do in her scene. She would start training them for a maypole dance tomorrow morning. For that afternoon she merely put them on to dance in two rings, one going one way and one the other. It did not, of course, look like maypole dancing but it gave some effect.

Philip made a big show of Phoebe's entrance. He got Mrs Mawser to lend him a tablecloth, which he pinned to her shoulders, and he picked some of the children to act as her ladies-in-waiting, and when it came to the crowning scene he picked a piece of convolvulus and twisted it together, and had Phoebe properly crowned.

'Of course,' he said to everybody at the end of the rehearsal, 'this is just a bare outline. By tomorrow I'll have everything worked out in detail,' he nodded at Miss Lipscombe, Mrs Miggs, and Partridge, 'together with what you three are to say.' Then he went up to Phoebe, who was still sitting on the garden chair which had been used as her throne. 'Well, how do you feel, Phoebe? This anything like what you wanted?'

It was, as a matter of fact, just the scene Phoebe wanted, crown, train and all, but she was not going to give in too easily. She stuck up her chin.

'I knew I was perfectly right when I said Augustus and Benjamin ought to be at my rehearsal. It's quite a difficult thing to carry a train nicely, and they haven't begun to learn.'

# CHAPTER SIXTEEN

———•———

## *Wardrobe Mistresses*

The dresses were lying on Mrs Day's bed. Mrs Day looked at them and shook her head.

'Shockin' old things. Comic to think we ever wore them.' She picked up a backless dark blue brocade. 'Imagine, I wore that at a Hunt Ball in mid-winter. Makes me shudder to think of it now. Die of cold.'

Mrs Andrews had one arm round Sally to prevent her pouncing on the clothes. She knew how careless Mrs Day was, and she was determined that she should not give away something that she would regret afterwards.

'There'll be Hunt Balls again next winter, most likely. You won't have the coupons to buy a new evening dress. But she'll have to go, won't she, Mrs Mawser?'

Mrs Mawser had been standing just inside the door. Now she came forward to the bed and looked down at the dresses. She thought the old evening dresses were a sad sight. She belonged to the date when people like Mrs Day put one on every evening no matter what was happening. She had much preferred those days, so much better, she thought, than the present, when Mrs Day would come and wash up in her kitchen. She picked up the blue brocade and held it out to Mrs Andrews.

'We shan't wear this again, madam. A very nasty burn, you'll notice, down the front breadth. There'd be no way to disguise it.'

Mrs Day held out her hands, which, as usual, were all over sticking plaster and bandages.

'Always was careless, wasn't I, Mawser? Burnt me clothes when I had any, now I burn me hands.'

Mrs Mawser gave the blue brocade to Mrs Andrews and picked up a black velvet.

'Moth. We shall never know how that occurred. Put away clean, moth-ball everywhere, and yet the whole dress is falling to pieces.' She gave the velvet to Mrs Andrews, and picked up a miscellaneous pile of shabby velvets and marocains. 'Just rubbish. We should have thrown them away before the war.'

Mrs Day pounced on a faded green velvet.

'Good gracious, Mawser! That old thing! I had that for the dinner party after Philip's christening. That takes us back twenty-five years.'

Mrs Mawser handed the rest of the dresses to Mrs Andrews.

'Many are older than that. If they can be of use in the pageant it would really make a very good end for them.'

Sally was fingering the clothes in her mother's arms. She was discarding her dream of flowered crêpe de chine and redressing herself.

206

'I could use the green velvet. I could have a green velvet Elizabethan top and some of the butter-muslin could be dyed for the bottom.'

'Shouldn't be green,' Selina reminded her. 'There are those green dancers from Linkwell that Philip's always talking about.'

Sally regretfully dropped the green velvet dress and held out the skirt of a dull crimson.

'That wouldn't be bad. Crimson with a pinkish sort of skirt.'

Mrs Andrews said:

'Don't forget I've got to make three sets of clothes for Augustus and Benjamin out of these. I should think this blue brocade would do for the Henry the Eighth scene and . . .'

Selina made a face at Sally.

'Oh, my goodness, we forgot to tell you. It's all changed. Phoebe's going to be the May Queen instead of Anne Boleyn.'

Selina saw the look of horror on Mrs Andrews's face, so she added hurriedly:

'I don't think it'll make any difference. Augustus and Benjamin will still be pages.'

Mrs Andrews looked from Selina to Sally.

'Do you mean to say that Phoebe's scene isn't going to happen? You know the letter was written last night about the costumes.'

Selina decided that it was best to break the news in one horrid sweep.

'They'll be wanted all right, only there'll be about ninety other dresses wanted as well. All sorts of people. It isn't fixed yet, but Philip said jugglers, tumblers, ladies-in-waiting on the May Queen, and children who dance round a maypole.'

Mrs Andrews felt quite weak in the knees at this bad news. She sat down abruptly on the bed and looked at the one person who might sympathize and understand.

'Pity me, Mrs Mawser. My husband says that half the cast will make their own clothes, but I know they won't. People simply haven't got the bits put away to make clothes out of. We're going to dress all Sally's dancers in butter-muslin, that will have to be dyed what Sally calls laburnum yellow, and I expect it will end in my having to do the dyeing. My husband says that all the mothers will make their own children's clothes, but I have a suspicion they won't. There was just one scene in this pageant that was fixed and nothing wanted doing about it, and that was Phoebe's. Four people taking part and all the dresses to be hired. Now you hear the news and you see how it's broken to me. Phoebe's to be a May Queen, which will mean white from head to foot, and we shall want about ninety other dresses as well. And when I get home and tell my husband the bad news, all he'll say is, "Oh, they'll make the dresses themselves."'

Mrs Mawser hated acting in the pageant. She had agreed to be part of the crowd in Christopher's scene, but she was only taking part because she felt it to be her duty. She thought it very unbecoming behaviour on her part to raise her voice and shout at Miss Lipscombe and throw mud, 'Not,' as she often said to Partridge, 'that I ever cared for the woman, but there is a long distance between not caring for somebody and throwing mud at them.' On the other hand, she approved of the pageant. She did not like to think of the Day family quietly slipping away from the Abbey when their family had owned it for so long. If go they must (and she supposed

Colonel Day knew what he was talking about when he said he must sell the place, gentlemen always understood figures) then they should go with style. It was difficult to go in style when the county could not pay farewell visits because of petrol rationing. The next best thing was to have a kind of public farewell. The pageant would be just that. Mrs Mawser saw in Mrs Andrews's anxiety about the clothes a way in which she could help the family to leave the Abbey in style with none of that nasty acting.

'If Mr Philip could spare me from the acting I could help over the clothes, madam.'

Mrs Day looked at Mrs Andrews.

'There's an offer for you. You two had better become joint wardrobe mistresses. Mawser's no end of a dab at cutting out, aren't you, Mawser?'

Mrs Mawser saw the Abbey being used as it should be used. She looked at Mrs Day.

'We could have working parties. Wonderful what a lot of work can be got through at working parties.'

Mrs Andrews felt as if a load were tumbling off her back. With real affection and gratitude she shifted the evening dresses to one arm and held out her other hand to Mrs Mawser.

'You are a dear. I feel a different person. It's not that I don't want to do everything I can to help but I've got such an impractical family. I'll have a talk to Mr Philip and get him to fix once and for all what is going to be worn, and I'll get him to decide who can be asked to hire their clothes and who can't. Then we shall know what's got to be made and we'll see if it's possible to raise the stuff to do it.'

Mrs Mawser was, for her, quite excited.

'Now, Miss Sally, you get me the yellow dye tomorrow and tell the boys to bring me up the butter-muslin, and I'll dye the stuff for your dancers. I can do it in the old copper; I'll have the water boiling quite early.'

Philip was in to tea. He was delighted to hear that Mrs Mawser would act as co-wardrobe mistress with Mrs Andrews, and agreed cheerfully to let her off acting in Christopher's scene.

'She was no good anyway. She looked like a rather superior Siamese cat at a meeting of common tabbies.'

Mrs Andrews sat in a chair beside Philip.

'Philip, can you give me half an hour after tea? I want to get the question of these dresses settled once and for all.'

'I can give you as long as you like, but we won't get them fixed once and for all today.'

Mrs Andrews sighed.

'What else are you changing? For goodness' sake make up your mind before I cut out Augustus's and Benjamin's tunics.'

'It's not changes.' He looked at Selina. 'I'll have to meet all the family in committee. It's time. I can't think how I was such a fool as not to time the scenes earlier. Do you know, with everything that we can put in, the pageant as it is won't play for much more than an hour.'

Selina asked:

'How long ought it to be?'

'Two hours at the least.'

Selina stared at him, made quite speechless with horror. At last she said:

'Do you mean that we've got to have exactly twice as much pageant as we've got now?'

210

He nodded.

'I worked out John's scene. There's about four minutes of monks chanting at the beginning, one minute's talking, about five minutes' horseplay, another minute's talking, and then another four of chanting by the monks at the end. And, mind you, that's stretching it. There's going to be a lot more chanting than most people'll want to hear.'

Sally said:

'Have you counted the extra dances from the Ballet School at Linkwell in my scene?'

'I've allowed for them roughly, and for the prologue and epilogue and bits in between. With all the doings we're putting into Phoebe's scene I dare say we shan't need to double the show. I reckon two long scenes will about fill the bill.'

Mrs Andrews murmured, 'Two long scenes.'

Philip turned to her, smiling.

'One of them at any rate won't need dresses. I think we should bring this pageant right up to date. We can have a scene during the war. The coming of the evacuees, and that time when the Americans took the Abbey.'

'Canadians had it, too,' Mrs Day reminded him.

Philip nodded.

'I know, but we couldn't raise any Canadians, there are none round here now, but we can use the Americans. It would make a fine finish. A whole lot of jeeps and stuff rushing on to the stage.'

The Colonel came in and heard what Philip said.

'Never sell the place if you have jeeps rushin' all over my grass.'

Mrs Andrews did not want Philip's mind distracted from clothes.

'I think it's a splendid idea. All they'll need to wear is their own uniforms; what could be better? What are you going to do for the other scene?'

Philip shook his head.

'I wish I knew; that's why I want a meeting of your offspring. One of them might have a good idea. And that's not my only headache. I've got Partridge, Mrs Miggs, and Miss Lipscombe on my hands. They were part of Phoebe's scene, and now I've altered it I've got to write a scene for them. Goodness knows what they are going to talk about.'

The Colonel helped himself to a bit of cake.

'Partridge won't care if you let him off.'

Philip got up to hand some food to Mrs Andrews.

'Too right, but Miss Lipscombe and Mrs Miggs will.'

Mrs Andrews took a bun from the plate Philip handed her.

'Well, do have your meeting to decide what the extra scene is soon, Philip. It's less than seven weeks to this pageant and, so far as I know, none of the actors have been told yet that they have got to make their own clothes.'

Philip gaped at her.

'Make their own clothes! Who said so?'

'My husband. You see, originally he offered to pay for the hire, but now, of course, it's such a big affair he can't afford it. He says that he'll hire a few, and anyone who can afford to hire their own should be asked to do so. The rest will have to make their own clothes. Well, I know that they haven't got the time and they haven't got the material, and it'll end in Mrs Mawser and myself doing most of it, but out of what?'

Philip put the buns back on the table. He ran his hand through his hair and it stood bolt upright.

'You can't make all the clothes. The hire cost should be deducted from the takings.'

'I should think it would use all the takings to hire them. We want to hand over a decent cheque to the Air Force Benevolent.'

Philip clicked his fingers.

'I know. You know there's this catch about the dress rehearsal. Thursday's early closing day and it's the only day that half the cast can get off. A lot of the people working round here, including your husband, can't be sure of making a dress rehearsal because it won't be on a Thursday. All the farmers taking part have been saying that they can't give two afternoons running. I've planned we have the dress rehearsal on Thursday afternoon and the real performance about five o'clock. Now why don't we charge for the dress rehearsal.'

The Colonel said:

'That ought to fit in fine. When I asked about the trains and buses to bring the audience in I didn't specify time.'

Selina thought of the people who were going to pay to see the dress rehearsal.

'I shouldn't think they ought to pay much to see the dress rehearsal. It's bound to be the most awful muddle.'

Philip threw her a comforting glance.

'We'll have a rehearsal or two in the clothes for the principals and the children and anyone who can turn up. We'll charge less for the dress rehearsal than we do for the real performance, of course, but we'll see that we get a full house for it, and the money taken will pay for the hire of the clothes.'

'Oh, Philip dear,' said Mrs Andrews, 'how simply splendid, but will you please walk back with us after tea and explain all this to my husband.'

There was not a rehearsal that evening so Philip came back with the family. First they had a family committee. It seemed funny having a grown-up there. John said:

'I usually sit here and run the thing, but this time, as you've got all the talking to do, would you?'

Philip was never a person to waste much time. He sat down and explained his troubles. He told them about the paid-for dress rehearsal. Then he explained about his scheme for putting in the evacuees and the Americans, 'But after that I'm stuck. We need one other good scene with plenty of action and dancing and stuff, to take at least twenty minutes.'

'Where did you want it to go?' John asked. 'I mean, between whose scenes?'

Philip took a piece of paper out of his pocket.

'Your scene's the thirteenth century. Phoebe's the beginning of the sixteenth century. Sally's the very end of the sixteenth, Christopher's the seventeenth. It looks as though we want one between John's and Phoebe's. Or a slice of Victorian England.'

Phoebe said:

'Oh, do let's do Queen Victoria when she was a little girl and said "I will be good."'

Philip shook his head.

'Much too small a scene for a pageant. And none of you are the right size for Queen Victoria at that age. Now, rack your brains, all of you. Think of something intelligent.'

Christopher was sprawling across the table. Now he looked up.

'We want something that happened to this village. Did anything ever?'

Philip stiffened, so they knew he had an idea.

'I wonder if we could do anything with the relief of Mafeking. Must have been very like VE Day. Bonfires, bells ringing, dancing and all of it.'

'How would they hear the news?' John asked.

Philip was gazing into space as if he could see Little Muchover in nineteen hundred.

'I should think it would come by messenger. A little place like this wouldn't have heard it very quickly. I think we might have a town-crier. We could have a record of bells and our old bell-ringers trundling across to go and ring the church bells. Then all the village pouring out and bustle and excitement. We might produce a bit of a comic band from somewhere, and finish up with a good dance. Lancers, polkas and all that kind of stuff.'

'I should think,' said Christopher, 'we could find lots of people who remember that night. There are plenty of very old people in the village.'

'Well,' said Philip, 'you go and ask them, but if they tell you that nothing happened at all, or that it rained that day so they didn't do anything, don't tell me about it, because in the Little Muchover in our pageant they rang the bells, lit the bonfires, and danced. Now, has anybody got any objections?'

'Who's going to be the chief person in the scene?' Phoebe asked.

'I don't know that we need a chief person. There wouldn't have been one, really. It's just all the village turning out.'

'Well, as long as there's none I don't mind, but I don't think it would be fair if somebody had two big parts. When we first planned the pageant we only had one scene each.'

'Don't listen to her, Philip,' John said. 'I don't mind if somebody else has two scenes. Nor does anybody else.'

'Well, I don't think we shall want anybody in that scene, but I tell you what we do want somebody for, that's a funny fellow to be Jack-in-the-Green in Phoebe's scene.'

Christopher looked up hopefully, for he was enjoying being funny in his own scene. Before he could speak Sally said:

'I was thinking about Alfie. We don't need him now for buns because, now it's the holidays, if we are asking people to tea we can fetch them ourselves.' She turned to Philip. 'I think Alfie might be Jack-in-the-Green. He's very good in Christopher's scene. He says "blasted she-goat" louder than anybody else.'

Philip looked at John, who nodded.

'He'd be very good, and I think he ought to have a part.'

Phoebe broke in:

'He took a lot of trouble teaching Mrs Miggs her poetry, which she isn't going to say.'

Philip hurried away from that subject.

'Will one of you see Alfie? I suppose you'd better, Selina.' Philip glanced down at his notes. 'Who shall we get for a town-crier? Do you know anybody who would do for that?'

Augustus and Benjamin did not seem to have been paying much attention to the committee. Benjamin had hummed all the time, and Augustus was playing with a puzzle where he had to get a piece of quicksilver broken into seven bits, and each of the bits had to form a button on a man's coat. Now he looked up.

'I think Mr Bins would make a very good town-crier.'

All the family looked admiringly at Augustus.

John said:

'He's quite right.'

Sally said:

'Mr Bins would be just perfect.'

Christopher said:

'You aren't such a fool as you look, Augustus.'

Selina, to save time, said:

'I'll go and see Mr Bins.'

'It's very suitable,' said Sally, 'that Mr Bins should have a part. After all, he brought the parcel to Selina, and if there hadn't been that parcel there wouldn't have been a pageant.'

Philip was not attending. He was writing a list of possible characters for the Victorian scene.

'I believe that's all unless anyone has got anything else they want to say. I shall need all of you in that scene, of course.' He looked at his watch. 'Do you think your father's nearly through with his surgery? I want to have that conference about hiring clothes.'

# CHAPTER SEVENTEEN

### ———◆◆—— ###

## *Sally at Linkwell*

Sally was so excited on the morning of her first ballet rehearsal at Linkwell that she felt sick and could not eat any breakfast. She had not to be at the school until ten-thirty, but she drove all the family mad, insisting that they were making her late.

'Hurry up, Benjamin. Dad, must I wait until Benjamin's finished? I shall miss my bus. Mum, don't encourage Augustus, he can't want another slice of bread. Phoebe, you are a guzzler.'

Neither her father nor her mother treated her complaints at all seriously. Dr Andrews said:

'My dear child, it's not yet half-past eight. If you catch the bus at nine-thirty you'll still be early for your rehearsal.'

Mrs Andrews said:

'You can't catch a bus until nine-thirty, Sally dear. A dancing rehearsal at ten-thirty is no excuse for getting you out of your share of the housework.'

Phoebe, Augustus, and Benjamin told Sally what they thought of her. Phoebe said:

'If you're silly enough not to eat your breakfast because of a stupid old dancing-class, that's no reason to call me a guzzler.'

Augustus said:

'I do want another piece of bread. I shouldn't wonder if I had five more pieces.'

Benjamin said, with earnest reproach:

'My dear, nobody likes being hurried when they're eating.'

Sally was appalled at the suggestion that the nine-thirty bus would do.

'It's the most dreadful risk, Mum.'

'Why?'

'If it's full, I shan't get there in time.'

'If you go to the bus stop by nine-fifteen,' said Doctor Andrews, 'you'll be at the head of the queue and there certainly will be room.'

Since the holidays had started and the rehearsals had been taking place every day, Mrs Andrews had stretched the invitations to tea. They might now have five people to tea two afternoons, or ten a week, always provided they ate buns. Three of Christopher's mummers were coming to tea that afternoon. Selina tried to help Sally.

'Couldn't Sally go in on the earlier bus and buy this afternoon's buns? That'll save Christopher going, and he could do Sally's washing up and beds.'

Sally looked gratefully at Selina and hopefully at her mother. Mrs Andrews thought that a good idea.

'All right. If Christopher is happy about it.'

There was never any question as to whether Christopher and Sally would agree. Christopher only said:

'But don't forget the buns. You'll have to go to the shop before your rehearsal, remember, or you won't get them.'

Sally was glad she had her attaché case with her in which to carry her practice dress. She would not have made a dignified entrance to a ballet school carrying bags of buns. Nobody could see there were buns when they were in an attaché case.

The Ballet School at Linkwell lay just outside the town. It was a large red brick building in a big garden. Sally was not quite sure where she ought to go. There was the front door marked 'Visitors' and a side door marked 'Students'. There was also a back door marked 'Tradesmen's Entrance'.

I'm not a visitor, I'm not a student, and I'm not a tradesman, she thought. In the end she rang the front door bell. It's probably the wrong thing to do, but it would be still worse to walk in at the 'Students' entrance and have to be told by the students that you've come to the wrong place.

One of the students answered the door; at least Sally thought she must be a student. She was about fifteen. She had bare legs and was wearing a black tunic. It did not seem likely that even in a ballet school the maids were dressed like that.

'I'm Sally Andrews. I've come for a rehearsal to do with our pageant.'

The girl was not a bit stand-offish.

'We knew you were coming this morning. We're rehearsing indoors as it looks as though it's going to rain. I'm taking part in the pageant. I'm one of the ghosts.'

Sally was puzzled.

'Are you? I didn't know there were ghosts.'

221

'Between all the scenes. They're pretty terrific really. Have you seen the designs?'

Sally grasped what the girl was talking about.

'I know, you're going to be a green dancer. Philip, he's the man who is mostly producing the pageant, said we'd have those, only I didn't know you were ghosts.'

The girl was leading her down a long corridor. She paused before opening a door.

'We're not going to be green. We're grey. Grey everything, grey veils, grey faces, grey clothes, even grey arms and legs. Madame Ramosova had a set of grey chiffon dresses. Then she's having some net dyed grey for head-dresses and hoops and things. We each have a different dress for each entrance, at least rather different.' She opened the door. 'This is the changing-room.'

The Linkwell Ballet School had uniform for practice, but there was no rule about that at Sally's school. She wore a tunic but it could be made of anything. Hers was the remains of an old blue frock. She had got the trunks of it on already, so all she had to do was to take off her sandals and her cotton frock and put on her tunic, and she was ready.

'Come on,' said the girl. 'Madame Ramosova is coming to class this morning, so we mustn't be late.'

The rehearsal took place in a large practice-room. Miss Faulkes was there and two other teachers. There were also about forty pupils. Most of the pupils were children, but some of them, old girls Sally supposed, seemed to be grown up. They all had black tunics like the girl who had answered the door. Sally felt most conspicuous in her blue. At the piano a thin, patient, anxious-looking woman was accompanying some

222

dancers, her eyes never leaving their feet. There were sixteen girls dancing. In the centre was one with glorious red-gold hair. Sally's guide touched her arm.

'Come and sit by the piano and you can see what they're doing.'

Sally was stunned by what they were doing. The dance was full of most difficult lifts. The Queen of the Fairies was always being elevated by the rest of the ballet, and in most difficult positions. Sally did not say anything to the girl beside her, but she did wonder whether a dance like that would not make the beginning part done by the children of the village and herself look pretty silly. At the end of the dance the Queen of the Fairies was carried right off the stage by her fairies, held by one leg, the other leg raised with a beautifully straight knee, her chin was up, her head back, she held both arms forward. As the dancers ran off with her the Queen's red hair blew backwards.

'My goodness!' said Sally. 'She does dance beautifully.'

The girl beside her had no time to answer, for at that moment Madame Ramosova came in. She saw Sally and beckoned to her.

'Did you see the first fairy dance?' Sally nodded. 'What did you think of it?'

'I thought it was terrific.'

'It will be effective. It is always difficult planning for dancing out of doors. There's so much that you cannot do. Now we have to rehearse where you come in.' She laid her hand on Sally's shoulder and led her across the room back to a seat by the piano. 'What I've planned is this. Your scene with the children as I saw it. Then the children pull you into the bushes and then we have my girls representing fairyland. Following the dance you've just seen there's a dance of gnomes and then Titania comes back with her fairies and there is general dancing, at the end of which your children come out of the bushes dragging you. I've only given them six bars of music. That just gives them time to run on, give you a push so that you fall at the Fairy Queen's feet and then they run off again. That finishes with the children.'

Sally fully sympathized with Madame Ramosova. Compared with what she had just seen their little dances seemed very unimportant, but she and the children had worked hard and had once been all the ballet, so she did not like to hear Madame Ramosova saying, in a pleased way, that all they needed was six bars of music and then they were finished. However, that was not the sort of thing you said to Madame Ramosova, so she said nothing at all but looked polite.

'Then,' said Madame Ramosova, 'the Queen of the Fairies beckons to her elves and they dance round you with flowers and tie you to a tree, from where you can watch the revels.'

Sally licked her lips, she did not like to interrupt, but it was necessary.

'There isn't a tree.'

Madame Ramosova clearly thought that a frivolous interruption.

'There will be. We then have a ballet of butterflies. I have used my best dancers for this. Then there is a scene of homage to Gloriana and, at the end, a procession of all the fairies, in which they carry the Fairy Queen off, and you are left alone. You have then four bars of music in which you struggle to be free.'

'And then I do my final dance?'

224

Madame Ramosova was seeing the whole effect in her mind's eye.

'I'm not quite sure about that. We must see the effect as a whole. I should think a very few bars to express joy and gladness at your freedom, a jeté and off.' Madame Ramosova got up. 'Now, I should like to see this from the beginning.'

Sally was glad to see the ballet from the beginning too. It was, of course, like seeing an entirely new ballet. The ballet she now saw was all to do with fairyland, and the most important person in it was the Fairy Queen. There were two places in the ballet where the Fairy Queen and all her fairies made obeisance to Queen Elizabeth. As Sally watched the ballet she could not help thinking how much better it would have been if she and the children were not coming on at all. They had very little to do and would look amateur beside these dancers. Madame Ramosova used several of her smaller children to represent Sally's fairies. They used the same simple tripping steps that her fairies used, then they swayed first backwards and then forwards, giving the effect of throwing her at Titania's feet. Then they danced off.

'That looked very well,' said Madame Ramosova. 'The six bars are just long enough.'

Sally was lying at the Fairy Queen's feet by that time, so the remark was not addressed to her, but inside she thought, It may look very well now with these girls doing it, but I'll never get my children to do it like that, not if I rehearsed them every day from now till the pageant.

There was, of course, no string of flowers and no tree, but Sally was bound to a chair with a length of wool. Then on came the butterflies. The butterflies, as Madame Ramosova had said, were her best pupils. They were, in fact, all professionals who happened to be free and were taking refresher courses during the summer months. Sally's eyes grew rounder and rounder as she watched them. Such elevation and such lovely plastique movements. Perhaps, thought Sally humbly, it's just as well that I'm only going to do four bars and a jeté and then off. I'd look pretty silly after this. At the end of their dance the butterflies sprang into the air and then fell fluttering to the ground. If Sally had not had her hands tied behind her she would have clapped.

Madame Ramosova said:

'Still very ragged. Lacks precision.'

The Queen of the Fairies came on again with her fairies and elves, and to the music of 'Greensleeves' they wove a mazy dance, lines working in and out of each other until, for their exit, they formed a long line running all round the stage, the fairies at the back carrying Titania.

There were, as Madame Ramosova had said, just four bars of the music left.

'You pull right, you pull left, and you pull centre, you break your bonds in time to the music,' said Madame Ramosova. 'You come down stage. Glissade, glissade, again glissade, glissade and grande jeté and off.' Sally carried out these directions as well as she could. Madame Ramosova smiled kindly. 'You have the music of that at home, I know, and you can practise that combination before the next rehearsal.' She got up. 'You girls will take the whole ballet through again. Good morning, Sally.'

Sally said:

'When will you want me for the next rehearsal?'

Madame Ramosova looked at the woman who was evidently her head teacher.

'When will you want her?'

The head teacher considered.

'One day next week. I think, madame, we'd better telephone. We need not trouble her to come too often, it's very
easy for one of the girls to stand for her. It's not as though she
were concerned with the actual ballet.'

Sally went quietly over to the girls who were acting as her
fairies. She hoped that her face had not got a snubbed look,
but she was feeling snubbed inside. Ever since Christmas she
had lived with her ballet. Ever since Madame Ramosova had
come to the Abbey she had been looking forward to rehearsals
at Linkwell. It was stupid to mind or be proud, but it did give
her a trodden-on feeling to hear, 'It's not as though she were
concerned with the actual ballet.'

The rehearsal went through from the beginning without a
pause. Sally was glad to find that though they were not very
well executed, she had the timing and the routine of her four
bars correctly.

'That will be all for today,' said the head teacher. 'You'll
now go to your ordinary classes.'

Nobody told her so, but Sally took it that she was done
with and sidled down the wall and made for the door. In the
doorway the girl who was dancing Titania was talking to a
friend. She smiled at Sally.

'I hear the ballet was your idea. Like it?'

Sally walked through Linkwell singing. What a glorious
world! A world in which real, grand dancers like the Queen of
the Fairies could ask her if she liked her ballet. Like it! It was
too gorgeous to be true. It was the most scrumptious ballet
that had ever been thought of. If only it was not so long to the
twentieth of September.

227

# CHAPTER EIGHTEEN

## *The Pageant Takes Shape*

In the next days the pageant began to take real shape. All sorts of things happened. Selina went to see Mr Bins. She did not have to go to his house, she only bounced out of the front door and caught him as he delivered the morning letters.

'Oh, Mr Bins, would you act a part in our pageant?'

Mr Bins was sorting the letters.

'Eight for the doctor, two for Mrs Andrews, and a postcard for John.' He handed her the post. Then, having done his duty, he began to consider the pageant. 'It's me time. You see, there's a lot of work to be got through. This is a big district.'

'I know, but it's the end scene we wanted you for, so you'd have done the afternoon post. We wanted you for the town-crier. You have to tell the people that the siege of Mafeking is over.'

Mr Bins pursed his lips and shook his head.

'It's me time. Shocking what a lot of time the post takes to deliver these days. It's all these parcels of food and that coming from abroad. Always having to wait for people to pay for this and that and nobody ever has the right money on them.'

'It's because of the parcels that we so want you to be in the pageant. You see, you brought a parcel for me last Christmas . . .'

'That's right, three pounds eighteen shillings and fourpence to pay, and Miss Lipscombe argufying. That woman would argue the hind-leg off a donkey.'

'That parcel was the beginning of the pageant. It had a party frock and shoes in it for me, and as there wasn't going to be a party suitable to wear it at we thought of the pageant instead. Oh, Mr Bins dear, wouldn't you like to announce that Mafeking was relieved?'

'Mafeking! I always fancied a visit to South Africa. Beautiful postcards I've delivered. Very nice bits of scenery they seem to have there. Have I got a piece to learn?'

'You will have. Squadron Leader Day is looking out the right words. You have a bell and you say, "Oyez! Oyez! Oyez!"'

Mr Bins turned away to continue his rounds.

'Well, you give me the piece and we'll see what we can do.' Then he turned back. 'Ought to be getting some good news for you. War with Japan will soon be over. Any day now I might bring you a letter.'

'I know. I keep thinking about that. Do you think it would be a letter, Mr Bins? I thought perhaps a message or a telegram.'

There was no need to persuade Alfie to be Jack-in-the-Green. He was delighted.

'I don't quite know what you do,' Selina said, 'but I believe you're all dressed up in green leaves and are funny.'

Alfie was fifteen. He was going back to London in the autumn to work in an uncle's shop. He had spent five years in the country with his grandmother, but he had never grown to like it. 'Give me London,' he always said. 'Dull, that's what the country is. Nowhere to go and nothin' to see. Take a walk and nothin' speaks to you but an ole cow.' He was quite unalarmed about what he might have to do as Jack-in-the-Green.

'If it's comic you can leave it to me. I know a sight of comic things to do. Used to go to the Empire regular before the war. Best music 'all for miles. See'd every comic that was worth seein', so I know wot's wot.'

Selina thought it best to let Alfie know in advance that he would not be able to decide in what way he would be funny.

'This is Squadron Leader Day's scene. He's producing it and he'll tell you what to do.'

'Righty oh! But he's only got to give an 'int. Make it Max Miller. Make it Tommy Trinder. Make it Bob 'Ope. 'E's only got to say the word and I'm there.'

Philip had got round the difficulty of what to do with Partridge and Mrs Miggs. In the May Queen's scene they were only part of the crowd, but in the new Victorian scene they danced together. The idea really came from Mrs Miggs. It was at a rehearsal of the May Queen's scene. Philip was just think-ing for a moment where to put his dancers, and in the pause Mrs Miggs said to the children round her:

'Proper dancin' there ought to be one day soon. You wait till we beat the Japs.'

She then picked up her skirts and began to sing and dance. She sang 'Knees up, Mother Brown'. She had just reached the line 'Under the table you must go' when Philip turned and saw her. He also saw Partridge's face. Partridge thought Mrs Miggs's performance most unsuitable and every inch of his face said so. Philip thought how funny it would be to put Mrs Miggs and Partridge to dance together. Mrs Miggs giving a nice abandoned performance as she did, and Partridge looking as depressed about it as he certainly would, he would not need to rehearse them at all. Just keep them well down stage where the audience could see them. He went over to Mrs Miggs.

'I've been watching you. You're a dancer, that's what you are. I shall have you dancing in this pageant.'

It had not been quite so easy about Miss Lipscombe, but at the second rehearsal of the May Queen's scene the right job for her had turned up. It was just as well it did, because she had been saying to everybody in a very angry voice, 'Some people seem to think I have nothing to do but to learn poetry, just to be told that I shall not be saying it after all.'

The May Queen's scene was elaborate. There were a great many things going on at once. Both Christopher and John were cheapjacks, and so were four other boys. Each of them had wares to sell and something to shout. Then there was a strong-man display. Philip had persuaded Mr Peters to be the strong man. He had nothing to do but to pretend to lift heavy weights, but he was a very good person to be the strong man because apart from the fact that he was big and strong-looking, he had a policeman's rather solemn face, and he could be trusted to keep his mind on what he was doing, and not be looking round watching the other performers.

There were several other booths and side-shows to be fixed and everybody had words to say, like 'Come and see the fat girl', or 'See the Eastern gentleman swallow a sword'. In and out amongst the stalls and the cheapjacks the crowd had to move, behaving like an ordinary crowd. Mothers, fathers, and their children out shopping. The children pleading for this fairing and that. Old friends meeting and shaking hands. Strangers arriving and being stared at by the village. As well, of course, as there would be at any fair, there were innumerable children on their own. Getting in people's way, trying to creep into the tents for nothing and showing each other what they had won at the side-shows.

The difficulty was that the children got so into the spirit of their parts that they became quite unmanageable. They looked very lively and very like children would look at a fair, but they got so excited it was quite impossible to get them to remember to be in the right place at the right minute. Then Philip had his big idea. Miss Lipscombe. She should be the schoolmistress. She should wear the dress that was all ready ordered for her as governess to Anne Boleyn, and walk about and pull the children into place, and say a few things from the rostrum to show that she was the schoolteacher.

Nobody could have been more suited to the job. From the very day that she took on the part of the schoolmistress the children began to behave better. Miss Lipscombe looked so severe it was quite difficult for them to remember that she was not really a schoolmistress, and when she said, 'You go where I tell you, Margaret Peters, or I'll send you straight home to your mother,' Margaret Peters forgot they were only acting and believed her.

It was a good thing that Philip had fixed Miss Lipscombe to be schoolteacher, because it got him out of another difficulty. It was found to be quite impossible to plant a maypole. It had to be brought on standing in a green frame, but it could not be fixed to the ground, and so the pole was inclined to wobble.

Philip arranged that Miss Lipscombe should hold it. What could be more natural? If she was the schoolteacher she would probably have taught the children to dance the maypole dance, so she was the right one to hold the maypole. Sally was the only person who objected to this arrangement.

'She looks so grumpy standing there, she spoils the look of my maypole dance.'

Philip would not listen to her.

'It'll spoil it a lot worse, old thing, if the maypole falls over.'

The next excitement was the programmes, posters, and tickets. Colonel Day said he would see to these.

'Know a feller in Linkwell. Have a talk with him. Very decent man. Shouldn't wonder if he wouldn't give us a cut charge as it's in aid of charity.'

Then, one afternoon when Selina came to a rehearsal especially called for Mr Laws, who would not remember where he had to come on, she found Philip talking to two American officers. Philip beckoned to her.

'This is the Commanding Officer from the camp, Selina.'

The colonel shook her hand and he introduced the other officer.

'This is Lieutenant Caldecott, but everybody calls him Bob.'

Philip said:

'The colonel thinks he can manage the band and the jeeps.'

The colonel nodded.

'I just don't know how we're situated. May be a cessation of hostilities any time now, maybe we'll be moved, but I've gotten an idea that we're likely to be hereabouts for some time yet, and, if that's so, we'll be pleased to supply the band and the drivers and jeeps.'

The colonel and Philip went off to discuss where would be the best place for jeeps to enter. Selina talked to Bob. He was very young-looking, with nice blue eyes and fair hair. She decided that she would take him into her confidence.

'Philip thinks it will be all right about the seats being sold. Every time I say is he sure they will sell, he says it's in the bag. Do you think you could sell any seats at your camp?'

'Why, surely. What's this pageant about?'

Selina explained about the Abbey and how long it had been in the Day family.

'Really, the only thing that we absolutely know happened at the Abbey is that the Abbot cursed it when Henry the Eighth turned the monks out, but we're not acting that. Colonel Day thought it might remind the monks to have a last fire before he left.'

Bob laughed.

'Well, I guess that's a risk I'd have taken.'

'Oh, no. It's been burnt down a terrible lot of times, and it's sure to be burnt again, but, of course, Colonel Day would rather it was burnt after it was sold than before it was sold.'

'I certainly can see his point there.'

Selina took Bob up to the Abbey and showed him round the outside.

'Of course the best thing that could happen would be that the people who buy it are monks or something like that, then the curse would be gone for ever.'

'Have this present family always lived at the Abbey?'

'Ever since Henry the Eighth gave it to them.'

'That's quite a while. Pity they have to go. I like all that tradition business. My family were British way back, which

235

surely gives me a right to take an interest in the pageant. How many seats did you figure to sell at the camp?'

Selina explained about the dress rehearsal and the performance.

'I think I'd sell tickets for the performance if I were you. I don't think the dress rehearsal will be very good.' They were back on the upper lawn. She saw that Mr Laws had arrived. It was extraordinary for Mr Laws to come to a rehearsal and be in time, and not an opportunity to let slip. 'I must go. That's the vicar. He's having a rehearsal especially for him because he can't remember when to come on. I've got to be my Uncle Jim this afternoon. He's a doctor and he can only come to rehearsals on Thursdays.'

Bob gave her a nice friendly smile.

'You count on me for those tickets. You tell me how many you want me to sell for each performance and I'll see they're sold.'

Selina thought this a very rash promise.

'But it might be hundreds.'

Bob laughed.

'Well, just think of that! Do you know, we've got thousands up at that camp.'

Seeing the American officers got Philip what he called 'revved up'.

'It's in the bag,' he told Selina triumphantly. 'Wonderful these fellows. They mean to fix up an electric buzzer or something to give the cue, and then the jeeps come swooping down the drive.'

'Won't it make rather a mess of the grass?'

Philip disliked being brought back to earth just as much as the cousins did. He looked at Selina severely.

'This is art, my child, and you can't consider grass when it's a matter of art.'

Selina did not say any more, but she wondered inside whether the Colonel would think that grass didn't matter in the cause of art. Philip was running over the scenes on his fingers.

'We get the dancing ghosts to show the passing of the years. Then the dark ages scene. Dancing ghosts again, and into May Day. Only one dancer that time because they're both in the same century, and along to Queen Elizabeth, bring on the ghosts again, William and Mary, another bunch of ghosts, Queen Victoria. The bells of Mafeking die out and we bring on one dancer to the trumpet-calls of war. The children stream in, labels round their necks, suitcases, they play games and march away again. We press the buzzer and up rush the jeeps. The Americans give some sort of display, then the band plays and they drive away. We bring my uncle on then, only he doesn't know it, smoking his pipe and walking with the dogs, wearing those shocking old clothes of his. Then he goes off, the Abbey's empty, the ghosts of the centuries come back, there's a new tenant coming, they beckon. How's that for a pageant, Selina?' Selina was just going to say, 'And you've got me as the spirit of England at both ends,' when Philip went on, 'And all this happens in five weeks and two days.'

Selina gaped at him.

'Five weeks and two days!'

The pageant had always been something that was going to happen in the future. Five weeks and two days! Was September the twentieth really as near as that? Her inside turned over. In five weeks and two days she would be coming on to the stage all by herself, wearing her cream organdie frock and satin shoes, and holding red roses, and she would say . . . suddenly she remembered the loudspeakers; she had not before thought of them in connection with herself . . .

'Philip, as it's five weeks and two days oughtn't we to get that rostrum up? And the loudspeakers?'

'It's in the bag. The rostrum is being fixed this weekend, and I hope to get the loudspeakers here the week after next.' He squeezed Selina's arm. 'You and I've got a lot of hard work in front of us, my girl. From now on we shall have to work as we never worked before, but it'll be fun.'

Selina felt rather like Alice when the Red Queen said 'Faster, faster'. Already something to do with the pageant was happening every minute of the day. There were rehearsals or people to see or properties to fix. In the Abbey scissors were clipping, needles flying, sewing-machines whirring. It was difficult to see how they were all going to work much harder than they were already, but she had faith in Philip; if he said so, it was sure to happen.

That night, at midnight, news came which stopped all work on the pageant for five days. The Japanese had capitulated. There was a public holiday for VJ Day.

# CHAPTER NINETEEN

❧

## *Dress Parade*

From the Monday after VJ Day the work on the pageant went faster and faster. Everything seemed to be happening at once. One day there was just the lower lawn and a few garden chairs for thrones. The next day the rostrum was in place, the lower lawn was a stage, thrones, canopies, trumpets, and all the other properties were placed in one of the stables and were carried down every day to rehearsals. Sally had been rehearsing her maypole dancers with a makeshift pole and bits of string, then one morning they arrived to find a gaily painted pole with coloured tapes hanging from it and a wreath of green leaves round the top. A piano appeared from apparently nowhere, and the mistress from the village school came to every rehearsal and was the band.

Sally said:

'Anybody can see by just looking that there's going to be a pageant. It makes me feel more pageanty every day.'

In the house Mrs Andrews and Mrs Mawser held their working parties. The dining-room had been cleared of everything except the dining-room table; this had been covered with blankets, and on it stood five sewing-machines, a miscellaneous collection lent by people from all over the neighbourhood. Along the wall Partridge had fixed lines of string supported at intervals from the picture rail. On this string line hung the dresses made in the wardrobe. A most impressive sight, starting with Sally's thirty yellow fairy dresses, with, next to them, Sally's crimson and pink frock. Then came Augustus's and Benjamin's little tunics, and the whole line finished up with rows and rows of monks' habits made out of black-out material.

'I don't mind,' Mrs Mawser often said, 'when I see the last of those monks. I never did care for that nasty black.'

Mrs Andrews looked at the monks' clothes with some respect.

'To me they're a frightful example of how often my husband is right. He said there were yards and yards of black-out material still buried in people's houses, and look how correct he was.'

All day long there were knocks on the dining-room door, and anxious faces peered in. Receiving everybody for fittings was Mrs Mawser's favourite job. She had a large exercise book, which she opened with an air.

'Now, Annie, let me see, you've fitted everything except your Victorian. Come over here, dear. Good morning, Miss Lipscombe, you've come in again about that witch. Perhaps you'll slip behind the screen and try it on. Oh, good morning, Miss Selina dear, have you brought Mr Laws for his fitting?

That's a good girl. Come this way, sir, we shan't keep you long, it's all ready.'

Mrs Day and the Colonel would sometimes look in. It could not be said that they were either useful or welcome, but you could hardly turn them out of their own dining-room. The Colonel would stand in the doorway smiling vaguely at the workers.

'How's everything? Gettin' along?'

Mrs Mawser or Mrs Andrews would say that they were managing all right. Then the Colonel would wander down the line of clothes, feeling them as he went.

'Marvellous! Wonderful what you women have made out of nothin'.'

Behind him would go Mrs Mawser clucking like a hen.

'Be careful, sir, lose a label off one of those dresses and we shall never be straight. Oh, sir, that string's not very strong. Oh, sir, please don't take them off the hangers, we shall get in a terrible mess.'

As the Colonel walked the eyes of most of the women would be fixed sadly on his clothes. He really was a terribly shabby man, and all of them wondered how Mrs Day let him go about in the state she did. If it was their husbands they would be ashamed.

Mrs Day usually came in with tea or lemonade. Her arrival made everybody get up. She seemed fated to put down the teapot or the jug of lemonade on a frock, or upset them on the nearby clothes. The moment she came in there was a chorus of, 'Let me take that from you.' 'I'll clear a space.' 'Put it there.' Mrs Day had to come for fittings. She had a perfectly beautiful Queen Elizabeth dress, but it needed what Mrs Mawser called 'making over'. It was gold, hung over a monstrous hoop with a great gold ruff, and a heavily jewelled and embroidered stomacher, but it had got rather creased and shabby. It was queer what a difference that dress made to Mrs Day. She would go behind the screen looking gaunt, shabby, and very bandaged about the hands; there would be shuffling and scuffling as Mrs Mawser put the dress on her, and out she would come, looking, in spite of the fact that she had not yet got her wig or head-dress, as the workers said to each other, every inch a queen. Mrs Day herself was completely unaware that she looked nice or dignified. She merely considered herself funny.

'Thing's too tight, Mawser. Should have thought I was near enough a human hop-pole without you squeezing me up like this. What a date! Who would wear this great wired ruff scratching the ears off them. Well, there's one thing certain, I shall be comic relief on the twentieth. No, Mawser, I'm not coming for another fitting tomorrow. Think I've nothing to do but stand about makin' a guy of meself?'

Somehow Mrs Mawser succeeded in getting every person for whom they were making or altering a dress to their proper fittings by the beginning of the first week in September. On the sixth, one fortnight before the performance, the hired clothes were to arrive.

'We have got to get every one of these dresses finished and put away, madam,' Mrs Mawser said firmly to Mrs Day. 'When you think of the hundreds we shall have to unpack on Thursday, and the hanging up and the labelling and the altering, it is clear that we can't have any of this lot of dresses cluttering up the room.'

Mrs Andrews agreed.

'It's also clear we're in for a very nasty time, but I suppose we shall muddle through.'

It was a case of muddling through. The Tuesday and Wednesday before the hired dresses arrived were a tremendous rush. Mrs Andrews got John, Christopher, Selina, and Sally to help. Two spare bedrooms were used and every finished dress had to be laid out or hung up and, for this move, each individual's dresses were being grouped together.

'It'll come easier in the long run,' Mrs Mawser said.

It did not come easier on that Tuesday and Wednesday, and everybody was very tired and cross before the job was done. There were continual shouts of:

'Has anybody moved Margaret Peters's maypole dancing dress? I've got all her others, and that's missing.'

'Has anybody seen Freddie Phillips's May Day suit? I've got his Victorian and I've got his Queen Elizabeth, but there's nothing for him for May Day.'

'One of Augustus's shoes isn't here. Are you sure you made him two?'

Selina was working so hard that she never had five minutes to herself from the time she got up in the morning to the time she went to bed. They were all terribly busy in those weeks before the performance, and the house had the merest lick of cleaning. Selina would rush through her share of bed-making and washing up, and fly up to the Abbey, where, as often as not, Philip was raging up and down saying, 'My word, you're late, Selina. These are the last weeks, my girl, and we've got to work.'

Selina was glad of the rush and excitement, because it stopped her worrying about her father and mother. Heaps of people were getting telegrams from their relations who had been in internment camps, but she had not heard anything. She suspected that her aunt and uncle were beginning to worry. Mrs Andrews often gave her an extra kiss in the morning or at bedtime, and, though she did not say anything, there was something in the way she looked at Selina that made Selina feel she would like to say, 'Don't worry. I'm sure we shall hear soon.'

Dr Andrews began making enquiries about ten days after VJ Day. He told Selina so.

'I dare say we shall hear in the ordinary way, but no harm in trying to get a bit of news in advance. You keep yourself busy with this pageant, and the days will pass quickly. It never does any good to sit around and worry.'

The clothes arrived in enormous baskets; each scene packed together. The children wanted to come and help unpack, but both Mrs Mawser and Mrs Andrews were absolutely firm in their refusal. The best they could do was to stand outside the dining-room window and stare in. It was the most exciting moment. Out of the baskets came armour for John's knights and for Dr Andrews. John nearly broke the window trying to see what he was going to wear, but he could not get a proper view. He saw Mrs Mawser lift up a bundle of brown and scarlet and he said, 'I bet that's mine,' but nobody was certain it really was his.

It was impossible to see from outside the window which reign was which when it came to Phoebe's scene and Sally's. All the clothes were tied in bundles and labelled, and as Mrs Mawser and Mrs Andrews unpacked them they laid them on the dining-room table.

'That enormous lot is mine,' said Phoebe. 'All those brightly coloured clothes are for the people in my fair.'

Sally stood on tiptoe.

'I believe they're mine. They're rich brocade, much more like courtiers for Queen Elizabeth than for fair people.'

Christopher stood on the window ledge to watch the unpacking of his scene. There was no mistaking which baskets held his clothes, because the first thing to come out was an animal's skin. Everybody looked at Christopher enviously and said 'Yours'.

When the last dress was unpacked it was six o'clock in the evening. Mrs Mawser bolted the dining-room windows, and not only locked the dining-room door, but hung on it an enormous card which said 'No Admittance'. Mrs Andrews came down to the lower lawn to have a consultation with Philip.

'We're starting the fittings and alterations tomorrow. I don't think, if we get enough helpers, that ought to take more than a week, because many of the women will see to the alterations of their own things. You could have your dress parade on Thursday next if you like. It suits everybody, being early closing, and it gives us another week after it for extra alterations.'

Philip called Selina.

'Put down a general call for everybody on Thursday, the thirteenth, for a dress parade, and see that everybody knows about it.'

There was no need for most people to be told about the dress parade. The news went tearing through the village. 'Putting on our dresses next Thursday.' 'You heard we're to wear our acting things next Thursday?' 'Everybody is putting on their costumes Thursday.' If the actors had not told each other, people who were not acting reminded them. The bus driver said, 'Be fetchin' you along Thursday. I hear you're wearing your clothes for the first time.' And the shopkeepers in Linkwell said, 'That right? You're wearin' the pageant dresses next Thursday?'

Thursday was luckily a fine day. Two large tents had been erected, one on each side of the stage. The men were to dress in one and the women and children in the other. It was crowded and noisy in the women's and children's tent, for the children were so excited at dressing up that they had to let off their feelings by rushing about, and there wasn't really room for that. Philip had called the actors in the different scenes for different times, according to when the largest number of people could get away, but it seemed to make no difference what time anybody was called; anybody who could come at the beginning came and stayed to the end, and everybody tried to get into their clothes at the same time. There never was such an orgy of dressing up.

Selina had wondered very much whether she should wear her lovely frock. It would, of course, be very nice to put it on, but it was likely to be a messy day, and it was the kind of frock that would spoil very easily. They discussed it at breakfast on the morning of the dress parade.

'Do you think I ought to wear my frock this afternoon, Aunt Ann?'

Mrs Andrews tore her mind from household work, what they were going to eat for lunch and what she knew was going to be an appallingly busy afternoon, and thought about Selina.

'I should think you ought just to put it on, darling, so that Philip can see how it looks.'

'I should think she oughtn't,' said Sally. 'It'll get in a frightful mess. She's sure to have to rush about. Very likely it'll get torn.'

'I don't see why she should rush about,' said Dr Andrews. 'I shouldn't think there's much for you to do this afternoon, is there, Selina?'

'Nothing at all,' said Christopher. 'Everybody just puts on their clothes and walks on to the stage. What's Selina doing?'

Phoebe helped herself to marmalade.

'Pinning. And pinning means kneeling on the grass, and then her dress'll get green and by the time it's passed on to somebody smaller it will get spoilt.'

'There oughtn't to be much pinning,' Mrs Andrews objected. 'Every dress has been altered and more or less fits.'

John cut himself a piece of bread.

'She'll be finding lost dresses. Everybody's sure to lose something.'

Mrs Andrews poured herself out another cup of tea.

'And there ought not to be any lost dresses. If everybody does what they've been asked to do and keeps their own pile in order, there should be no muddle, everything's labelled.'

Dr Andrews passed his cup up to be refilled.

'Don't you wait on them, Selina. You make them look after their own things. Anybody who can't find their clothes will have to come on without them.'

Mrs Andrews filled the doctor's cup.

'But I should be glad if you could help to dress Augustus and Benjamin. I don't think that ought to make you in a mess.' She looked round the table. 'I think just for today everybody who's finished might go. There's a lot to do and we may as well get started.'

247

Sally got up.

'If I were you, Selina, I should ask Philip. If he doesn't want you to wear the frock, I shouldn't. It's a great pity to spoil it.'

Selina had not liked what Phoebe had said about her frock passing on to somebody smaller. Almost every day she looked at the frock and stroked it, but she had never put it on since it came in December. She had tried on the shoes and they still fitted, but only just; how too awful to contemplate if the frock did not meet. She did not feel as if she had got any fatter, but you never knew. It was not a thing to risk.

'I shall put it on just to let Philip see it, and to be sure it fits. Then I'll change. Mrs Mawser will look after it.'

Long before the dress parade started the upper lawn was covered with people. They had all got dressed early and had taken up good positions to watch the other dresses paraded on the lower lawn. It was a queer sight. All the periods together. A monk chatting to a fairy, a knight lighting the cigarette of one of Queen Elizabeth's attendants, Miss Lipscombe, dressed as a schoolteacher in the time of Henry the Eighth, talking to the Colonel, who was just wearing his ordinary everyday clothes.

As everybody had arrived the dresses were paraded in the order in which they would appear in the pageant. Of course everybody could not be there at the right time, but anybody who was late was to display their dresses at the end. Selina wore an overall over her frock, and she was glad she had the sense to put it on, because she was kept very busy. Besides, though she had not told anyone, it was a wee bit tight. Under the overall she had the tightest hooks undone.

'Selina, go and see if the dancers are ready.'

'Selina, go and tell everybody to keep off the lower stage until they're called.'

'Selina, go and see if my aunt has got her togs on yet. Remind her that Queen Elizabeth and the courtiers come on straight on top of the ghosts.'

Selina held up her frock and ran about with her messages. All the time she was turning over something in her mind. Ought she to carry her red roses? She had brought them in case. They were not very good red roses, she had picked them in the garden that morning, just enough to show what her flowers would look like. Were her roses part of the dress? When she returned to Philip after her messages she said:

'Do you want people to carry things if they're part of their costume?'

'What sort of things?'

'Flowers, or trumpets. Things like that.'

Philip considered this carefully. He held his megaphone to his mouth.

'If anybody has a property that is part of their dress, such as trumpets or flowers, will they bring them on. Now, will everybody concerned with the prologue and the first scene please go to the back of the stage.'

It was extraordinary, even after months of rehearsals, how difficult it seemed for people to know for certain what scene they were in. At least half the actors asked if they were in the prologue or the first scene. While they were finding out that they were not monks or knights, Mr Laws, John, and Dr Andrews went to the back of the stage. The dancers had not been on the upper lawn. They had a corner to themselves in the dressing-tent, where two of their teachers were in charge of them. When Philip called for the prologue the ghost dancers left the tent. They had not got make-up on, but they looked queer and unearthly in their grey dresses and grey head-dresses and veils.

Selina went to the back of the stage. She took off her over-all and laid it behind a bush. She did up the waist of her frock. She changed into her satin shoes. Then she picked up her roses. She shook out her organdie skirt and felt rich all over as she heard her underskirt crackle. John was standing near her.

'Do I look all right?'

John, like everybody else taking part in the pageant, was far too interested in his own clothes to have any time for anybody else's. He barely looked at her.

'Wizard.'

Selina knew he had not seen her, still it was nice of him even to have pretended.

'Quiet, please,' roared Philip through his megaphone. 'Now, if everybody's ready, we'll start. Prologue.'

Selina took a deep breath, held her roses in both hands and walked to the middle of the stage. It was silly to be nervous, she thought. She would just stand perfectly still until Philip told her to turn round. Nothing happened at all. Philip did not say anything. Nobody said anything. The pause at last became awkward. Philip raised his megaphone.

'I said prologue. Do get off the stage, Selina, you're hold-ing everything up.'

Selina flushed. She raised her voice so that Philip could hear.

'But I am the prologue, Philip.'

Philip sounded annoyed.

'Don't be silly, ducky, hop off and get out of the way, and let the prologue come on.'

Selina did not remember afterwards how she got off the stage. She found herself pulling on her overall and throwing down her flowers. John was speaking.

'You silly ass! Why did you let Philip order you off like that? You are the prologue.'

It was very difficult for Selina to lose her temper, but she lost it that afternoon. Her voice shook with anger.

'He's a beast. I hate him. He's always treated the prologue and epilogue as if they didn't matter. Now he's made me look a fool in front of everybody.'

'Well, tell him off.'

'How can I tell him off? There are hundreds of people here, he wouldn't listen.'

John picked up her roses.

'You're standing on them. Don't be an ass. Go and make a row. Don't care who's there. I wouldn't.'

'Not in front of everybody. He wouldn't listen, but after the dress parade's over I shall tell him everything I think.'

Philip's voice boomed through the megaphone.

'Selina! Selina! Everybody for the first scene, please. Selina!'

'Are you going to answer, after he treated you like that?'

Selina nodded.

'Somebody's got to run the messages, but I shan't speak to him. I shall just save it all up inside until afterwards.'

Philip was so busy during the afternoon that he did not notice that Selina did not speak to him. Monks' robes were too short. Knights' armour was wrong and they could not get on to their horses. Phoebe kept everybody waiting because

Philip had said 'Carry flowers, if you carried flowers in a scene'. She refused to go on to the lower lawn until a bunch of white flowers was picked for her. Miss Lipscombe complained that her schoolteacher's dress was too tight. The attendants on Queen Elizabeth had got their clothes mixed, a fat woman was wearing a thin one's dress, and one of the men complained that he could not find his ruff. Mrs Day looked absolutely superb, except that she had a bandage and three pieces of sticking-plaster on her hands.

'You'll have to see you don't burn or cut yourself between now and the twentieth,' Philip roared at her.

'Can't promise that,' she roared back. 'Look a shockin' guy anyway. What's a bit of sticking-plaster more or less.'

Alfie had got his Jack-in-the-Green cage of leaves on the wrong way round, and it took three people to pull him out of it, Mrs Miggs dragging at the top and two men pulling at his legs.

''Ow was I to know which was the front?' Alfie said. 'There ain't no markings.'

The William and Mary clothes passed without much complaint, but everybody grumbled about the Victorian. They had not got this and they had not got that, and this was too tight, and this was too loose. Mrs Mawser and Mrs Andrews took pages of notes.

At last all the dresses had been seen. Philip raised his megaphone.

'Will everybody tie their dresses up in bundles, see that the label is on each, and take them back to the library, where Mrs Andrews and Mrs Mawser will check them.' He turned to Selina. 'What an afternoon! I'm thirsty, what about you?'

Selina was even angrier than she had been earlier in the afternoon. Philip had again insulted her. He had called for the epilogue and never turned to her and said, 'Don't you bother, we know your dress is all right', or something like that. He had just looked at the dancers, and said, 'OK. That's fine.'

'I think you'd better speak to me alone.'

Philip was very fond of Selina. He was sorry that he had made her angry, and he could see that she was very angry indeed. He said, in an extraordinarily meek voice for him:

'All right, anywhere you like.'

They went into the vegetable garden because there was nobody there. Philip lit a cigarette and waited for Selina to explain. She had so much to say that all the words wanted to fall out of her mouth at once.

'I think you're the meanest man I ever knew. I know you've been wounded and all that, but that's no excuse for being rude to me.'

'How have I been rude to you?'

'Pretending you don't know! Wasn't this pageant got up just so that I could wear my frock? Didn't I write pages and pages about being the spirit of England? You've always been rude about it. Every time I asked you if I might rehearse it you wouldn't let me. You've got so grand and conceited, you think you can say anything you like to anybody. You called for the prologue. I came on at once holding my roses, like you said I was to, and in front of everybody you said, "Get out of the way", and "Hop off", just as if I wasn't in the pageant. I was the only dress this afternoon that you didn't bother to look at.'

Philip said, in a very gentle voice:

'Will you believe me when I tell you that I have not the faintest idea what you're talking about? What frock was the idea of the pageant?'

Selina tugged at the buttons of her overall and threw it on the ground. She held out the skirt of her despised party frock. She shook it to make him notice it.

'This.'

Philip looked at the frock.

'And very nice too, but I didn't know it was anything to do with the pageant. I just thought it was what you were wearing this afternoon.'

Selina knew that must be a lie.

'People don't come to dress parades in taffeta and cream organdie and satin shoes, you must know that.'

He spoke more gently than ever.

'If you would stop being angry and explain the whole situation to me I expect we can sort things out, but, believe me, I never heard of you wearing a frock in the pageant until this minute.' He put his good arm round her shoulders. 'Come and sit on that seat and tell me all about it.'

It was quite a long story. The arrival of the parcel from America, the meeting to decide how best she could wear the frock, the plan of the pageant, Sally's idea of a girl dreaming a ballet, and John's changing it to a girl dreaming a pageant. The trouble of writing a prologue and an epilogue. The anxiety she had been in in case the frock had grown too small. She made him put his finger inside the sash so that he could feel for himself how nearly that danger had come true, how she had put it on that afternoon partly to be sure it fitted, but partly for his approval. How she had asked him herself if she should carry her flowers and how he had said yes. Now, when she had come on, he had insulted her. As she finished speaking she looked up at him. Then she had the worst insult of the afternoon. He was not listening. He was gazing down the kitchen garden, with his stiff, having-an-idea look. It was more than she could bear. It was a very undignified thing to do. It was a thing despised in the Andrews household. She burst into tears. Philip did not seem to notice that she was crying. He prodded her with the fingers of his good hand.

'Go over there to the end of that path.'

Selina was crying so much that her voice came out in a howl.

'I won't. You've spoilt everything. I won't ever run any messages for you again.'

It was Philip's turn to be annoyed.

'Don't be an ass. Do what I say; go to the end of that path. It's an idea.'

Selina could not find her handkerchief, so she took her overall with her and rubbed her face on that. She did not want to obey Philip, but she had got so used to running for him that, somehow, she could not stop doing it. Half-blinded with her tears, and hiccuping as she went, she ran up the path.

'That'll do. Now turn round. Drop that overall. Throw it away somewhere. Now start the words you were going to say.'

It was a wretched time to choose. Selina knew her voice was wobbly with tears. Nobody could ever have looked less like the spirit of England. Her nose must be shining, her eyes red, and on one side of her were cabbages, and on the other cauliflowers. Still, she had asked Philip to look at her and hear her prologue, so it was no good not doing it when he was willing to hear it.

'I am the spirit of England and . . .'

Philip began to laugh.

'No, darling. You'd need a couple of lions and a trident for that.' He went up to her. He put his arm round her and led her up and down the winding paths of the kitchen garden. He said that he had been worried for some time about the beginning and the end of the pageant. He thought it wanted something to pull the whole story into shape. Hearing what Sally's original idea had been he thought they could use it. 'You, my pet, will dream the pageant. Don't ask me now where you sit, stand or what you do. You can't be on the stage all that time, so I shall have to get you off. Besides, you're too useful as stage manager to be spared. But we'll have you on again at the end.' He turned her to face him. 'If I gave you something important to learn, would you have the courage to say it through the microphone?'

'You'd teach me?'

'Of course. It's too early yet to tell you what I want you to say, and maybe it's something that'll never happen, but I'll have you saying something at the end in any case.' He smiled at her. 'Friends?'

She flung her arms round his neck.

'I'm sorry, Philip, but honestly I thought you knew. Truly I'm sorry.'

He held her chin.

'Come on in. You've got a dirty face and I could do with a drink.'

Selina felt so happy that it hurt. It was extraordinary to have been so miserable for hours and hours, and then to find that there was nothing to be miserable about. She was going to wear her frock. She was going to be the prologue and the epilogue. They came out of the kitchen garden on to the lower lawn. The dress parade had gone on until after six, and now it was after seven. It had been a nice day, clouds of gnats were flying around, the sun was moving over to the west and the Abbey threw a great shadow across the lawn. Suddenly Selina gave a gasp and clutched Philip's arm. There were three windows above the dining-room. They were all open. Out of the middle one was pouring grey smoke, and now and again there was a flicker of fire.

# CHAPTER TWENTY

———— •• ————

## *Fire*

I t did not take Philip a second to make a plan of action.
'Run and get my uncle and aunt, Partridge, and Mrs Mawser.
Tell them where the fire is. I'll telephone the Fire Brigade.'

Mrs Mawser and Partridge were in the kitchen. Mrs Mawser
was quicker than Partridge.

'Call the Colonel. Get the stirrup pump, I'll get the buckets. That old monk. I knew he'd get us.'

'Can I help fill the buckets?' Selina asked.

Mrs Mawser looked at her over her shoulder.

'Take off that frock and those shoes. There's a pair of gum-
boots of Mrs Day's outside. They're too big, but they'll be
better than nothing.'

Selina struggled out of her frock.

'I left my shoes on the lower lawn.'

Mrs Mawser was pouring water into a bucket.

'No time for them now. Over the dining-room. My goodness,
my dresses.'

259

Partridge and the Colonel came hurrying in. They picked up the buckets of water in so calm a way that Selina could see how used they were to fires.

'Mrs Day's taken the stirrup pump up,' the Colonel said to Mrs Mawser.

They all trooped up the stairs, except Mrs Mawser, who was filling more buckets. Philip met them at the top of the stairs.

'Seems to have started in the wall. The bed's on fire and the curtains. Have to try to keep it under until the Fire Brigade comes.'

The passage was full of smoke. It made tears pour down Selina's cheeks, and her eyes and throat ache. Mrs Day was there uncoiling the stirrup pump.

'Lucky I did me fire drill.'

Selina could not see that fire drill had been very much good to Mrs Day, because she did not seem to understand a stirrup pump very well. She uncoiled it in such a way that it got twisted and writhed about like a snake. Philip took it from her.

'Come on, let me do that.' He unwound it and gave the Colonel the pump end. He himself took the nozzle. 'I'll go in.'

The Colonel looked round at Mrs Day, Partridge, and Selina. He was already pumping before he spoke.

'I'll begin the pumping, but when I go down to get the buckets filled I'll have to leave the pumping to you, Partridge, and Miss Selina.' He turned to Mrs Day. 'Telephone the Andrewses and get them to send the children round the village asking for help. We could do with a ladder and a string of buckets until the Fire Brigade comes. Always said we ought to have a Fire Brigade in this village.'

Mrs Day hurried off.

Philip's voice came from the fire in a very muffled sort of way.

'I'm going in on my hands and knees. Whatever you do, keep the water going. It'll be a miracle if we stop this fire from spreading.'

The first bucket was empty. The Colonel put the pump into the second bucket and picked up the empty bucket. He gave the pump to Partridge.

'Steadily and evenly, Partridge.' He beckoned to Selina. 'Push him away and pump yourself when the bucket's half-empty. He easily gets tired.'

Selina watched the water in the bucket anxiously. Even in the middle of a fire Partridge was not the kind of man you pushed. But when the water was nearly halfway down the bucket Partridge began to pump more slowly and he panted as he pumped. Selina put her hand on the pump beside his.

'Let me. Colonel Day said I was to do it for half the bucket.'

'It's all right, Miss Selina,' Partridge panted.

But Selina was firm. She even gave him the little push the Colonel had directed and she took possession of the pump, but the change over had stopped the flow of water. Philip, his face black with smoke, crawled on his hands and knees out of the burning room.

'What on earth? For goodness' sake keep the water going. The whole house will burn down if you aren't careful.'

Selina pumped desperately. She had been holding the pump when Philip had complained about the water, and obviously he thought it was her fault. Pumping water looked so easy when Colonel Day did it, one foot on each side of the part of the pump that went on the floor to hold it steady, and a handle at the top to lift up and down, but when she came to do it she found it was terribly hard work.

'I won't think about my arms,' she told herself. 'I shall think only about the pageant dresses and then I won't mind.'

Pump, pump, pump. Steadily and evenly the Colonel had said. How difficult it was to keep pumping steadily and evenly. What a long time it took to pump half a bucket. The Colonel touched her on the shoulder.

'Well done, old lady. Now, keep on pumping until I say when and then jump out of the way, and I'll start on the new bucket.'

It seemed to Selina that they had been hours outside the burning room. Bucket after bucket of water was carried up by the Colonel. Each time he brought two full buckets. He pumped the first bucket, and then ran with it down the stairs to where Mrs Mawser had two more full buckets waiting for him. Selina and Partridge shared the second bucket. Pump, pump, pump. There never seemed time for her arms to get rested before it was her turn to pump again. And they were not apparently being very successful. Smoke gushed out of the burning room. Their eyes streamed and they choked. It was very difficult, Selina found, to have enough breath to pump when your inside was full of smoke.

Mrs Day, between telephoning for help, came up now and again. Selina heard her say to the Colonel, 'Isn't it too much for that child?' and she heard the Colonel answer, 'She's being splendid. Hang about in the drive and see they get the ladders as soon as help arrives.'

The little party working in the passage to keep the fire under did not see the excitement outside. Almost everybody in the village came up to help. A ladder was put against the window and the window was opened by Philip and a chain of buckets was passed up. One of the farmers, who was taking part in John's scene, was at the top of the ladder and other men stood on the ladder and passed buckets up to him. Then, from the bottom of the ladder right the way up to a tap in the kitchen garden people stood in two lines, one passing full buckets up and one passing empty buckets back. John and Christopher looked after the tap. First John, and then Christopher, filling a bucket and sending it on its way.

Sally was working quite near the bottom of the ladder on the empty bucket side. She had a terrible feeling she was going to be sick. For all they were doing the fire was not getting any better. No sooner did a flame disappear from one side of the window than another flame sprang up on the other side. She saw in her mind all the clothes for the pageant being burnt to a cinder. No pageant, no ballet. Too awful to think of.

Dr Andrews, Mrs Andrews, and several of the village women had been talking in a group. Their faces were very grave and they kept shaking their heads. Presently they disappeared, probably to have a conference with Colonel Day. Rumours ran up and down the line of workers. The Fire Brigade could not come because it was out at another fire. The Fire Brigade could not come from Linkwell, because the fire engine had broken down on the road. The farmer on the top of the ladder was shouting to Philip inside the room. He turned and said something to the man behind him, and the man behind him said something to the man behind him, and they all began to climb down the ladder.

Oh, goodness! thought Sally. It's no good their going on. They can't stop the fire. Oh, why doesn't the Fire Brigade come?

Upstairs Selina knew quite well what had happened. A second room had caught fire; flames were pouring out of a wardrobe against the wall. The buckets and pump were moved back. Philip, indescribably dirty, came out to his uncle shaking his head.

'Proper furnace. Must have been going for hours. Probably started in the wiring in the wall. Afraid the floors are going to fall in.'

Selina's heart missed a beat. She was glad Partridge was pumping, for she was certain to have stopped pumping at Philip's words. 'The whole floor's going to fall in.' Fall in! On to what? On to the pageant dresses below.

The Colonel stopped Partridge pumping.

'Not safe to stop here any longer. We'll take this contraption out into the garden. The Fire Brigade should be here any minute.'

The night seemed full of clanging bells. It was not only the Fire Brigade from Linkwell, but four fire engines roaring up the drive. The firemen did not wait for the engines to stop, they no sooner reached the upper lawn than they were rushing out lengths of piping and fixing hoses in place. The chief fireman had gone forward to see what was happening. At once he roared:

'Back, everybody, back.'

They all moved back, pushing and jostling down the lawn. There was a crack and a great sheet of flame shot up into the air, and the three rooms over the dining-room caved in. The whole of the centre part of the house was in flames.

Sally could not bear it. She could be of no further use now the Fire Brigade was there. She went down on to the lower lawn where nobody could see her and she cried and cried.

'Oh, why had the fire to start just there? Why had it to be over the dining-room? And now it's all fallen in and the dining-room's in flames. No pageant! No pageant at all.'

Selina found Sally. She had come to fetch her shoes. She looked the most disgraceful mess. Her face all over soot, her overall gaping in front and showing her knickers, and her legs half-lost in Mrs Day's gum-boots. She heard Sally's sobs before she saw her.

'Don't cry, Sally. The Colonel says it might be worse. That wing was burnt before. It was not very nice and he doesn't think it'll make a great deal of difference to selling the house.'

Sally was sobbing so much it was difficult for her to speak.

'I don't want to be mean, I'm terribly sorry for the Colonel and Mrs Day, but I'm not crying about them. It's the dresses. No pageant. No pageant at all.'

Selina put her arms round Sally and shook her.

'Don't cry. It's absolutely all right. The dresses aren't hurt.'

Sally felt as if she were coming up from the bottom of the sea.

'Not hurt!'

'No. They were all carried out by Uncle Jim, Aunt Ann, and some of the women and put on the stone floor in the kitchen. Mrs Mawser's looking after them. She's looking after my dress too.'

Suddenly it was darker. For a moment the two girls did not realize what had happened, then Sally said:

265

'My goodness! The flames are going. The fire's nearly out.'

Voices were shouting on the upper lawn.

'Selina. Selina.'

Selina tumbled her way up the lawn. She was carrying her shoes and she found it very difficult to walk in Mrs Day's gumboots. As she came near the house everybody spoke to her.

'You're wanted.'

'Your uncle wants you.'

'Mr Bins wants you.'

They made a lane for her. Dr Andrews was standing with Mr Bins. He held out his hand to Selina.

'There you are, niece.'

Mr Bins felt in his breast pocket.

'I was coming to you when I heard about the fire. It's quite safe.'

He brought out a cable and held it out to her. There was very little fire left, but enough flames to read by. Selina read the cable through twice before she took in the sense of what it said. Then she looked at her uncle.

'It's from Dad and Mum. They're safe and well. They expect to be home soon.'

The news went round the lawn as quickly as if it were another fire.

'Selina's mum and dad are safe.'

'Selina's heard from her mum and dad.'

'Selina's mum and dad are coming home.'

The Colonel climbed up on to one of the fire engines. He shouted for silence and everybody gathered round.

'You've heard the good news. Mr and Mrs Cole are safe. I may tell you Selina deserves a bit of good news tonight.

Worked like a brick at that stirrup pump. Suppose we give her three cheers.'

The fire was almost out, the pageant dresses were safe, and Selina Cole had good news. There was so much to cheer about that the noise could be heard down in the village.

'Hip, hip, hooray! Hip, hip, hooray! Hip, hip, hooray!'

# CHAPTER TWENTY-ONE

## *The Twentieth*

None of the family slept late on the morning of September the twentieth. The first to wake up was Sally. She was peering out of the window at half-past five. Was the sky red? 'A red sky at morning is the shepherd's warning.' It had been such a dreadfully wet summer, it would be so easy for it to rain. It had been decided that if it rained as much of the pageant as possible would be done in the village hall, but nobody could pretend it would look nice in the village hall. Sally sniffed at the morning and her heart began to beat quickly with excitement. It was not raining. It was not going to rain. The sky was not even faintly red.

Sally sang.

'Oh, splendid, glorious day! This is pageant day. It has come at last.'

Phoebe was disturbed by Sally. She sat up in bed and rubbed her eyes.

'What time is it?'

269

Sally bounced across the room and flung her arms round Phoebe.

'It's just struck six. I've been awake for hours and hours. Do you know, it's pageant day?'

Phoebe shot out of bed and went to the window.

'Is it fine?'

Sally joined her.

'Absolutely. Don't you think it's going to be the most gorgeous day we shall ever know?'

Phoebe put her hands on her diaphragm.

'Do you know, I feel most peculiar inside. Every time I think that today is the day my inside goes round like it does when you twist yourself up in a swing and then unspin very fast.'

Sally thought about her inside.

'You're absolutely right. Mine feels very queer too. I wonder if the others are awake. Do you think they feel queer?'

They looked in on John and Christopher. Christopher was half-awake. Sally sat down on his bed.

'Does knowing it's the pageant today make your inside feel queer?'

Christopher had not been awake enough to remember it was the pageant day. He sat up.

'Is it fine?'

'Absolutely.' She persisted with her question. 'Do you feel queer inside?'

Christopher was going to say 'No' when he suddenly remembered how he had to play about amongst the crowd, making them laugh, how he had to shout jokes, and they had to roar with laughter. There were days when he felt like a stuffed pig. Was today going to be one of those days? As he thought this he felt as if his inside had moved.

'It does feel odd.'

John opened his eyes.

'Jabber, jabber, jabber. What time is it?'

Phoebe sat down on his bed with a bump.

'It's six o'clock. It's pageant day, and it's fine, but we all feel very queer inside. Do you feel queer when you think about the pageant?'

John sat up. Did he feel queer? He thought of his scene. The horses arriving, his father and the Abbot talking, then his coming out from the back of the stage on to the rostrum. He remembered the loudspeaker. He hated the loudspeaker. 'Don't shout,' Philip said. 'Up here you're making such a noise you sound like ten schoolboys instead of one.' He liked the part that came next when he and his father pretended to fight on horseback. Neither he nor his father rode very well, but it was fun, and Philip said it was quite effective. If only there were not that loudspeaker. The mere thought of being heard through a lot of loudspeakers by masses of people made him feel as if he had influenza. He lay down and shut his eyes.

'I hope it's only the pageant, but I shouldn't wonder if I'd eaten something bad. I feel sick.'

Selina had woken up very soon after Sally. She, too, had stood at the window and seen that the day was fine. But she had not, like Sally, got excited about the day. She had at once felt miserable and wobbly about the knees. The beginning was easy. Just to walk down the stage reading, and walk off, just as the music for the ghosts started.

It was the scene at the end that made Selina's mouth go dry and her knees shake. She had to come back still reading, and walk up the stage on to the rostrum. All alone on that awful rostrum. Nobody but herself and Philip knew what she was going to say. If only it was the same thing at the dress rehearsal as at the performance, but Philip was determined that the special speech was only to be made at the performance. He did not know how awful it was to have to learn two speeches and not to have said the important one at the dress rehearsal. How dreadful if she did not say the words clearly. If people did not know what she was talking about. How dreadful if she lost her voice. People could lose their voices from fright. She had read about it. It would spoil everything. Philip would be furious. She heard the rest of the family talking. She thought she would feel better if she had somebody to talk to. She went into John and Christopher's room.

Mrs Andrews heard the family moving about. She put on her dressing-gown and went to see what was happening. She found a very mournful gathering. John was still on his back with his eyes shut. Selina and Sally were sitting on the end of his bed, Selina holding her front and Sally with her head in her hands. Christopher was sitting on his bed holding his knees against himself because he said he felt better that way. Augustus and Benjamin had joined the party, and Phoebe, cross and nervous, had taken a sheet off Christopher's bed and was giving them a last minute rehearsal in carrying a train. Because it was the pageant morning and everybody was in a fuss Augustus got in a fuss too. In the ordinary way he did not mind in the least what Phoebe said, but this morning it was all too much for him. As Mrs Andrews opened the door she heard him say, in a voice choked with tears:

'I am trying, Phoebe, and it's not my fault if I do it badly; it's Benjamin, his legs are shorter than mine and we don't walk the same.'

Mrs Andrews seemed to think it was an ordinary morning. She kissed Augustus and Benjamin and said they were very nice pages, whether their legs were short or long. She took the sheet away from Phoebe's shoulders and said she thought that Phoebe's scene was much too good to need any more rehearsing. Then she had an idea.

'Suppose, as you're all awake so early, that you cook the breakfast for me. You can go down and do it in your dressing-gowns. As it's a special day we'll have boiled eggs.'

It was queer how much better everybody felt by the time they had cooked the breakfast. It was great fun having breakfast in their dressing-gowns; they had never done that before. Even Dr Andrews and Mrs Andrews wore dressing-gowns. Dr Andrews made them laugh about his. He said that they had all got to hide him if Miss Lipscombe came before he was dressed. If Miss Lipscombe saw him in his dressing-gown he would never have the nerve to face her in his surgery.

After breakfast they got dressed and did what housework was to be done. Mrs Miggs, most unexpectedly, turned up.

'I never would 'ave done,' she told Mrs Andrews, 'seein' it's the pageant an' all, but young Alfie's that above himself and obstreperous. "There's nothin' else for it," I said to meself, "but to get out, or there would be words spoke which I should regret."'

She then dashed round the house doing a great deal of work and singing 'Rule, Britannia'.

When the work of the house was done Mrs Andrews called all the family into the dining-room.

'Now, darlings, two of you are to go and fetch the programmes from the printers. Benjamin and Augustus, will you go and pick up all the windfalls in the garden. The rest of you had better go up to the Abbey and help Mrs Mawser about the tea. I want everybody back here by twelve o'clock sharp. Lunch is at a quarter past.'

The morning passed wonderfully quickly. Sally and Christopher went to Linkwell for the programmes. Every shop in Linkwell had a poster about the pageant, and everybody they met said they were coming to the performance. In the end it had been decided that the dress rehearsal at two o'clock would be for children. Most of the boarding schools were not back, but all kinds of organizations were bringing children over. Junior Red Cross and St John's, Girl Guides and Boy Scouts, Boys and Girls' Training Corps, parties from churches, and, as well, innumerable individual children. In all, startling though it seemed, nearly a thousand children were expected. There could, of course, be no seating. Everybody, both for the dress rehearsal and for the real performance, had been asked to bring a rug or a cushion to sit on. There were a few seats right at the top of the lawn, up against the Abbey, but most people would prefer to be nearer to the stage.

The programmes were ready. Bundles and bundles and bundles of them. They were done up in two big paper parcels, but the printer knew Christopher and Sally and, of course, realized that they were simply bursting to see a programme, so he undid one of the parcels and took out two programmes for them to look at. They looked too splendid for words. Every scene put down under its date, and the names of all the principal people taking part in a row under each scene. Selina was down at the beginning and the end as 'The Dreamer'. At the end of the programme was the name of everybody acting, in alphabetical order. There were so many names that they took up the whole of the back side of the programme.

Up at the Abbey the rest of the family were so busy that they forgot to feel worried. There would, of course, be no time for the actors to get away to tea between the dress rehearsal and the performance, and so there was tea for everybody at long trestle tables behind the men's dressing-tent. Every woman in the village had spared a pinch of tea and a little bit of sugar, and the farmers between them had sent the extra milk. The buns had been made in Linkwell. They had just been delivered when Selina, John, and Phoebe arrived. Boxes and boxes of buns. All to be carried to the tea-table and laid out on plates.

Selina did not spend her whole morning helping with the buns for Philip called her away. There was nothing really that he wanted her for, but he wanted someone to talk to and to go round with him and see that nothing was missing. Everything was in perfect order. The wooden platform for the band. All the props ready on their right sides of the stage. The mounting-block, by which the knights got on to their horses, waiting under the trees. In the dressing-rooms everybody's clothes were lying neatly labelled and ready in piles. At the far end of each tent were make-up tables. Philip looked at his watch.

'The make-up men ought to be here at any time now. I told them they'd have to start making up at one o'clock. It's nearly twelve now.'

Selina was surprised it was so late.

'Oh, goodness, I must get the others. We're having lunch at a quarter past twelve, and we swore we wouldn't be late.'

Philip was clearly in that sort of mood when he hated to think of any actor leaving the Abbey grounds. He wanted them there all the time.

'Be sure to be back here at one o'clock sharp. I shall be wanting you for any amount of things.'

It was when they got back to the house that the sick feeling of the morning returned. Quite suddenly they all knew they did not want any lunch. They told Mrs Andrews.

'I don't feel hungry, Mum,' John said. 'I think I'll skip eating. I'm on in the first scene, I'd better go and get made up.'

'I'd really rather go up to the Abbey,' said Sally. 'I expect my children will be early and they might be wanting something.'

Christopher said:

'I'll go with her.'

'I take hours and hours to put on my May Queen dress,' said Phoebe. 'I think I'd better go now.'

Mrs Andrews opened her oven door and looked in.

'Nobody is going to the rehearsal unless they eat their lunch.' There were murmurs and expostulations, but she paid no attention. 'I know how you all feel. You couldn't eat a mouthful, but you don't know what I've got in my oven. We've had a present. It's roast chicken.'

It was surprising what happened to that chicken. The moment they saw it they all began to feel hungry and, though Dr Andrews served it very carefully, it only just went round for two helpings each. When the carcass was taken away there was not, he said, enough to feed an ant. While John and

Christopher were removing the chicken carcass and bringing in the stewed apples and custard, the telephone rang. The telephone would not be ringing about a patient on a Thursday, so they all held their breaths. What had happened? Was some important person ill? Had something gone wrong at the camp so that the band and the jeeps could not come? Dr Andrews came back smiling.

'That was Dr Wilson. He said he doesn't care if there's an outbreak of bubonic plague this afternoon, he's not going to miss seeing me act. He still insists I'm going to be Henry the Eighth.'

It was not very easy to swallow the apples and custard, but as Mrs Andrews passed each plate she said, in a voice that was meant to be obeyed:

'It's got to be eaten and then you can go.'

John finished first. He got up. Dr Andrews said:

'You go on and get your make-up on. I'll bring Selina and Mr Laws in the car.' He turned to Mrs Andrews. 'What about you and Augustus and Benjamin?'

'What about me?' said Phoebe.

'And me?' said Sally.

Mrs Andrews shook her head.

'Selina and John are on at the beginning and they've got to go now, but Sally, Christopher, Phoebe, Augustus, and Benjamin have plenty of time. We're going to clear the lunch things and wash up.'

Sally was appalled.

'Oh, Mum, not today. It's more than I can bear to be here when so much is happening at the Abbey.'

Mrs Andrews began collecting the dirty plates.

'I know exactly how you feel, darling, but it's going to be more than the make-up men can bear if everybody's clamouring round them at once. It isn't one o'clock yet. We'll clear away and wash up and even then you'll be at the Abbey by half-past one.'

# CHAPTER TWENTY-TWO

———◆◆———

## *Dress Rehearsal*

The audience were arriving. The lawn seemed to be covered with children all talking at once and all terribly excited. In the tents there was an uproar . . . The make-up men were the only people who were absolutely calm. They went on saying methodically:

'What are you meant to be?'

To the children they gave a dab of rouge and a little bit of lipstick, but all the grown-up people they made up most carefully. Mrs Day had been specially made up and the effect, when she was finished, was startling. She looked incredibly like pictures of Queen Elizabeth.

In spite of all the care that Mrs Andrews and Mrs Mawser had taken everybody lost bits of their clothes. There was a continual roar of 'Who's taken my hat? I know I put it down here.' 'Has anybody got on a pair of tights that doesn't belong to them?' Then suddenly there came a sound which silenced everybody. The band was playing the overture.

Philip, using his megaphone, went first to one tent and then to the other, and outside each he called:

'Stand by, everybody. Overture and beginners.'

Philip wanted to see the dress rehearsal from the front, so he had arranged that after the first call Selina should see that all the actors got on.

'It'll be all right, ducky,' he said. 'Keep shouting at them. They all know which scene they're in and you ought not to have any trouble. They've been rehearsed enough, goodness knows.'

Selina knew that everybody had been rehearsed enough, but she also knew that did not mean that they knew when they ought to go on to the stage. It was never any good arguing with Philip, but she did wish he did not want to see the performance from the front, and could be behind and shout to the actors himself. Philip came over to where she was standing ready to make her entrance. He put the megaphone down beside her.

'There you are, my pet. It's all yours. I'm going to the upper lawn now. Don't let anyone miss an entrance or I'll skin you alive.'

The overture was coming to an end. Selina opened her book. This was the easy entrance, but even so her heart missed a beat. The music stopped. She took a deep breath. She was on the stage.

It was over. She was off. The music had started, the ghosts were dancing. Sally was hanging about the side of the stage with her maypole dancers. She looked quite lovely. A wreath of roses round her hair, her vividness accentuated by rouge. Her stiff velvet Elizabethan bodice, her ruff and her floating skirt slit up at the side, showing almost the whole of one leg, suited her beautifully.

'Oh, Selina, what was it like? Are there a lot of people there?'

Selina could only mutter.

'Couldn't look. I had to read my book.' Then she picked up the megaphone, and was counting the actors. She went out to the back of the stage, and raising her megaphone, shouted to her uncle, 'Are you all there? And the horses?'

The doctor was already up on Lucky. He cantered over to her.

'We are three short this afternoon. We expected to be. Philip knows three of the farmers couldn't get away. They'll be here for the performance.'

Selina found an intelligent monk.

'Are you all here?'

'Two short the other side, but they'll be here for the performance.'

Selina knew that John and Mr Laws were ready. The doctor had delivered Mr Laws himself and she had seen him made up in a tonsured wig looking extraordinarily handsome. John had promised to see that Mr Laws was at his entrance at the right moment. Selina gave a thankful sigh. That was one scene accounted for. Now she had to find Phoebe, her pages and ladies-in-waiting, and Miss Lipscombe. Sally could be trusted to look after her own maypole dancers, but there was all that crowd. They would be sure to need rounding up. John rushed up to her.

'Selina, I've lost Mr Laws.'

The first music was coming to an end. There were loud-speakers fixed at the back of the stage so that the actors knew where the pageant had got to. The moment the ghost music stopped the monks would process on, chanting. When they had finished and gone off the knights would come on. Selina turned a desperate face to John.

'You had him last.'

'I know. He was standing beside me. I just turned to speak to somebody and he was gone.'

Selina did not waste time telling John what she thought of such carelessness.

'Go back to the entrance and wait. I'll find him. If he isn't there in time you warn Uncle Jim he's missing.'

The ghost music came to an end. The ghosts glided off. One of the monks pitched a note, and the others took up the chant. With heads down, two and two, they came on to the stage. John could hardly stand still, he was in such a fuss. Would Selina find Mr Laws in time? The chant was coming to an end, the leading monks were off the stage. There was a pounding of hoofs, Dr Andrews and his knights were on.

Dr Andrews reined in Lucky at what was supposed to be the door of the Abbey.

'Halloo there.' He turned to his companions. 'Knock on the door, one of you.'

John knew he ought not to be seen, but he had to poke his head through the entrance.

'Dad, Dad, Mr Laws isn't here yet.'

Dr Andrews was splendid. He might have been expecting Mr Laws to be missing and to have rehearsed what he would do if he was. He started a kind of mock battle with one of the knights, and while he was fighting he said to the others:

'Shout and make a noise. The Abbot's missing.'

Selina was desperate. Where was Mr Laws? He was not in the men's dressing-tent. He was not in the ladies' dressing-tent. Nobody had seen him. Everybody was looking. Then suddenly Selina had an idea. The sunk rose garden. There were not many roses in it, but you could see a rose or two from the back of the stage. It was just the sort of thing to have tempted Mr Laws.

He was standing gazing down at a rose. Even in the state of mind that she was in Selina could see how extraordinarily like an abbot he looked. She gripped his arm.

'Quick. You ought to be on the stage.'

Mr Laws looked at her with a distant air.

'Curious, Selina, this little fellow is an old-fashioned moss rose. You seldom see them nowadays.'

Selina could have shaken him. Looking at moss roses in the middle of a pageant! She took his hand.

'Run. For goodness' sake, run.'

There was one thing about Mr Laws, he could not be put out by a thing like having missed his entrance. He came on to the rostrum with his monks behind him with as much dignity and calm as if it was the right moment in the pageant for him to have come on. Selina just waited to hear him say his first words, then, throwing up her eyes and making a most expressive face at John, she rushed off to find the actors in Phoebe's scene.

She did what Philip had done. She went first to the men's dressing-tent and then to the women's and called out through her megaphone:

'Everybody for the May Queen scene.'

Then she went into the women's tent to see that Phoebe and Miss Lipscombe were ready. She had no intention of any more of her leading actors missing their entrances. The moment she got inside the tent she could see that something was wrong. Phoebe's face was scarlet, much more scarlet than any rouge would have made it. Her eyes were blazing and she was beating Benjamin with her bouquet.

'You did it on purpose. I know you did it on purpose. You're hateful and mean and now I can't be May Queen, and it's all your fault.'

Benjamin was always a very sweet-looking little boy, but in his miniature Henry the Eighth suit he looked absolutely enchanting. As usual he was quite unperturbed, in fact he did not at first seem to notice that Phoebe was hitting him with a bunch of white daisies, because he was humming. Selina saw that Phoebe would not be able to answer a sensible question. She looked at Augustus.

'What's up?'

Augustus pointed to crimson marks on Phoebe's train.

'Benjamin's nose bled. We hadn't got a handkerchief, so we used that.'

'Dirty beast,' raged Phoebe. 'He made it bleed on purpose. Now I can't be the May Queen.'

Benjamin looked at her in a very superior way.

'My dear, nobody can make their nose bleed a' purpose.'

Miss Lipscombe had so got herself into the part of being the schoolteacher, and ordering all the children about, that she was being a schoolteacher off the stage as well as on it. It came in very useful at that moment. She had a large handkerchief and four safety-pins.

'Be quiet, Phoebe, disturbing everybody. I shall just pin this handkerchief over the stains. They'll never show.'

Mrs Andrews had been in the other tent helping some of Queen Elizabeth's courtiers to dress. She asked what had happened. Phoebe began to tell her. She was so sorry for herself that while she was telling the story she was almost crying. Mrs Andrews knew that she was excited and worked up about the pageant, so instead of telling her not to make such a fuss, as she would have done ordinarily, she gave her a kiss.

'It'll be all right, darling. I will make a spray of white roses before the performance and I'll sew them on so that the stains will never show.' She knelt down beside Benjamin to see that his face was clean. 'If your nose bleeds again, don't use Phoebe's train.' She took her handkerchief out of the pocket of the overall she was wearing. 'I'll tuck this inside your tunic, Augustus. If Benjamin's nose bleeds, give it to him.'

The ghosts were on again. Selina relaxed. Everybody was ready. In this scene not one actor was missing. Alfie, Miss Lipscombe, Phoebe and her Court, and all the village. If only, she thought, they do this scene nicely, and there isn't much to go wrong, it may make up for the muddle in the last scene.

Selina was being too optimistic when she thought there was nothing much that could go wrong. It was quite true, Phoebe's was an easy scene. Everybody liked acting in it, and it was full of gaiety and movement. The children in the audience obviously adored it. They clapped and clapped when Phoebe came on, and they roared with laughter when Alfie was playing around as Jack-in-the-Green. Then came the maypole dances. Miss Lipscombe brought on the maypole and stood it in its proper place. She even looked quite nice holding it in spite of the fact that she had forgotten to take off her pince-nez. The band played a chord and all the children took hold of their proper ribbons. The maypole dance began.

It is easy for a maypole dance to go wrong. Sally had rehearsed her children carefully, and they knew the dance well, but the excitement of the dress rehearsal must have been too much for them. The ribbons, instead of being a plait at the top of the pole, began to get tangled. Selina, who was rounding up Mrs Day and her courtiers, was not aware that anything was going wrong, but she saw that something must have been when she went over to Sally to ask if she had her dancers ready. Sally's eyes were tight shut. She spoke in a voice of unutterable despair.

'I can't look. I can't look. I know what's going to happen.' Before Selina could look there were screams of laughter from the audience. Sally's voice was more desperate than ever. 'There, it has happened. I knew it would.'

Selina looked at the stage. The ribbons, which should have looked so charming at the top of the pole, had got in a mess lower down. This meant the dancers had very short lengths with which to dance. Their faces were pretty grim, but they were obviously determined to finish the dance in spite of the fact that with every skip they bound Miss Lipscombe tighter and tighter to the pole. The audience seemed to think this was part of the performance. They screamed so loudly with laughter that you could hardly hear the music. It was not very easy to see Miss Lipscombe's face, because it was partly hidden by coloured tapes, but, from the bit she could see, Selina knew what Miss Lipscombe was thinking about being laughed at.

'How will she get off the stage, Sally? Her feet are tied together.'

Sally had realized without looking exactly how tied up by now Miss Lipscombe would be.

'She'll have to be carried.'

'What! Tied to the maypole?'

'Yes.'

It was John who saw what was best to do. He had finished crying his wares as a cheapjack. He moved across the stage to Christopher.

'She's tied up in knots. We'll have to carry her off.'

Christopher went one way and John the other. They found seven fairly strong people and Mr Peters. When the maypole music stopped they rushed forward, and, as if it were part of the scene, laid Miss Lipscombe and the maypole on the ground, and, between them, picked her up with the pole and carried her off the stage. They laid her down behind the hedge.

It was always a relief to Selina to hear the ghost music. Whoever else went wrong the Linkwell dancers would be perfect. Selina did not trust Mrs Day to be ready for her entrance. She collected her and her courtiers, and she even held Mrs Day until it was time for her to go on. Nothing very much went wrong with that scene, except that Mrs Day forgot that she was sitting by the microphone and that every word she said could be heard by all the audience. Fortunately most of the things she said were complimentary, but they were not a bit like Queen Elizabeth.

'Wonderful good-lookin' girl that carrot top. Bit skimpy about the clothes, what? Glad they don't expect me to stand about in nothin'. Not the weather for it.'

Selina was told by all the actors that she ought to tell Mrs Day not to talk, but she knew it would do no good if she did, anyway she was Philip's aunt, and he was sure to tell her himself before the performance.

Christopher's scene was a muddle from start to finish. The procession came on at the wrong moment and had to go off again. The crowd forgot to make a path for it to go through, and, worst of all, somebody got rough and tore Miss Lipscombe's wig off. Miss Lipscombe had a long grey wig and very good make-up, and she was really acting beautifully, so it was unlucky about the wig. It was particularly unlucky as she had been so unfortunate in Phoebe's scene. She had been forced to lie behind the hedge, been rolled over, which was very uncomfortable because of the pole, while she was unplaited, and it had not helped that everybody seemed to think her being carried out very funny. If she had not been in such a hurry to get dressed and made-up as the witch, she would have told them all what she thought of them. It was the height of bad luck that her wig came off, because the children in the audience screamed with laughter.

She won't like that, thought Selina. She's meant to look frightening.

It was Mrs Miggs who upset the Victorian scene. She always had been rather funny at rehearsals dancing her barn dance with Partridge, but that afternoon, because there was an audience, she started overdoing being funny. It was not altogether her fault, because the moment she began to dance the audience started to laugh, and that went straight to Mrs Miggs's head. She danced more and more wildly, lifting her skirt higher and higher and showing more leg, and doing a dance that was much nearer 'Knees up, Mother Brown' than a barn dance. Partridge was dreadfully shocked. In fact, so shocked that he looked at Mrs Miggs as if she was something that had disagreed with him. Of course the more Partridge looked like that the more the audience laughed. It was when the barn dance came to an end that Mrs Miggs particularly disgraced herself. She had always been one, as she said, to like people to have a good time. If laughter was anything to go by they were having a good time that afternoon, so the moment the barn dance finished she shouted to the band:

'Give it us again, boys. Give it us again.'

The band had been told no encores, and while the band leader hesitated, Philip called out:

'Straight on, no encores.'

It was then Mrs Miggs did the worst thing of all. She yelled:

'Ole spoil sport,' and put out her tongue in the direction of Philip's voice.

By the time that Selina was waiting to make her own entrance she was trembling so much that her knees knocked together.

I'll never remember the words, she thought. She heard the shouts of the evacuee children and the jeeps starting up. She tried to think of her lines. 'I have dreamed a dream . . .' Oh, what did come next? The children were singing . . . Now, what was it came next? 'I have dreamed a dream and . . .' The audience were thrilled by the jeeps. They climbed up off their rugs and clapped and waved. Many of the American soldiers they knew quite well. It was bringing the pageant right up to date. When they went off everybody cheered. John had promised to push on the Colonel. The Colonel was in his shabbiest clothes, smoking his pipe, his dogs at his heels. He was doing so exactly what he did every day, just taking a stroll, looking at his land, that he was quite natural. His back was to the audience when the ghost music started again. As the Colonel and his dogs wandered off the stage the ghosts beckoned to the future. Selina opened her book.

It seemed a terribly long way to walk from the bottom of the lower lawn to the rostrum, and there was a queer stillness after the music, applause, and cheers. On the rostrum she closed her book.

'I have dreamed a dream. Seven hundred years I've seen . . .' She stopped. 'I've seen, I've seen . . . I've seen . . .'

She heard a rustle behind her. John's voice:

'Say anything, just say goodbye.'

Selina jumped to the end of her speech.

'Our pageant is over.' She opened her book. 'A new page is to be written.' She looked at the audience. 'What will the future bring?'

Everybody was very depressed. They gathered round the trestle tables and waited for the teapots to arrive, but out of the corners of their eyes they were watching for Philip. What on earth would he say? After all the work he had put in. A rehearsal like that!

Tea had arrived before Philip came. He was with the American officers. They were talking together and did not at first notice how silent the actors were. Then Philip looked up. He raised his eyebrows to Selina in a question.

'What's up?'

Selina, John, Christopher, Sally, Phoebe, Miss Lipscombe, and Dr Andrews gathered round him, all talking and explaining at once why the rehearsal had gone wrong. How dreadful it had been and what ought to happen to make it right before the performance.

Philip took his megaphone from Selina. He raised it to his mouth.

'Silence, everybody. Thank you very much. Considering everything that was not at all a bad dress rehearsal, but it showed me one thing . . .' He paused, and in the pause everybody was asking 'What?' Philip was smiling. 'There's nothing for anybody to worry about. We're going to give a first-rate performance. It's in the bag.'

# CHAPTER TWENTY-THREE

## *The Pageant*

People were coming. The drive was full of cars. All along the road buses were parked. There were jeeps in the field beside the drive. People who had come by train were walking in great parties across the railway footpath.

Sally folded her arms and hugged herself.

'I can't believe it's true. I just can't. We're going to act our pageant at last. Eight hundred and fifty people have paid to come, not counting the children this afternoon. Oh, glory! Glory!'

They peered through the entrances on to the stage. It was not allowed, but they simply had to look.

'It's like an ant-heap,' said John.

'An ant-heap,' Christopher corrected, 'wouldn't have ants walking about selling programmes.'

The members of the Women's Institute, who were not acting in the pageant, were the programme sellers. Selina watched their progress anxiously.

'I do hope they've remembered that people can, if they like, give more than sixpence. They are so used to saving that it's difficult for them to turn round and say "spend".'

John peered over her shoulder.

'You don't want to worry about the programme sellers. You want to worry about your speech.'

Sally defended Selina.

'She wasn't the only one who went wrong this afternoon. What about Mr Laws? Or my maypole dancers?'

Selina was very conscious of her speech, but not about the one that she ought to have said at the dress rehearsal. It was the performance one that worried her. That was Philip's secret. It would have been so nice if she could have told the others. It was so difficult not being able to ask anyone to hear it. Thinking of Philip made her go and look for him. He was standing at the back of the stage talking to Colonel Day and the American officers. He beckoned Selina over to join them. He put his arm round her.

'Have you got your words right for tonight?'

She flushed.

'Oh, Philip, I do hope so. It was simply awful this afternoon.'

He laughed.

'Not a bit of it. The kids never noticed. It's the one tonight that matters, but you haven't got to worry about it. I've gummed it into your book. You don't want to read it if you can possibly help it, but it's there if you forget what you've got to say.' He looked at the three men. 'It's important, isn't it?'

The American colonel nodded.

'Very important.' He looked at Bob. 'If you get it wrong this young man'll come up and say it for you.'

'I shan't get it wrong. Not if it's written out. Just having it there will give me great confidence.'

Philip looked at his watch.

'We'd better get everybody rounded up. Can you lay your hands on Mr Laws?'

There was no muddle this time. Selina could, of course, not watch Mr Laws herself, but John got Christopher to help him, and long before it was time for him to go on they had the Abbot waiting at his entrance.

Everybody was very keyed up and nervous. Even Mrs Day was shaken out of her usual casualness.

'Feel shockin', Selina. Philip says I made a proper ass of myself this afternoon. Don't want to sit on that dais lookin' like a stuffed dummy, but it seems every word I spoke was heard all over the whole place. Nasty contraptions, these loudspeakers.'

The audience seemed to be in a very nice mood, prepared to like everything. They clapped the moment the band started to play, and when it finished the overture there was such a roar of applause that, had encores been allowed, they would have had to have given one. As the applause finished, Selina came on. She was not feeling nervous. The whole pageant lay between her and having to speak, and having walked safely through her first entrance at the dress rehearsal she had got confidence, and had stopped feeling shy. What did confuse her, and almost made her look up from her book, was that the audience clapped her. This was a great surprise. After all, what had she done to be clapped?

As she came off she turned for a moment to watch the ghost dancers. They came gliding out of the trees in their grey frocks

and early English head-dresses. They looked quite lovely with
their grey arms and grey faces against the green hedges. They
danced in and out of each other, twisting and weaving until one
century was left alone, beckoning as she danced off. The monks
began their chant.

Sally was watching from the opposite side of the stage. As
the last ghost drifted off she said, in a whisper:

'Lovely! I wish, oh, how I wish I danced like that.'

She had not known anyone was listening. She was surprised
to feel a hand on her shoulder. It was Madame Ramosova.

'I have been talking to your mother over tea, Sally. She
tells me you want to take up dancing as a career.'

Sally nodded.

'More than anything in the world.'

'I have told your mother that after Christmas I shall have
a vacancy and I can make special terms for a promising pupil.'

Sally could not believe that she could be hearing correctly.
Madame Ramosova could not mean that she might be going as
a pupil to Linkwell Ballet School.

'You don't mean . . .'

Madame Ramosova smiled.

'Yes. I was telling your mother I see great promise in the
little dance you do. I think it will be arranged.' She saw how
shining were Sally's eyes. 'It's a hard career you've chosen, my
child. Endless work and endless disappointments, but I think
we shall make a dancer of you.'

Sally felt as though she were flying. She ran round the
stage looking for Christopher. It was too marvellous. She must
tell Christopher or she would burst. Christopher was talking
to Mr Bins. In spite of a coat with many collars, a cocked hat

and a lot of brass buttons, and that he was carrying a bell instead of a post-bag, Mr Bins still looked every inch a postman. Sally clutched Christopher by the arm.

'Christopher, the most marvellous thing's happened.'

Christopher looked rather disgruntled.

'Who told you?'

'Madame Ramosova.'

Mr Bins shook his head.

'Don't know how she came to know. I only see'd it myself just as I left the Post Office.'

Sally was so in the clouds that it was difficult for her to come down to earth, but she did grasp that Christopher and Mr Bins were not talking about her going to the Linkwell Ballet School.

'What's in the Post Office?'

Christopher said:

'A parcel from Washington, and Mr Bins has read the declaration form. It's your tights and my skates.'

Sally could see from Christopher's face that she ought to be thrilled, but when you have reached the top pinnacle of happiness you can climb no higher. She was saved answering by Selina.

'Are your maypole dancers ready?'

In a moment Sally was back on the earth. She still was lit up and glowing with happiness, but the pageant was happening and she had to keep her mind on it. She did not bother to answer Selina but ran off to collect her children.

Nothing went wrong with Phoebe's scene. Mrs Andrews had done what she had promised and there was an enormous spray of roses sewn over the bloodstains on her train. Benjamin and Augustus behaved beautifully. They carried the train with such pride that they got a round of applause all to themselves. Nothing this time went wrong with the maypole dance. The ribbons were plaited, and the audience clapped the maypole dancers so hard, trying to make them do it all over again, that Philip had to call them to curtsy. The scene was real fun for everybody. It felt like being at a fair. The cheapjacks roared their wares, Mr Peters lifted his weights as though they weighed hundreds of tons, the barkers shouted so loud that they could be heard to the back row of the audience.

Sally's scene was a riot. The children looked sweet in their yellow frocks and yellow wreaths of flowers; they had relations in the audience, and it would not have mattered if they had done the dance wrong or even fallen over. As it happened, they danced beautifully. Sally danced better than she had ever danced before. It is easy to dance when you are so full of happiness that you feel as though you are floating, and Sally felt just like that. The Linkwell ballet was really exquisite and anybody who knew anything about dancing was enthralled, but all the relations and friends of the children nudged each other and said, 'Just as soon see our kids and Sally any day.' Mrs Day was a sensation. Almost everybody in the audience knew her. The whole time she was on the stage programmes rattled, and people whispered, 'That's never Mrs Day! My! She looks every inch a queen.'

Christopher and his mummers, led on by St George, had the time of their lives. They joked with the audience, played with the children, and really looked like a procession on some great day. Miss Lipscombe was terrific. Her wig stayed on and her screams were so terrible that she made the children in the audience shiver.

'Isn't it awful,' said Christopher as he came off, 'to think we shall never act this scene again?'

Miss Lipscombe heard what he said.

'I must say, I've enjoyed myself.'

The Victorian scene was perhaps the best of all. Mr Bins rang his bell and announced the relief of Mafeking as if nobody had heard the news before. The bell-ringers walked across the stage to ring the bells, and everybody who knew they were real bell-ringers told everybody who did not know. The recorded bells sounded grand, as they ought to have done, as they were really the bells of St Paul's Cathedral pealing at the coronation. Of course the village knew they were hearing a gramophone record, but they did not think the bells anything special. 'They're not our bells, but very like. Ours are a bit sweeter.' Because the pageant had gone well there was real gaiety in the crowd scene. People wanted to dance and they looked as if they did.

Mrs Miggs behaved very well. Philip had said to her, 'Just a bit less spirit, otherwise it's grand.' Mrs Miggs thought this was generous seeing she had put her tongue out, so she toned her performance down. Toned down, her dance with Partridge was really funny. It did not matter to the audience that Philip had said no encores. They clapped, whistled, and shouted 'encore'. Philip laughed and signalled to the conductor, and Partridge and Mrs Miggs danced their barn dance all over again.

When the scene was over everybody flocked round to congratulate them. Mrs Miggs took the applause as her right.

'Always was one for a bit of dancin'.'

'You were good, Mr Partridge,' Phoebe said.

He shook his head.

'Thank you, Miss Phoebe, but I must admit to being glad it's over. Not the sort of thing I care for.'

The ghost was on. No longer dressed in floating draperies but a grey air-raid warden's suit and grey tin hat. She had a dramatic dance calling nineteen thirty-nine. A record reproduced the wailing of a siren. Two and two, with labels round their necks, and gas masks on their backs, and suitcases in their hands, the children marched on singing 'Roll out the barrel'. They marched off through the back, took off their labels, put down their suitcases and gas-masks, and ran back on to the stage and played games.

Every woman in the audience had looked after evacuees, and they nudged each other and said, 'That was a time, that was', or 'Colonel and Mrs Day only had two rooms for themselves, the children had all the Abbey.' It was nice after so much history of the past to come to a bit which they had lived through and been part of. Then the children had gone. Philip pressed the buzzer. The band played 'Over there', the jeeps raced along the path on to the stage. That scene went even better than it had with the children at the rehearsal. Of course the entrance of the jeeps could not be done twice, but the audience would have liked to have seen it again, and clapped and clapped to show how they felt.

The Colonel was on. Sauntering across with his dogs. Mrs Mawser watched him from the side of the stage. There were tears in her eyes. Nor were Mrs Mawser's the only tears. Almost everybody in the audience knew and loved the Days. This was the sad part of the pageant. The Colonel saying goodbye to the Abbey.

The ghosts were on, beckoning to the future. Selina's hands were damp and she felt sickish. This was it. This was where she had to speak. She opened her book at the typed page Philip had gummed in.

He was beside her. He squeezed her arm.

'This is fun. Speak up clearly. Give them all a surprise.'

Selina was on the rostrum. She was by the microphone. She knew she had the typed sheet, but she knew she would not need it. There was dead silence. Her voice reached everybody clearly.

'Seven hundred years you've seen. Years of change. Years of gladness. Years of suffering. One thing has remained unchanged. The English heart. The English love of the old customs, and the old ways. This pageant sees an end of an old way of life. For more than three hundred years the Day family have lived in the Abbey. Now it passes away from them, but the family will still be here.'

Everybody, both in the audience and round the stage, was whispering, 'Still be here?' 'What's she saying?' 'The Days aren't going?' 'What's that?' 'Isn't the Abbey being sold?'

'The Americans have wished not to drive away and leave no mark. They have bought the Abbey as a hostel for the youth of America, so that they can visit here. These are the Commanding Officer's words. "To keep alive for ever the bonds of friendship forged in these last years."'

Selina's voice was drowned in a roar of applause.

'Don't speak through the clapping, ducky,' Philip called. 'Wait for it.'

The audience saw that Selina had not finished speaking. They said 'Sssh'.

'Colonel and Mrs Day will live in a few rooms and act as host and hostess.' She raised her voice as Philip had taught her. 'The Abbey, therefore, passes to a purpose the abbot and monks, dispossessed in the reign of Henry the Eighth, would approve. If a curse has rested on this place, it is lifted now.'

Was it Selina's fancy or did she hear a sigh? A tired sigh, as if someone very old had worked too long and was glad to rest.

All the actors came on. The dancers were called for and curtsied beautifully. Mr Laws, John, and the doctor took a call. Phoebe, Benjamin, and Augustus were called for and Phoebe curtsied and the boys bowed. There were cheers when Sally came on with her dancers. They were in Victorian dresses, of course, but the audience remembered what else they had been and said, 'That's the one that danced, and those are the children that danced with her, and some was the maypole dancers', or 'That's Margaret, third from the left', or 'That's little Annie, doesn't she look a duck. Danced ever so sweet'. Miss Lipscombe, still dressed as a witch, had a special call all to herself. So did Alfie, who had no intention of being forgotten and put on his Jack-in-the-Green outfit while Selina was speaking. So did Mrs Miggs, because Partridge absolutely refused to take a call. Christopher and his mummers bowed in a long row. Then Mrs Day came on alone. She got such an ovation that she went off again and fetched the Colonel to bow with her. She said to him between bows:

'Let's get off or I'll make an ass of meself. Aren't people kind?'

Last of all the Americans made their bow and they were cheered so loudly the Abbey seemed to shake.

Then the audience called for Philip. He came on to the rostrum and made a speech. He said he had come to introduce some people who needed a good clap. The wardrobe mistresses. Mrs Andrews and Mrs Mawser came on hand in hand. The family were all standing together, and they clapped so loud that Mrs Andrews heard them and blew them a kiss.

Philip was speaking again.

'There is one other person you must meet. A person too often forgotten. Selina.'

Selina, very red about the face, joined Philip on the rostrum.

'This is the stage manager. The frock she is wearing, a gift from America, inspired her and the Andrews children to write the pageant. As you saw for yourselves, she wears it as prologue and epilogue. As well, she has been a magnificent stage manager. We could not have done without her.'

The audience and the actors clapped and cheered. Selina felt a tug at her skirt. It was Benjamin. He was carrying a bouquet of red roses.

'My dear. These are for you from Philip.'

'Authors. Authors.'

Everybody was shouting.

John, Sally, Christopher, Phoebe, and Selina came forward. The boys bowed, the girls curtsied.

The band played 'God Save the King'. The pageant was over.

'What do you think?' said John. 'The Americans say we can borrow the Abbey and do the pageant again next year.'

'And I can use the pond next holidays to skate on if it freezes,' said Christopher.

Sally danced a few steps.

'I don't even mind the pageant being over. I'm going to the Linkwell Ballet School. I feel as if I were made of very good tasting chocolate cream.'

Selina was so happy she too danced.

'Mum and Dad are coming home. And I've been given a bouquet.'

Phoebe was half-crying.

'Don't be so cheerful. I feel as if nothing nice will ever happen again.'

Selina undid her waist.

'That's all you know. I've grown fatter and taller since Christmas. I haven't said anything before, but I've felt all day as if I was going to burst.'

Phoebe was jumping with excitement.

'You don't mean . . .'

'Yes. I'm passing down to you the party frock and shoes.'

# About the Author

NOEL STREATFEILD was born in Sussex in 1895. Her father, a clergyman, was Vicar of St Leonard's-on-Sea and then of Eastbourne during her childhood. She was one of five children and found vicarage life very restricting. At a young age she began to show a talent for acting and was sent to the Academy of Dramatic Art in London, after which she acted professionally for a number of years before turning to writing. She won the Carnegie Medal for her book *Ballet Shoes*, and was awarded an OBE in 1983. Noel Streatfeild died in 1986.